LINEAR TACTICAL SERIES

SHADOW

USA TODAY BESTSELLING AUTHOR
JANIE CROUCH

Cover by Deranged Doctor Design.

A Calamittie Jane Publishing Book

SHADOW: LINEAR TACTICAL

This book is dedicated to my Bat Signal Group.

For all the times I've sent up the signal and you've come speeding to my rescue.

The profession is crazy, man. Let's stick together.

PROLOGUE

Today was the day Heath Kavanaugh was getting his answers.

Finally.

The man he was following was the one who had given Heath the codename *Shadow*. He had taught Heath to live in the shadows, survive there, destroy there. So it was fitting that the shadows hid him from his prey now.

Shadow walked out of the shadows.

Nobody spared him a second glance at the bank in Rome, Italy. It was late afternoon, and everyone was rushing to finish up their business before heading home.

Dr. Timothy Holloman sat in the bank manager's office. Heath wasn't exactly sure what Holloman was doing—transferring money? opening an account? asking for a date?—but it didn't matter.

All that mattered was that the man was here, Heath was here, and they would damn well be leaving together.

If you want answers, I'm the only one who has them. You're going to have to let me go.

Just the thought of Holloman's taunt that day six weeks

ago made Heath's trigger finger itch. And the fact that the words were true was the only reason Holloman had walked out of that port in Oregon that day.

Holloman had developed and run Project Crypt—a covert US government agency used for missions that needed to be conducted with the utmost precision, discretion, and lethality. He'd made Heath and the other dozen Crypt agents into deadly super soldiers.

All fine and good, except Holloman had left out a few key points.

Like that Crypt missions weren't actually US government sanctioned.

And that they'd brainwashed some of the Crypt agents in order to force them to perform sleeper missions without their knowledge.

And that they'd done something to Heath's mind.

Not brainwashed him like the other agents, but they'd *put* something in there. Put endless gibberish in his mind that never seemed to go quiet.

And Holloman was about to tell Heath what the cacophony in his mind meant. Whether he wanted to tell Heath or not.

Because, hell, after what Holloman had done to Heath and his friends, it wouldn't hurt Heath's feelings if he had to pull out a few of Holloman's teeth in order to get him to talk.

Heath smiled at a young bank teller, talking to her fluently in her native Italian. She smiled at his compliments about how she really should be outside on a beautiful day like today rather than trapped in the old bank building.

He kept one shoulder facing her, still able to keep Holloman in his line of sight, as she mentioned a nearby restaurant she was hoping to visit soon that served one of her favorite bottles of wine.

Any other time, Heath would have been quick to find out more information—about her, about the café, about the wine. The woman was definitely his type . . . tall, leggy, confident.

But today she was just one more shadow he was hiding in.

He chatted with her a couple more minutes, then said his goodbyes when Holloman walked through the manager's office door, casually strolling toward the front of the bank.

Heath followed discreetly. Holloman didn't seem aware of his presence, but he didn't want to spook the man. Heath's van was parked a quarter block away. A gun at Holloman's back ought to be all the incentive needed to get Holloman in. If not, he'd go to the backup plan—sedate him, then shuffle Holloman to the vehicle, pretending like Holloman had hit the bottle too early.

But either way, today was the day Heath was finally going to have some answers after a decade of wondering what the hell was going on in his head.

By the time Holloman was ten feet out the door—thankfully going in the direction of the van—Heath was on him. Keeping his gun in his pocket, Heath grabbed Holloman by the shoulder and pulled him up against the weapon rather than the other way around.

"Good evening, Doctor," Heath whispered against Holloman's ear. "I've been trying to catch up with you for quite a while."

Holloman stiffened but didn't try to pull away. "Shadow. I have to say, you're not who I expected to find me here today, if I was going to be found."

Heath kept the gun against Holloman's waist. "You've got so many people hunting you, you can't even keep track of them all? Since you successfully eliminated most your little Project Crypt pets, I would've thought I ranked higher on your people-who-want-to-kill-me list."

Holloman actually smiled. "Yes, well, that's just it, isn't it? You don't want to kill me. At least not yet."

"I hope you don't think for even a second that means you're safe. Some of the most sadistic bastards on the planet trained me how to both survive and dole out unbearable pain. Oh wait, that was *you*. I'm sure we're about to have a lot of fun."

Holloman stepped away from Heath's grasp. Heath let him go. There was nowhere he could run that Heath wouldn't be able to catch him. Holloman turned to face Heath. He hated how calm the man looked.

Always so damn calm.

"Now, Shadow, you'll want to be careful not to break me. Without me, you're never going to get your answers."

The damned thing was, Holloman was right.

But Heath didn't let any of that show. He was an expert at masking his emotions. "Oh, I think I can find the right balance between making your life pretty damn miserable and getting the answers I need."

Holloman gave him a smirk, his mouth opening for some smart-aleck remark—

—and his head exploded right in front of Heath.

He heard the rifle shot not a split second later.

Heath caught what was left of Holloman's body as it fell to the ground.

"No," he whispered.

Then his training kicked in.

Heath dropped Holloman and rolled behind one of

the small cars parked on the street. He drew his weapon and peeked out, looking up toward the third-floor apartments across the road where the shot must have come from.

There. Third apartment down, northeast corner. Heath raised his weapon and shot, careful to make it a shot to distract or wound, not to kill.

Whoever had killed Holloman was now Heath's only chance for answers.

He was being so conservative, the bullet barely hit the window frame. Panic built on the streets around him. Civilians ran, screaming and ducking for cover.

No one shot back. Holloman had been the target, not someone the assassin had deemed disposable. But more importantly, he hadn't been aiming at Heath. Holding his weapon low and to his side, he moved out from behind the car and into the surrounding panic. He kept one eye on the window as he weaved in and out of the frantic bystanders. Sirens sounded in the distance; Heath was running out of time. There could be any number of people who could place him standing right next to Holloman at the time of his death.

The cops would have too many questions Heath couldn't answer easily. The purpose of his own gun being primary.

He darted around a woman sobbing into her phone while pushing a stroller and ran toward the door leading up to the apartments.

Inside the building wasn't any less chaotic. People weren't sure what was happening—some darted outside to see if they could find out what was going on; others rushed inside. Rapid, excited Italian echoed off crowded stairwell's walls.

And to Heath's trained eye, none of them seemed out of place—like a killer trying to quietly make an escape.

Heath moved upstairs, keeping his face averted as much as possible. The sirens grew louder. He could hear them all the way from inside. He didn't have much time.

Seconds later, he arrived at the apartment door where the shot had originated. He didn't hesitate, turning and kicking with the back of his foot to force the door open, then instantly spun with his weapon drawn.

The apartment was empty.

He did a thorough sweep to make sure before coming back to the window the shooter had used, which was still cracked open.

But there was nobody here.

Whoever had shot Holloman was gone.

And so were all of Heath's answers.

CHAPTER ONE

"Look, the man is my best friend, but Finn is unfocused and not ready for this. We can take him."

Heath never expected to hear words like that come out of Zac Mackay's mouth.

But Zac was right, things *had* changed at Linear Tactical. Heath had seen it the past six weeks, ever since he'd made his way back to Oak Creek from Italy, trying to piece his world back together.

But this was pretty cutthroat. Heath had worked at Linear Tactical for years, mostly in overseas negotiation and kidnap/ransom cases. Until recently, he hadn't spent much time at the Linear home office here in Wyoming, mostly because according to the US government, Heath didn't actually exist.

A shadow, if you would.

But *damn*. Heath had never thought he'd see the day when Zac would turn against his childhood friend and brother like this.

Heath looked at the man and shook his head. "Really, Zac? You sure this is how you want it to go down?"

It was a much more feminine voice that broke their stare. "Are you kidding me right now, Mackay?"

Violet Collingwood, Aiden Teague's girlfriend, smacked Zac on the shoulder. "Finn's wife is exactly 427 months pregnant, and you're going to use that *against* him? Were you this ruthless in the Special Forces?"

Zac crossed his arms over his chest, eyes still narrowed, face still grim. "In the Special Forces, we weren't playing for all-you-can-eat dessert from the Frontier Diner."

The man had a point.

Heath nodded. It was time to take charge. "Fine. Zac, if you think you can get around Finn, do it. Otherwise, Violet, you and Jordan distract Aiden and Gabe—don't be afraid to play dirty. Everybody else just try to get open. I'll throw to whoever will get us into the end zone. This is it. Last play. It's now or never."

And the damnedest game of football he'd ever been a part of, not that there'd been that many in the past decade. The special agent business—for or against the government you thought you worked for—didn't leave much time for community pastimes.

This was nice. One, because the physical activity of the game helped silence the damned gibberish in his head for a couple hours. But beyond the football too. The whole settling down, starting to make a life for himself here in Wyoming. It was not something he would've ever thought he wanted, but it had helped him in the past month when he thought he might go completely crazy.

He was never getting his answers. Holloman was dead, there didn't seem to be any leads, and Heath was stuck with this jabber in his mind forever.

The sounds—*almost* like words, but nothing that made sense in any language— constantly bombarded his thoughts unless he pushed them out. Like the nonsensical clamor a baby made when talking to himself. Useless. Static. Noise.

And inescapable.

Nothing to do right now but breathe in, breathe out, and move on.

Or in this case, throw the damn football.

Heath tamped down the muddled voices in his mind trying to break through as the team moved out of the huddle. Heath hiked the ball, getting ready to throw. Zac ran out, spun, then cut to the left for a long pass. Heath grinned as Jordan distracted her fiancé, Gabe, with a kiss that had the big man wrapping his arms around her and completely forgetting the game. Violet dropped and swept Aiden's leg with her own—a fighting move he'd probably taught her in the past year. They both laughed as they began mock sparring right there on the makeshift football field.

But Zac had underestimated Finn. Pregnant wife or not, the man was covering Zac too closely for a Hail Mary throw. Nobody else seemed particularly open, but all the shenanigans had cleared a path for Heath to run the ball himself.

He cut to the left, tucked the ball into the crook of his arm, and sprinted downfield. He thought he was going to make it until a flying tackle blindsided him and sent him and the tackler down hard into the grass.

"Not today, Satan."

Heath chuckled and rolled onto his side. Gavin. "Should've known you'd be the only one fast enough to catch me blind. And this is supposed to be a game of touch, not tackle, you jackass."

Behind them, Gavin's team cheered their win, everyone good-naturedly accusing everyone else of cheating.

Gavin hopped up and offered Heath a hand. "As soon as I saw Jordan kissing on Gabe, I knew you guys were playing dirty. I was planning to help double-team Zac if Finn couldn't cover him, but then I saw you had an opening. Knew you wouldn't miss it."

He and Gavin had known each other a lot of years, even if they'd never played football together before. "Hey, for all-you-can-eat desserts, you do what you have to do."

"Absolutely. I'm a little surprised you didn't . . ." Gavin's grin faded as a car pulled up to the side of the Linear Tactical office. "Crap."

"Trouble?"

"Federal agent. If needed, do your Shadow thing, make yourself scarce without looking like you're doing so."

Heath nodded. The man was already on them.

"Agent Franklin." Gavin reached out to shake the other man's hand. "What brings you to Oak Creek? Hopefully not looking for any more international criminals."

Franklin gave Gavin an easy smile, but the agent's eyes took in everything around him. He was in his mid-thirties—Heath and Gavin's age—with sandy-brown hair and a face that was saved from being too pretty by a scar that ran over his right eye and the downward pull of his lips.

"Why?" Franklin said. "Got any around here?"

Gavin laughed but didn't answer. Considering Heath could be labeled a criminal for some of the things he'd unknowingly done for Holloman and Project Crypt, not saying too much was probably wise.

Gavin turned to Heath. "Heath, this is FBI Agent Craig Franklin. He and I met about three months ago when I was working a case that led us to a port in Oregon. Big brouhaha. I think you were out of the country at the time?"

Or Heath had been right in the middle of said

brouhaha. "That's right, I remember you guys telling me about that. Bad guy got killed."

Actually, a lot of people had been killed that day. But the particular "bad guy" Franklin thought was dead happened to be living happily in a cabin with the love of her life about two hours from here. She'd also been a part of Project Crypt with Heath.

Heath reached out his hand to shake Craig's. "Nice to meet you. I do a lot of overseas work for Linear Tactical, so not often in the mix here."

Craig looked back and forth between Heath and Gavin. "Actually, I'm aware of who you are. You're part of the reason I'm here."

Heath forced himself not to stiffen. If Agent Franklin knew exactly who Heath was, he wouldn't be standing here talking to him; he would've come in with a SWAT team.

"Why don't we take this over to my office?" Gavin said. "We can drive into town and make everything official."

"Actually, I prefer to keep this unofficial if you don't mind."

Heath glanced over at Gavin. He had no idea how well Gavin knew this guy, but Heath was willing to hear him out unless Gavin had reservations. Heath gave Gavin a tiny nod.

"Okay, why don't we go into the Linear office then? We can talk about whatever is on your mind."

Everyone else had started heading home. Gavin led the way to the office, Craig between them so there was no chance for Heath to communicate. It was fine. Heath knew Gavin had his back.

Gavin opened the door and Heath made his way to the fridge, grabbing a sports drink for himself and tossing one to Gavin. "Drink, Agent Franklin?"

"Craig, please. And no, I'm fine."

"What's on your mind, Craig?" Gavin took a chug of his drink, then took a seat behind the desk he hadn't used much since becoming the temporary sheriff of Oak Creek almost four months ago. Heath perched on the corner of the desk, and Craig took a seat on the couch in front of the window.

"The government contracts out research money to different universities across the country depending on their specialties. We've got some biomedical engineering faculty members selling state secrets at Wyoming Commonwealth University."

A sports drink bottle hit the desk behind Heath with a thump. "You're aware that my sister studies at WCU?" Gavin asked.

Heath stared at Gavin over his shoulder. "You have a sister? How is it I've only met your two dumb brothers?"

"One, because you've been out of the country for the past half-decade, and two, Jacquelyn—Jackie—isn't hot on my job here. For Linear Tactical or for the sheriff's department. She's not big on military or law enforcement careers in general."

Heath whistled through his teeth. "Sucks to be her."

Especially since damn near everybody in Gavin's family was connected to the military or law enforcement. All three brothers were. Hell, even the two of Gavin's cousins he'd met—Noah and Tanner Dempsey—were involved with the military or law enforcement in Colorado.

Gavin's father was the governor of Wyoming, having run for office after an established career in, that's right, *law enforcement*. Jacquelyn Zimmerman had picked the wrong family to be born into if she didn't like cops or soldiers.

"Do I need to pull her out, Franklin? Jackie has health issues—a heart problem. She's working on a master's degree in hospitality, but I don't want her in the middle of anything."

Craig shook his head. "WCU is huge with multiple departments. We're looking into the biomedical engineering department, nothing to do with hospitality majors."

Gavin shrugged. "I think she was looking for a major as far from law enforcement as she could get."

Craig nodded. "Well, that should do it. The math and science buildings are on the opposite side of campus, and there's no reason to think you should be concerned for her safety in any way."

Gavin folded his arms over his chest, all business. "Okay, if you're not here as a courtesy call about getting Jackie out, why are you here?"

Craig let out a sigh. "I'll be honest with you. I wish I weren't. I need your help. I have reason to believe there's a leak in my department. I don't know how far up it goes, and I don't have a lot of time to flush out the mole. Making sure this technology doesn't fall into the wrong hands is of primary importance."

Craig turned to Heath. "It's my understanding that you studied at Wyoming Commonwealth University for a couple of semesters."

Heath crossed his arms over his chest. He wasn't surprised Craig had found that information. It was part of the information docket someone would find if they searched his ID. A lot of the info in the docket was completely false, but not this particular detail. "That's right. I'm sure you guys will snicker at this, but actually, I studied languages and international communications."

He'd been recruited straight into Project Crypt from WCU.

Gavin shook his head. "Your ability to speak every language on the planet has saved me more than once."

"I don't think eight counts as every language on the planet." He spoke eight fluently and at least another dozen enough to get by. Heath turned back to Craig. "I don't know enough about WCU anymore to be particularly useful in a sting op. Definitely not in the math and science department.

"I'll be honest, it's less what you bring to the table as a former student and more the fact that you're part of Gavin's inner circle. That means he can trust you. You've got a basic understanding of the campus, you're not the mole in my department, and I'm hoping you might be between assignments and willing to work undercover."

Heath glanced over at Gavin again. His friend shrugged.

Maybe this was the kick start he needed. Since Holloman's assassination, Heath had been floundering—trapped with the murmurings in his head and no chance for answers. Kendrick Foster, the resident Linear Tactical computer specialist, had been trying to recover what data he could from a damaged hard drive Heath's friends Dorian and Ray had obtained a few months ago. But so far, nothing of any use.

Heath had been in a damned holding pattern. He'd been passing the time teaching his assigned Linear Tactical classes each day. As much as he loved self-defense, survival, and weapons training, his heart hadn't been in it.

It was time to find a new baseline for normal. Make peace with what his life was going to be like now.

Undercover work with a bunch of college kids should give him a chance to get his head on straight. He wouldn't mind playing the role of professor for a while. Maybe he could even pull out the glasses he owned and had used for undercover work before, even though he didn't need them. People tended to be less suspicious of guys with glasses.

Maybe it would block out some of the gibberish in his head for a while. Something to concentrate on besides the fact that he wasn't ever going to have answers.

It was time to stop bemoaning that fact and learn to live with what he couldn't rise above.

"I'll do it. Tell me more."

CHAPTER TWO

"You're a strong, independent, black woman who doesn't need any man."

Lyn Norris was actually *none* of those things.

Okay, yes, she was a woman.

And her grandmother had been born in the Caribbean, so the black part was at least partially true. Although Lyn's European heritage didn't tend to make that noticeable.

But the strong, independent part . . . definitely nothing true about that.

But she was trying. That was the important thing—she was *trying*.

"What are you mumbling about being a black woman over there?" Zuri Greenbank, Lyn's friend and *actual* strong, independent, black woman, shifted the box of books she was carrying.

"Merely reminding myself that I can do this."

Zuri grinned and pressed the up button on the elevator. "Move the last of these manuscripts into your office?"

The other woman knew damn well that wasn't what Lyn was talking about. "Dad called to check on me today to make sure I was doing okay. The Brothers have all video called me a least once in the past two weeks. Usually they just text incessantly, not actually wanting to talk."

It was so much easier to mislead them when she was texting rather than having to see their faces. She loved The Brothers—thinking of them as one entity rather than three individuals was easier, especially since they tended to gang up on her—and Dad—but they were all damn observant. She'd learned a long time ago she could hide a lot more in a text than a phone call or video chat.

Dad was in Cheyenne, hours away, thank goodness. Tristan and Andrew were both deployed for the navy and out of the country. Gavin was closest, less than an hour away, but he was busy with his temporary sheriff's position in Oak Creek.

All just far enough away to rarely drop by unannounced, which suited Lyn perfectly.

Lyn was here at Wyoming Commonwealth University getting her doctorate in what she'd always wanted to study: linguistics and philology.

Her family thought she was getting a master's degree in hospitality and that, for some reason, it was taking her five years.

Could you even get a master's degree in hospitality? And why would someone need five years to do it?

Not that she had anything against a hospitality major— it had even been part of what she'd studied in undergrad. The major her father had actually known about and been thrilled she'd chosen.

After all, if he needed someone to play hostess at the governor's mansion, a daughter with a degree in hospitality would certainly fit the bill.

Never mind that hosting functions would be Lyn's definition of hell.

Just leave her alone with her ancient languages and how they applied to contemporary times. That's what she really loved and was studying now.

"Your dad and The Brothers care about you." Zuri leaned back against the elevator door as it opened so Lyn could enter.

"I know. They care too much. Always too much. It's that alpha-hero gene all of them got in spades. Please change the subject."

Zuri followed Lyn inside the elevator and pressed the button for the eighth floor. "Fine. Saussure's views on the subject of synchrony and diachrony have to do with the question of how different people use the term morpheme. That needs to go in your introductory chapter."

Lyn tilted her head, considering Zuri's point. "Actually, you're probably right. That should be included as part of my initial premise."

Zuri winked at her. "Of course I'm right. I know you've missed me since I've been gone."

"Longest seven months of my life."

Zuri knocked into Lyn with her hip. "I've missed you too, kiddo. Just think, finish your dissertation this year and you'll be out in the real world also."

The thought didn't actually bring Lyn any peace. It was difficult enough for her to make friends here in the university's closed environment. She couldn't imagine that would get any easier on the outside.

And it would mean telling her family she didn't plan to play hostess for the rest of her life. That she wanted to travel, experience different cultures and their languages firsthand.

That was going to go over splendidly. And was why she'd taken an extra year to work on her dissertation rather than pushing through and finishing like she was more than capable of.

The elevator door opened; Lyn shifted the heavy box of manuscripts in her hands and began walking down the hall. She was a little out of breath before they got halfway to her office.

"You okay?" Zuri asked, waiting while Lyn had to stop and get her heart rate under control. "It totally sucks that you have to be over here with the nerds."

Lyn laughed, appreciating her friend's subject change. "You were just debating a comparativist's view on synchrony and diachrony with me, and you're going to call the math and computer science guys *nerds*?"

Zuri winked, then started walking slowly again. Most people would attribute Lyn's breathlessness to carrying the heavy boxes since she was a little on the heavy side. And that was partially true. But most of it was because of the heart defect Lyn had lived with all her life: supraventricular tachycardia.

Wolff-Parkinson-White syndrome, to be exact. A really drawn-out way of saying her heart didn't always work the way it was supposed to. Sometimes it started beating too fast and couldn't pump blood effectively to other organs.

Her tachycardia was why her family thought she was studying hospitality. Because someone with her condition shouldn't have dreams of traveling the world and learning how the use of language affected societies and made them better.

No, she was much better suited to hosting functions for her father and making small talk with politicians and businessmen.

Sorry, Dad, not in this life.

Lyn wasn't good at making small talk with anyone. And the career she was interested in may take her out of Wyoming, but it wasn't dangerous. She had no idea why she hadn't just told Dad a month ago when he'd come to visit that she was working on a degree in linguistics.

Maybe because he'd had all three of her brothers with him. They'd been wrapping her in cotton wool since the day her mom had died of a similar heart defect. For twenty-three years, since Lyn had been five, four alpha males—six, if she counted her cousins Noah and Tanner, who could be just as bad—had done everything to make sure her life was as gentle and easy as possible.

It had never actually occurred to them to ask her if she *wanted* gentle and easy.

"You doing okay?" Zuri asked again

Lyn nodded. "Yeah. Let's get these in."

They zigzagged their way through the complicated hallways to finally get to the back. Lyn set her box down to unlock her office door. The room wasn't much bigger than a supply closet, and it was in the middle of the math and CS division, but at least it was hers.

"Okay, this isn't so bad." Zuri looked around. "At least you don't have to share, and there's probably little chance of it flooding like the linguistics PhD offices. You didn't carry all this stuff yourself, did you? I know you like proving to yourself that you're tough."

"A couple when I first moved in two weeks ago, but maintenance moved the rest." Lyn gestured to the boxes she and Zuri had set on the ground. "Thanks for helping me carry these. I wanted to transfer the more valuable manuscripts from the library myself. Heath offered to help, but I told him I could do it."

Zuri raised one beautifully shaped dark eyebrow. "Heath?"

Paska. Why had she used his name?

Zuri laughed out loud. "Did you just curse in Hungarian?"

"No, of course not." Lyn picked up a box and turned away to put it on her desk. "It was Finnish." Collecting curse words in other languages had become a sort of hobby of hers.

Zuri laughed again. "So who's Heath?"

"Nobody. A friend. Nobody. Um, he's the maintenance guy who does the cleaning and stuff. You probably haven't met him since he's new."

She was babbling.

"You're on a first-name basis with the *janitor*?"

Lyn could feel heat rising on her face. "Yeah. He's really nice." And really handsome and kind. Several times over the past two weeks, he'd taken time to help her: once when she'd gotten locked out of her office and once, gah, when she'd gotten lost in this unending maze of hallways.

"*Nice*?"

Lyn fought the urge to cover her face with her hands. "We've had coffee and donuts a couple of times before my morning theory class." A *couple of times* being at least half a dozen. "He heard me say a naughty word in Spanish that he happened to know, and I've been teaching him curse words in other languages."

And it had been the highlight of the past two weeks.

"Okay, girl." Zuri held her hands out in a show of surrender. "Nothing wrong with a little janitor crush."

"It's not like that."

Zuri's eyebrow rose again. They both knew it was *exactly* like that.

"Well, I say you should ask him out," Zuri continued. "You spend too much time in your books, and coming from an ex-fellow linguistics doctoral student, that's saying something. When was the last time you had a date?"

Lyn began placing the manuscripts from the box into their appointed spots on her shelves. "Undergrad." And even that hadn't been serious. Most college guys weren't into *plump*. And the ones who had been interested had made a rapid exit after her dad or The Brothers had made an appearance. It had kept Lyn's lovers to a grand total of three.

Her family claimed they were just *looking out* for her. They called it the military/law enforcement gene.

Lyn called it a pain in the neck.

"Undergrad is way too long ago. Tell me about this Heath."

What was she supposed to say? That compared to all the academic types and undergraduate students barely out of their teens that Heath seemed more . . . manly? That he was over six feet of muscular body that spoke of hard work rather than just time in a gym?

That the other day when he'd said hi and asked her about the class she'd just finished teaching, she'd been staring at his wrists, nice and tanned under his rolled-up sleeves, as she'd tried to put a coherent sentence together?

She'd gotten turned on by his wrists, for goodness sake. His *wrists*.

Cachu.

"Seriously, now you're cursing in Welsh? I say ask your hot janitor out." Zuri handed her another book.

"I think 'facilities maintenance technician' is the correct term."

"Fine. Ask your hot *facilities maintenance technician*

out. Unless you're too good to go out with someone with that profession."

Lyn grunted, reaching up to reorganize a manuscript on a higher shelf. A custodian might be the opposite of a career in linguistics, but so what? Lyn had an impressive list of faults: hips too wide, lips too big, head always in a book, but judging others based on their careers wasn't one of them.

Unless he was some sort of alpha-male, law-enforcement type. She'd had quite enough of those in her life.

As best she could tell, Heath was kind, reasonably intelligent based on their brief conversations, and . . . Lyn didn't like to objectify someone based on their looks, but as Zuri had picked up on, Heath was *hot*.

Chocolate-brown eyes and dark-brown hair. A face that looked like it had a perpetual five o'clock shadow. Not the kind some of the guys on campus carefully cultivated. Heath's seemed more natural, like he really did need to shave twice a day to keep his jaw smooth.

What would Zuri say if Lyn told her she'd already imagined how that scruffiness would feel against her skin?

Her friend would probably go ask Heath out for Lyn herself.

Zuri was right. It had been quite a while since Lyn had pulled herself out of her studies long enough to really be interested in a man. Years. She'd been burned more than she'd thought when the last guy had decided plus sized wasn't what he wanted.

"I don't care about his profession. I'll ask him out if the time is right. Maybe he totally goes for the awkward, scholarly type." Lyn tapped the glasses perched on her nose.

"Excuse me, we call that *sexy librarian* around here. And if he's got a good, solid job, that means your father and The Brothers can't chase him off, can they, Ms. *Norris*?"

Lyn cringed. Her parents had hyphenated their last names when they'd gotten married, Norris-Zimmerman, but The Brothers all went by Zimmerman. When Lyn had transferred to the linguistics department, she'd dropped the Zimmerman and kept the Norris. Jackie Zimmerman had been reinvented as Lyn Norris without ever having to change any official paperwork.

Maybe a little drastic, but easier to keep from her family.

She hugged Zuri. "I miss you. How dare you finish your studies, get a successful career, and leave me behind to teach undergraduate courses and finish my dissertation by myself."

"And now you're in the math and engineering division! How will you ever survive?"

"I have no idea." Lyn was only partially kidding. "But the biomedical engineering geeks have been pretty nice. I actually hung out with a group of them last week for a glass of wine at Baxter's. It was nice, even though I have no idea what they're talking about when they start discussing research."

"Don't they have anything better to talk about?"

Lyn grinned. "We discussed my research for a little bit. Then they had no idea what *I* was talking about. But at least it sounded all exotic and mysterious to them. I'm sure they'd be impressed that I can cuss in twenty different languages."

"Maybe you needed some biomed peeps to appreciate you."

Lyn shrugged. "Maybe. At least it's some new faces. New conversations."

Zuri bumped her hip against Lyn's again and slipped an arm around her shoulder. "You like having a new language to learn and study—and don't tell me you're not studying the way those biomed engineering nerds are speaking."

Lyn snickered. "Guilty as charged. A group of us is supposed to hang out again tomorrow night. Drinks and stuff. I've met a couple of grad assistants, Veronica Williams and Troy Powell, they're nice. Dale Hudson—"

"Associate professor. I've met him a couple of times. Follicly challenged and likes to hear himself talk, but otherwise not too bad."

Lyn shrugged. "There are more too. I just don't know them yet. I'll meet them tomorrow."

Zuri grinned. "Look at you. You've got new nerds wanting to hang out with you. Sounds like the sort of event you should invite a big, strong, sexy janitor to. See if he can help you figure out the engineering language. Or, if not that, maybe you two can come up with a language of your own. And by language of your own, I mean—"

Lyn slapped a hand over her friend's mouth. "I know exactly what you mean. We'll see if there's a good time for me to ask him. I might not even see Heath again before tomorrow."

But she hoped she would.

CHAPTER THREE

He was a damned janitor.

Heath really should've gotten all the details of this mission from Craig Franklin before he'd agreed to it. When the man had said he had the perfect means for sending Heath in, Heath had assumed it would be as a professor or even a nontraditional student.

Not a damned janitor.

He picked up another wastebasket and poured its contents into the larger trash can he'd been wheeling around all evening, trying not to cringe as a half-full can of soda spilled out onto the floor. Heath grabbed his mop.

But as much as he might dislike it, the role was good for undercover work. Nobody had paid him much attention for the nearly three weeks he'd been here. He had a key to almost every office and lab. People spoke around him as if he weren't there at all.

But damned if these college kids weren't the biggest jerks on the planet. And the professors? Not much better. None of them ever spoke to Heath, ever made eye contact with him, or picked up after themselves. Most of them were deliberately rude behind his back or even sometimes to his face.

Heath wasn't here to make friends; he was here to keep important information from being stolen. So he kept his head down, and when some bratty professor or kid muttered some asinine statement about him probably having a criminal record or not even speaking English, he didn't even look up.

Definitely didn't pull his gun on them like he was tempted to do and explain that he had an IQ over 140 and had spent the past decade protecting the country. Sort of.

Instead he just dumped another trash can.

Sending him in as a student wouldn't have given Heath the access to offices and labs he needed. Sending him in as a professor might have, but even Heath knew that wouldn't have worked. Academics were close-knit and would heavily scrutinize an outsider suddenly showing up and wanting information. Not to mention, they would expect him to know detailed data and particulars about biomedical engineering.

So custodian, or *facilities maintenance technician*, as the job read on paper, it was.

The job—both the undercover work and the maintenance duties—had kept him busy for three weeks. Access to the biomedical engineering and technology labs had been more widespread than either Heath or Craig had expected. Which was why the illegal sale was going on in the first place: someone had recognized there was a big gap in security and had decided to take advantage of it.

Heath's job had become twofold: figure out who was planning to sell the nanotechnology data and, in the process, shore up the security of the labs themselves.

When he wasn't emptying the trash and cleaning the

classrooms. Which, unfortunately, gave the gibberish in his head way too much time and volume—a literal constant headache. One that he ignored as much as possible.

What other choice did he have? Especially right now—there was nothing he could do about it. Kendrick Foster, Linear's part-time computer guru, was back in Oak Creek digging up what he could about Holloman's murder. Maybe it would lead somewhere. Anywhere.

But for right now, Heath was behind a janitorial cart.

When he wasn't, he was poring over the lab's logins—seeing who was coming and going when. He'd also installed tiny cameras throughout the halls of the building and in the labs themselves. Watching that footage took time.

They needed a team working on this case, and Craig was doing what he could to help, even looking through some of the footage himself. But if there really was a mole in his office, sending in someone else to help Heath could tip off the perps.

That meant for now, Heath was on his own and working twenty hours a day.

He'd been so busy, he hadn't made it over to the south side of the campus where the hospitality classes were taught to check on Gavin's sister, Jackie, like his friend had asked. But since none of the danger was anywhere near the building where little Jackie Zimmerman studied, getting eyes on her had been moved to the back burner.

It was getting late now. Evening classes were letting out. Heath decided to head up to the eighth floor, where the biomedical research labs were situated. He had to wait a long time since one of the three elevators was out of service, and none of the students or instructors would make room for him and his cart, even when there was space available.

It was like they were afraid they might catch janitor cooties if they were in an enclosed space with him for too long.

Heath promised himself he would learn the names of every custodial staff member in any building he worked in from now on. He would say hello, ask about their day. Not treat them like they were invisible.

Because they weren't undercover, so they weren't trying to be invisible.

Finally, an elevator opened—empty—and Heath was able to wheel his cart into it. Once he made it to the labs, he kept his head down and pulled out a dry mop.

This floor was where he would catch his perp. So here more than anywhere else, it was important that everyone think he was "just" a janitor.

Heath had narrowed his suspect pool down to six, but he had his money on one associate professor, Dale Hudson. The guy was in and out of the lab at weird hours. Beyond that, he seemed shifty. Heath had spent the past ten years, first for his work in Project Crypt and then in his work for Linear Tactical, dealing with people, reading them, sizing them up.

Dale Hudson had secrets. What remained to be seen was whether those secrets involved selling technology to enemies of the United States.

But he wasn't the only possible suspect. Hudson's two graduate assistants—Veronica Williams and Troy Powell—both tended to keep odd hours at the lab and had access to the data in question. The head of the department, Jane Porter, had also made an unexpected visit to the lab in the middle of the night last week.

There were another couple of people Heath was also

keeping an eye on. They hadn't been in the lab at odd hours, but maybe that was because they were smart enough to know it would draw attention.

Heath was narrowing it down, but he wasn't doing it fast enough. He was running out of time.

Between passing conversations—since he was invisible and all—and the info he'd gathered from offices as he'd cleaned them, he'd learned enough to piece together that the nanotechnology project was near completion. The data would soon be ready to transfer if it wasn't already. Whoever was making this play would make it soon.

Heath needed to figure out who that was.

But the woman standing at the end of the hallway struggling to get the key out of her office door was definitely not one of his suspects.

Lyn Norris.

Lyn was the only person he'd met so far who didn't ignore him. She never sidestepped him in the hall as if he had some sort of communicable disease. She never attempted to make jokes or comments that she thought would go over his head. She never talked down to him as if he had a learning disability.

She was *aware* of him.

At first, he'd thought she was onto him, that he'd blown his cover. She was observant and intelligent—a potentially dangerous combination.

But he'd soon realized that those big brown eyes followed him everywhere because she was aware of him as a *man*, not as an undercover agent.

Sweet almost-Dr. Norris had a crush on him.

She was so *not* his type. He preferred leggy blonds over short brunettes with ample curves and shy eyes. Not to mention the pile of books she always carried around.

But damned if he'd been able to get her out of his mind from the first moment he'd seen her.

And then he'd heard her muttering curse words in Spanish. Since it was one of the languages he spoke fluently, he'd asked her if she spoke it too. But no. Evidently, she collected curse words in other languages.

That had led to several mornings with them sharing coffee and donuts and her teaching him curse words in different languages. Many of which he already knew.

But he liked it. And soon found he would enjoy getting to know sweet Lyn better.

To explore what almost-Dr. Norris looked like without her glasses and peeled out of those button-down sweaters she liked to wear.

To kiss the mouth that stammered every time she talked to him about anything that wasn't a foreign curse word.

Watching her now as she held a full conversation with the keys stuck in the doorknob, Heath wanted to walk over to her, help her get the door open, then lift her and her luscious curves onto her desk and make out with her until neither of them could see straight.

Or hell, he would even settle for just talking to her. Taking her out to dinner.

But that wasn't going to happen. Not now, not while he was undercover. And even afterward, he couldn't either. Not while he was still trying to figure out all this Project Crypt stuff in his head—still as inescapable now as it had been the day Holloman had been killed.

As much as he might be tempted, and *damn* he was tempted, Heath would not be asking the pretty grad student out.

He had to keep his head down and focus on the job. Catch the bad guys and get out. As long as he didn't make any romantic moves toward Lyn, he was certain she would be too shy to make any toward him.

And he tried to remind himself that was a good thing.

~

L yn had cursed at her keys in every language she knew. How difficult could it be to get a key to come out of a doorknob?

Damn it, why were normal things so hard for her? And despite what she'd said to Zuri earlier, hanging out with all new people in this building was hard too. Interesting, maybe, but stressful.

And even if she saw him, there was definitely no way she was going to be asking out—

"Hey, looks like your keys are stuck. Can I help?"

—*Heath*.

That voice, smoky and deep. It had Lyn releasing her grip on the keys, smoothing her sweater over the too-generous curves of her waist, and shifting back and forth on her low heels.

"Heath. Hi! My keys are stuck!" *Scheiße*. That's exactly what he'd just said except with an appropriate amount of enthusiasm rather than that of a circus ringmaster. She took a breath. "I mean, yeah. If you could help, that would be great."

Looking into his eyes was hard, so she dropped her gaze.

And then couldn't stop staring at his wrists. They were so sexy. She just wanted to wrap her fingers around them, hold on to them—preferably while he was cupping either side of her neck to kiss her.

She popped her eyes back up to his and found him studying her with an easy smile.

Oh no, did he know she'd been fantasizing about his wrists? What she was thinking? *Mierda*.

"It's no problem. I just need you to step out of the way so I can get to the keys."

"Oh! Yeah, of course." She stepped back so he could get to the doorknob, feigning a smile that had to look ridiculous since she was gritting her teeth.

"You're just coming back from class, right? Everything go okay?" He grabbed the knob and wiggled the key. Lyn forced herself not to ogle his wrist like some arm perv.

"Oh, it was fine. Hard to interest lower classmen in elements of comparative philology, but I try."

Was she really talking about linguistic theory with Heath? He probably had no idea what comparative philology was. Most people didn't.

"I'm sure you're great at making it interesting."

Lyn was much better at researching and reading than she was teaching, but teaching some undergraduate sections of language theory was part of her doctoral program fellowship, so she did it.

She shrugged. "I'm not sure my students think so. A lot of them went to the Adil Garrison talk instead. More interested in learning get-rich-quick possibilities than in attending class."

"Yeah, Garrison was touring this floor yesterday. All the people following him around made for quite a big mess to clean up." He twisted the key one more time. "Here you go, got it open for you."

Of course he had. She'd been trying to get the door unlocked for ten minutes, but he'd done it in ten seconds.

"Thanks." She sighed as he handed back her keychain and held the door open.

This was her chance to ask him out. She needed some sort of segue to start the conversation.

Think of something interesting to say. Think of something interesting to say.

"Do you know that the Chinese language has fifty thousand characters but you only need to know about two thousand to read a newspaper?" Oh dear God. How was she possibly going to segue into asking him out from *that*?

"What?"

"Never mind."

How could she be twenty-seven years old, so familiar with the intricacies of communication and language, and still be so *bad* at talking to an attractive man?

Heath nodded and took a step back. "I guess I should get back to work."

"Right. Yeah."

"Did you see this?" Heath reached down and picked up a note that had fallen to the floor.

It was from Veronica, reminding her of tomorrow night, since Lyn had almost forgotten last time.

"Oh, this is from a friend. The biomed engineering graduate fellows invited me out for drinks tomorrow at Baxter's. She wanted to make sure I'm still going."

"Are you planning on it?" Heath looked genuinely interested.

This was her chance. If Zuri were here, she would've already been nudging Lyn closer. Lyn had been trying to get up her nerve all day.

She wondered if he would laugh at her if he knew she'd developed a script of sorts for asking him on a date. Things she could say and possible responses he might have so she would know how to reply.

She'd even looked through a few textbooks on interpersonal communication, searching for common signs of attraction in a person's nonverbal body language and codes.

Lyn may almost have a PhD in linguistics, but when it came to romance, she was pretty bad at it. Finding the right words was difficult for her. Researching how to ask Heath out had made it seem viable. All she'd needed were the right words.

Easier said than done, now that he was standing here beside her. Whatever script she'd developed had flown out of her mind. She shifted her weight back and forth again, pulling her book and computer bag closer to her chest.

Just say it.

"Yes, I'm going out with them. I was hoping maybe you might want to go with me." The words came out all in a rush.

And then silence.

Not good silence. Awkward silence.

You didn't have to be a linguistics or interpersonal communication expert to realize that. Any given five-year-old could.

"Lyn . . ."

He was going to say no. She could tell by the grimace that crossed his face before he carefully schooled it back into a neutral mask. "*Ttong.*"

He tilted his head to the side. "Korean?"

She didn't care how he knew she'd said "shit" in Korean. She just wanted to melt into a puddle on the floor.

What had she been thinking? Heath wasn't interested in going out with someone like her. Just because they'd joked about cuss words in different languages and had coffee and donuts—and he'd probably thought she should skip the donuts—didn't mean he wanted to *date* her.

He probably thought she was a plump bookworm who

didn't do much besides academic work and had very little experience when it came to men. He'd be right.

She should stick to her ancient languages. They weren't ever going to hurt her.

CHAPTER FOUR

He could've told her a half dozen even more foul words in Korean, one of the languages he spoke fluently. And he was ready to use them all right now.

He couldn't say yes. There was nothing he'd like more than to go out with Lyn Norris. But doing so now, under these circumstances, when he was pretending to be someone he wasn't and investigating the people around her? He couldn't do it.

But damned if he knew how to get out of this situation without it detonating.

"Lyn . . ." he repeated. He reached a hand toward her.

"No." She took a step. "Don't worry about it. You're not interested. I understand. Have a good night."

She left a wide gap as she moved past him down the hallway. She didn't even close her office door.

Just let her go, Kavanaugh.

It was better this way. For everyone. He wouldn't be here much longer anyway. He had a job to do that took precedence over everything else.

But that look on Lyn's face. That stiff upper lip hiding a world of hurt. And she'd left her office door open.

He hadn't known her long, but he knew how shy she was. He'd observed her with other people, and she was always quiet. Kind, but quiet.

Heath couldn't imagine what it had cost her to ask him out. He should've told her he needed to work. That would've solved the whole problem, rather than making her think he was personally rejecting her. For once his head was throbbing and it had nothing to do with the gibberish.

Just his own idiocy.

He turned, but she'd already rounded the corner in this maze of a hallway.

He couldn't let her leave like this. Couldn't stand the look in her eye. He pulled her office door closed, flicking the lock on the inner knob as he did.

"Lyn," he called out, rushing after her with his cart. He turned the corner.

"Lyn, hang on." She didn't even slow down, so he left his cart and began jogging down the hall after her. She got to the elevators and pressed the button without even looking at him.

And, of course, the damn thing had no delay for her. The same elevator that had been out of service fifteen minutes ago was now fixed.

"Lyn—"

She stepped in, then turned and pressed a button, still not looking at him. He picked up speed and leapt through the doors without touching them as they closed. He reached over and pulled the emergency stop button, ignoring the buzzing it made.

Now she looked at him. Probably because she thought he was crazy, chasing her down the hallway right after refusing to go out with her. They both started talking at the same time.

"Look, I just want to say—"

"Heath, it's okay. You don't—"

They both stopped. Lyn gestured with her hand for him to continue.

"I just wanted to say, I didn't say no because I wasn't interested. I can't go out with you tomorrow night because I have to work."

The pained look on her face eased. Heath felt like he could breathe again. "Oh. I guess I didn't even think of that. Maybe we could do it some other time. This weekend or something."

See, dumbass? This is why you should've left it alone. Now what are you going to do?

Heath knew one thing for certain: he didn't want to put that hurt look back on her sweet face.

"Um, yeah. I just need to check on some things. Let me get back to you."

It wasn't exactly a lie. But it was definitely misleading.

Lyn nodded, obviously skeptical but at least not hurt. "Okay, that sounds good. I guess we can talk about it some other time."

He wanted to reassure her that he'd love for them to go out. Hell, he'd like to back her against the elevator wall and kiss that plump bottom lip until she was absolutely sure he wanted to go out with her.

But since he *couldn't* actually go out with her, he should probably *not* do that.

"Did you need anything from your office?" He hit the button to open the door.

The elevator lurched a few feet before stopping, then

everything went dark. Lyn screamed, and he bit back a curse.

"Heath?" Her breath sawed in and out.

He reached over and found her, wrapped an arm around her shoulders, and drew her next to him. "Some sort of equipment malfunction. It's okay, the emergency generator should kick on in a second."

But it didn't. And that was really weird. If the elevator was out of service—which it had been when he'd tried to take it up here not even twenty minutes ago—then the door shouldn't have opened at all. And since the door had opened, then obviously the elevator had power.

Heath may not be a real custodian, but he knew this wasn't right.

He pulled out his phone to use as a flashlight, shining it in Lyn's direction first. She was still breathing heavily and now patting the front of her pants at the hips.

"You okay?" he asked.

"I . . . I have some pills. Beta blockers. I should probably take one, but they're not with me."

Beta blockers. Was that like Xanax or something? He hadn't pegged Lyn as dealing with anxiety, but that wasn't always readily noticeable.

And hell, anxiety while being trapped in a lurching, dark elevator was completely understandable.

She took her pulse. He moved his fingers over hers on her neck. He definitely didn't need her passing out.

"Hey, it's going to be all right. Breathe with me." He wrapped his fingers around hers at her neck so she couldn't feel her own heartbeat. Knowing her heart was beating too fast wouldn't help her calm down. "In. Out."

After a few moments, she started breathing at his pace,

more calm and even, getting her anxiety under control. "Good girl."

She nodded. "Did power go out in the whole building maybe?"

He shrugged. "Even if it did, the backup generator should be on in here. Let me use the emergency phone."

He opened the small door that held a phone with a direct line to campus security or emergency services if the line was commandeered. But when he picked up the phone, it was dead too.

Okay, that *really* wasn't right. The elevator shifted again, dropping a few more inches, the terrifying lurch causing Lyn to gasp.

He turned the light off on his phone and turned it around to make a call. He needed to get help here right now.

"Elevator phone isn't working, so I'll use my cell to call security and get a maintenance team over here."

"Yeah, that's a good idea," Lyn whispered. She stood right next to him. Heath didn't blame her. The elevator's eerie silence—coupled with the very real possibility they could be taking their final breaths—filled the air between them with tension.

He found the number for campus security, then hit send. The call immediately died, so he tried again. Same thing.

"What's wrong?"

Heath shook his head. "I don't know. My phone seems to have a signal, but the call drops every time."

"Want me to try mine?"

"Yeah." He read her the number, and she punched it in, but the same thing happened.

"Okay, I guess we'll try 911." An emergency call would bounce off any cell phone tower regardless of their carriers.

But the call dropped again.

Heath tried one more time to be sure, but he already knew what was going on. The power, backup power, emergency phone, and cell phones all not working or being blocked.

Someone was deliberately sabotaging this elevator.

Had the perp figured out he was investigating them? Had he blown his cover, and they were trying to take him out?

That seemed extreme. Not to mention, killing undercover law enforcement near where you were already committing a crime would bring *more* law enforcement, not less. Not a good plan.

Good plan or not, he needed to get them out of here.

The elevator shimmied again, and Lyn gave another little screech, but at least she didn't start hyperventilating again.

"You claustrophobic?"

"I wasn't until I got in this elevator." She was keeping it together. "Did you ever see *Mission: Impossible*? All of them were my brothers' favorites when I was growing up. I've been forced to watch that elevator crash scene in the first film a hundred times."

"That's not going to happen. There are security measures that will keep us from crashing."

The elevator lurched again, and Lyn jumped closer, clutching his arm. "Security measures like the backup generator and the emergency telephone?"

He slipped his arm around her shoulders again. "Well, that elevator crashed into the ceiling, not the ground. Wrong direction. We'll be fine, Dr. Almost."

She smiled, albeit tightly, at the title. She refused to be called doctor until her dissertation was finished and defended. Which was never going to happen if they didn't get out of here right now.

"What do we do?" she whispered.

"Do you have anything in your bag that's thin enough to fit between these doors? If I can get something wedged in there to get it started, I should be able to pry them open."

He shined his light into her bag as she searched through it. "You need something strong, right? I have pens, notebooks, a clipboard . . ."

"Let's try the clipboard." It wasn't perfect, but it might be strong enough.

The elevator trembled again when Heath took a step toward the door, pulling Lyn with him. He slid the hard-plastic clipboard into the crack and twisted it slowly, not wanting to break it.

"Let me twist it so you can grab the doors once they open," Lyn murmured. She shifted her weight slowly—neither of them wanted to experience the sickening jolt of the elevator falling again—and moved so she stood in front of him.

Heath had to push his body all the way against Lyn's with his arms around her in order to get the leverage that he needed. She repositioned herself, bringing her luscious curves more in contact with him, to turn the clipboard.

Was he really getting turned on when they both might plummet to their deaths any moment? *Get a grip, Kavanaugh.*

"Turn on three, okay?" He placed his fingers at the edge of the door.

"Will it crush your fingers?"

"No. Once I can get them in there, there shouldn't be any pressure pushing the doors back together."

He hoped.

"One, two, three."

Lyn turned the clipboard as hard as she could, twisting both the top and bottom edges. It was enough. The doors slid open a crack, and Heath was able to get his fingers in.

"Got it," he told her through gritted teeth, using all of his forearm strength to pry the doors apart. Good thing his arms had been getting a pretty sizable workout over the past few weeks with his custodial duties.

Instead of escaping under his arm like he expected, Lyn slipped her fingers into the crack also and added her strength, as limited as it was, to his efforts. The door cracked a few more inches.

"Okay, good," he told her. "Let me get in here and use other muscle groups."

Now Lyn slipped out under his arm, and he wedged his shoulder between the doors. Putting his back and legs into it, he was able to get the door open another foot. Enough for them to fit through.

The elevator had dropped far enough that the floor of the level where they'd entered was now up to his chest.

"Hand me the clipboard."

She did so quickly, gasping as the elevator groaned again. Heath placed the clipboard in the crack of the outer door attached to the building, not the elevator. Thankfully, this door opened without as much effort.

The easiest way to get them both out would be to climb up himself and then hoist Lyn. He didn't waste any time. Without jumping—the sudden movement could send the elevator into freefall , which at best would trap them, at worst would crush him—Heath used his upper-body strength to pull himself up and onto the floor outside the elevator.

Immediately, he turned and stuck his arms back down to Lyn.

"Give me your hands," he said.

She hesitated. "I'm too heavy for you to pull up."

Heath rolled his eyes. "Honey, trust me, I could bench-press those perfect curves of yours a dozen times over without breaking a sweat. But now might not be the time to show you, okay?"

She needed to get out of that elevator. Now.

He felt her small hands grip his arms, not like they were shaking hands, but grasping his wrist; he grasped hers. A much more secure grip. Smart.

"Good girl."

True to his word, he hoisted her easily out of the elevator. He slid back along the ground as she came up so that they both ended up on the hallway floor in a tangle of limbs, Lyn half on top of him.

Both of them just lay there for a few moments, breathing hard. Heath was well aware of every place Lyn's body touched his, from chest to thigh.

And he wasn't making any attempt to scoot her away.

"You okay?" he asked, hoping she'd think the huskiness in his voice was a result of the danger.

Not that he was about to thread his fingers into her dark hair and pull her lips down to his.

She nodded. "Yeah, I think so. Thank goodness you were here. If I had been in that elevator alone . . ."

He wrapped an arm around her waist and pulled her closer. Neither of them wanted to finish that sentence. He couldn't stop his fingers from trailing up and down her back.

The elevator hadn't gone crashing down to the ground yet, but it still could at any second.

"We should probably go report this to security—"

Heath's comment was interrupted when a number of the biomedical engineering faculty, some of the same people Heath was investigating, stepped out of another elevator.

All their chatter stopped when they saw Heath and Lyn jumbled on the floor, sprawled in front of the elevator.

"Lyn, what in holy hell is going on?" A female voice, Veronica Williams, said. "Somebody call security. The janitor has attacked Lyn."

CHAPTER FIVE

"Oh my gosh, so you both almost died in the elevator?"

Lyn was surrounded by most of the biomedical engineering group at Baxter's Bar & Restaurant the next evening, telling the story again. Everyone seemed fascinated, although Lyn tried to downplay the whole thing as much as she could.

Lyn had never liked to be the center of attention. She'd never been able to make her father understand that.

It didn't take her audience long to disperse once it became obvious she wasn't going to give them a lot of juicy details—not that there were that many. Everyone moved on to other, more interesting things. Lyn may love languages, but that didn't mean she was good at telling stories.

Especially ones that started with the janitor rejecting her for a date and ended with her lying fully on top of him, surrounded by a half dozen of her colleagues.

Troy and Veronica flanked her on either side as the others moved away. They still wanted to talk about what had happened.

Veronica popped an olive from her drink into her mouth. "All I'm saying is that the janitor guy—"

"His name is Heath."

"Whatever. Janitor guy was holding you pretty protectively there on the ground," Veronica finished.

Lyn could feel herself blushing. She wished she were talking to Zuri about this rather than Veronica. She'd still be blushing, but at least she was comfortable with Zuri. She didn't know Veronica at all. "It's not like that. He's not interested in me."

The other woman rolled her eyes. "How do you know? You're pretty, in an academic sort of way."

Veronica was pretty in a no-matter-what-job-you-have way. Tall, slender, blond. Basically, everything Lyn wasn't.

Lyn had made peace with her figure a long time ago. Her dress size was never going to be in the single digits. It wasn't that she was fat so much that she obviously didn't starve herself.

Troy seemed focused on something else and not even involved in their conversation, thank goodness. Lyn's flush grew deeper. "I sort of asked him out. To come here, tonight."

That got Troy's attention. "You did?"

"Look, I don't want to talk about it." Lyn wanted to talk about this even less than she wanted to talk about the elevator incident.

When Veronica looked like she wasn't going to let it go, Lyn jumped out of her seat. "Excuse me, I need to go to the restroom."

Before either could answer, she fled upstairs to the bathroom and splashed some water on her face. She needed a few minutes to pull herself together. Peopling was so *hard*.

She was tempted to hide in a stall but forced herself to

come out. Rather than go back downstairs, she headed to the outdoor seating on the balcony, letting out a sigh as the cool summer evening hit her cheeks.

She looked out over the Grand Tetons, letting some of the tension roll off her. She'd miss WCU and the rugged beauty of Wyoming in general when she left. This would always be home, but her future jobs wouldn't be here if everything went the way she was hoping. The Center for Ancient Languages had already contacted her about doing research in Egypt once her dissertation was finished.

They wanted to *hire her*, already recognizing that her findings concerning the Sahidic and Bohairic dialects and their application to modern society had real benefits. It was a huge honor and so freaking exciting.

She hadn't told anyone about it. Not Zuri, and especially not Dad or The Brothers. Even if her family did accept that she'd changed her entire course of study without telling them, they were never going to accept a career opportunity that required she work deep in Africa, often far from cities.

And hospitals.

She'd have to deal with that—and her family's complete freak-out—when she got to it. The situation at hand was enough to deal with right now.

Leaning back on the railing, she glanced inside the bar. Troy and Veronica seemed to be arguing—or at least discussing something pretty intense. Dale Hudson, in all his follicly challenged glory, had also joined their debate.

Normally, she'd be interested in the nuances of their heated discussion—to see if the words they chose were different when they were challenging each other. After all, they were, in essence, speaking their own language. Would engineering and math terms automatically fall into their debate? Would they be more rational and reasonable because they dealt with hard data every day?

But she turned away to look out at the Grand Tetons again. She'd had enough excitement for the week already. She wasn't interested in joining the engineering drama club, even if it might give her some linguistic insights.

She shouldn't have come here. She thought she fit in with these people, but she really didn't. She would rather be alone than making awkward small talk—it wasn't worth the effort.

Unless maybe it was Heath. He never made her feel awkward, and talking to him always seemed worth the effort.

But the truth was the truth. She didn't kid herself into thinking he was going to track her down so they could schedule a date. She'd seen his face when she'd asked him out: something akin to panic.

Not the expression she'd been hoping for.

Then the whole elevator incident couldn't have possibly helped the situation. She hadn't panicked—although she'd been pretty *sakra* close given that she'd been sure they were going to plunge to their death any second.

Then he'd had to lift her out of that elevator.

Spanx were a girl's best friend, but they just kept everything from bulging out. They didn't actually make her weigh any less.

I could bench-press those perfect curves of yours a dozen times over without breaking a sweat.

They might never go out, but those words in Heath's deep, husky voice were going to play front and center in her fantasies for a long time.

And then he really had lifted her without any difficulty and before she'd even had a chance to be embarrassed.

"Hey Lyn, you doing okay out here?" Troy's voice pulled Lyn out of her fantasy.

"Um yeah." Lyn nodded. He was too close to her, but there wasn't much room to move with the other people along the railing. "I'm fine. Just enjoying the view."

He scooted even closer, their shoulders now touching. "Yeah, for a bunch of science geeks, everybody in the biomed department sure can talk a lot. I just wanted to say I'm glad you're okay after what happened in the elevator. That had to have been scary."

Was that his hand running up the back of her sweater? She tried to step away, but he kept her pinned with his arm.

"Troy—" She didn't want to make a scene, but she wasn't interested in him in this sort of way.

"I know you're embarrassed about asking out the janitor and him turning you down." His tone lowered and took on a ring of false intimacy as he leaned down to whisper in her ear. "But believe me, I can provide whatever you need if you've got some *frustrations* you want to get out."

"What? I'm not mad."

"I'm not talking about that sort of frustration. Obviously, you have needs if you're asking the janitor out." His hand on her back dropped to her hip. "You and I could work something out. No need to go slumming."

Lyn was insulted on so many levels, she didn't know which to address first. And Troy's hand was still trying to turn her toward him as he leaned closer.

He actually thought she wanted to kiss him. Unbelievable.

She used the momentum he was providing with his hand to curve around toward him, but then ducked under his arm. He obviously wasn't expecting that and stumbled before shooting her an annoyed look.

"No need to play hard to get, Lyn. You're obviously looking for some company if you're propositioning the janitor."

Heath may not have the advanced degrees Troy had, but Lyn would vouch for his character over Troy's. She would wager Heath had never coerced a woman or taken advantage of her delicate state because of a life-threatening event.

"Look. I'm not interested." Her words were too gentle, her voice too soft. Lyn rolled her eyes at her own inability to say the much harsher things she wanted to. Things about equality and not judging a book by its cover. But she didn't. She was terrible at confrontation.

Troy said something, trying to get her to turn her attention back toward the mountains, but a large, completely bald man wearing a suit—not balding like Dale Hudson, but totally bald—stood just inside the door, watching her. As soon as she met his eyes, he looked away and took a sip of his drink.

Okay. Creepy.

"Lyn . . ." Troy took a step toward the bar inside, then immediately stepped in front of her and spun around, blocking the guy from her view.

Troy kissed her before she could figure out what was going on, his arms coming around her like tentacles, moving up and around her back and shoulders, nearly knocking her purse to the ground.

Creepy was everywhere tonight.

She was too shocked to do anything at first, but then she pushed against him, hard, prepping to use any number of the self-defense moves her brothers had taught her over the years. She may not like confrontations, but that didn't mean she was going to let someone grope her.

She was moving into a fighting stance when Troy took the hint and backed off.

"Not feeling it this evening? No problem, another night then." He had the nerve to wink at her. "Don't make me wait too long."

He turned and walked back into the bar.

Lyn resisted the urge to wipe her hand across her mouth. Barely. But at least when she looked back up, Troy was gone. And the scary bald guy was nowhere to be found. Maybe the creeps had decided to hang out together.

That was it, she was going home. She'd had enough excitement in the previous twenty-four hours to last her the rest of the year. She straightened herself from the railing and walked inside, hoping she wouldn't find Troy wanting an encore.

Because there definitely would not be one. Regardless of whether Heath wanted to go out with her or not, Lyn was *not* interested in Troy. She had hoped to be friends with him, but now she wasn't even sure she could be that.

Damn it, now things would be awkward around the offices. She couldn't believe how differently he'd behaved tonight than last week. He'd acted so friendly and normal before.

Maybe she could sneak out of the restaurant without saying goodbye even though it'd get her an earful from Veronica. She'd pull the shy-linguistics-instructor card. Scurrying off without saying goodbye was considered a quirky part of her nature.

But Veronica caught her and dragged her over to a table.

"Hey, are you okay?" she said. "You were outside for a long time."

Lyn shrugged. Add what had just happened to the list of things she didn't want to talk about. "When I came back from the bathroom, it looked like you and Troy and Professor Hudson were in a pretty intense conversation, and I didn't want to interrupt. Then Troy came outside and we were . . . talking."

Veronica sighed. "Yeah, there's some crazy mess going on in the lab. Missing elements and mislabeled data. So frustrating. But I don't want to talk about that. Let's have another drink and just talk about girl stuff."

Girl talk. An even worse version of small talk. Lyn had to get out of here. "Actually, I'm pretty tired. I'm going to take a rain check."

"Oh. My. Gosh." Veronica was looking at something over Lyn's shoulder, her jaw nearly hit the floor.

"What?"

Veronica just pointed, mouth still agape. Lyn turned and saw Heath walking through the door.

Now someone might have to scoop *her* jaw off the floor.

He wasn't wearing his green work coveralls and cap like he'd been every other time she'd seen him. Now he was wearing a black T-shirt—one that fit snug enough to show off the excellent physique underneath—tucked into black jeans. He walked over to the bar, where the female bartender fell all over herself to get the bottle of beer he ordered. He paid, then began walking in Lyn and Veronica's direction.

"How in the world did I miss *that*?" Veronica murmured.

Looking at Heath now, who was infinitely more attractive out of his plain work uniform, Lyn was amazed he hadn't laughed at her outright when she'd asked him for a date yesterday. The man walking toward them was quite at ease with himself and this sort of social situation, drawing the attention of several females in the room—including Veronica. He was *way* out of Lyn's league.

But he was still heading directly toward them.

"Ladies," Heath murmured, his deep voice making her want to take a step closer. He was looking at Lyn even though Veronica—with her blond hair and long legs—was definitely the more attractive of the two women. He had to see that.

"Heath, is it?" Veronica asked. "I'm Veronica Williams. I work in the biomedical engineering department."

Heath stopped looking at Lyn and held out his hand to Veronica. "Heath Smith."

Smith. Until now, Lyn hadn't known what his last name was. She didn't want to ask and seem like she was prying. Smith. Even with it being so common, she never would've imagined that was his name.

"I thought you had to work." The words burst out of her before she could control them.

He turned to her again. "I decided I would come in early tomorrow and worry about it. I'd rather be out here with you tonight."

"Actually, I was just leav—"

"She was just about to get another drink for us both," Veronica interrupted. "You two sit down. I'll get us another round, Lyn."

"Thanks," Heath said, then touched the small of Lyn's back and led her to a group of low love seats by the window near where Professor Hudson and some of the other biomed faculty and staff were sitting.

Heath's touch seared her skin through her thin sweater. Unlike Troy's deliberately intimate touch, which had only made her want to move away, Heath's almost absent gesture made her want to move closer.

She introduced him to the faculty members and lab assistants as her friend. Obviously, none of them placed him as the same man who swept the floors and emptied the trash in their building, so Lyn didn't mention it. Neither did Veronica when she returned with their drinks.

Lyn sat next to Heath in one of the love seats and watched as he talked easily with the people around him. Even when they talked about work-related stuff, he listened and nodded. Everyone seemed to like him. When they asked what he did, he said something about being a maintenance technician. Nobody questioned what that meant.

They did obviously question what he was doing here with someone like Lyn. She could see it in their eyes, could tell in the way that some of the women tried to shift his focus to them. But she had to admit, Heath never left her side, drawing her into the conversation as much as possible, but still, no one quite knew why he was there with her.

Lyn didn't really know either.

She reached for her antiarrhythmic medicine. She had a feeling this night was going to be tough on her heart in more ways than one.

CHAPTER SIX

Heath couldn't seem to stop touching Lyn even though he knew it made him a bastard. He was using her. Was at this bar because he needed info as quickly as possible.

He'd spent most of the day looking into the elevator incident. They'd kept it roped off all night, and Craig had arrived first thing this morning to go over the scene with Heath.

They'd brought in Charlie Hill, head of the maintenance department, who Craig had thoroughly vetted himself. Charlie was one of the few people at WCU who knew Heath was working there as more than just a janitor.

The three of them had gone up into the elevator shaft to look around.

"Definitely not an accident," Charlie had said in his gruff, Southern accent. "No way power would've blown from both the primary and secondary source at the same time."

Heath nodded. "That's what I figured too."

"Plus, the emergency phone line being damaged? Not

sure when that happened, but it had to have been since inspection three months ago." Charlie had already shown them where the elevator phone's cord had been cut through.

Heath grimaced. "Plus, the cell phone blocker."

"Yep." Charlie nodded. "It was definitely specific to this elevator. Believe you me, everyone freaks out around here if cell coverage goes out. We'd have heard about it."

Craig turned from the elevator wiring he'd been studying. "So, it was definitely sabotage."

Charlie shrugged. "Looks that way."

Heath walked over to study the cables himself. "Do you think it would've fallen to the ground? Killed us?" He glanced at Craig. "Maybe somebody found out what I was doing and was trying to get rid of me."

Charlie walked across the top of the elevator and pointed at some of the elevator's mechanics. "Could be, but the backup brakes weren't blown. If someone had been trying to kill you, those would've been tampered with too. Not to mention, it would've all happened pretty quickly. Blocking a cell phone wouldn't have been necessary."

Craig nodded. "Plus, how would they have known you'd be in this particular elevator?"

Heath studied the backup brakes. Charlie was right, there was no sign of tampering. "Yeah. Honestly, I wouldn't have been in it at all if I hadn't gotten in to talk to Lyn Norris."

If he hadn't run after her, she would've been trapped in there alone. Heath ground his teeth. Even if the intent hadn't been to kill someone, she would've been scared to death.

Although, she'd kept it together like a champ last night, stepping in front of him to try to help pry open the door even though it might crush her fingers. He really shouldn't still be able to feel her curves against him, but hell if they weren't far from his mind.

Charlie stepped back from the emergency brake system. "In my personal opinion, which, granted, doesn't count for much in this situation, I'd have to guess that the purpose here was to trap and scare someone. Most people wouldn't have been able to do what you did, Heath. They would've been stuck here for hours, wondering if their next move might send the box straight down."

Craig glanced over at him. "Hell, this might not have anything to do with the case at all."

But they both knew this was too big of a coincidence not to be connected somehow.

They all got out of the elevator shaft, and he and Craig left Charlie so the man could call the repair technicians. The elevator would have to be inspected again before it could be used. Campus security—and Heath—would be keeping a much better eye out for anyone spending unnecessary time near the elevators.

He'd walked with Craig back out to his car. "This Lyn Norris who was in the elevator with you—could this sabotage have been meant for her? Is she one of your suspects?"

"No. Definitely a case of wrong place, wrong time. She's not part of the biomed engineering faculty and doesn't even have access to the labs. She's a linguistics doctoral student."

"Languages. Right up your alley. Want me to run her background?"

"No, let's concentrate on the real suspects. I don't know what this elevator incident means exactly, but things are escalating."

Craig nodded. "It's not only the sellers we need. It's the buyers. We want to let this go all the way to the sale so we can catch the buyers too."

"Yeah. But first, I've got to figure out who we're dealing with on this end. If that elevator mishap wasn't meant for me, who was it meant for?"

Heath had thought about that all afternoon after Craig had left. Maybe there was more than one bad guy. Or maybe the perp was having second thoughts about selling the nanotechnology, and the elevator situation had been the buyer's way of nudging him or her back on track.

Nothing helped focus people like being trapped inside a steel box that might crash to a terrifying death at any moment.

Whatever it meant, something was happening *soon*. He needed more information about his biomed suspects fast.

And he happened to know exactly where they'd be.

So here he was, *gathering intel*. He was treating this like a real date to keep the conversation flowing naturally, since no one except Veronica had recognized him from WCU.

And soft, sweet Lyn just looked bewildered.

Not that treating this like a date was any hardship. Even knowing he shouldn't, he couldn't seem to keep his hands off Lyn's lush body. He made sure their arms and legs were touching on the couch. He leaned into her whenever she said something, which wasn't often but was usually dryly funny or insightful.

But he was also keeping a strict eye on what was happening around them.

There was definitely tension between Veronica and Dale Hudson, number one on Heath's suspect list. Both of them had the means to steal the microchip. So did Troy Powell, who he hadn't seen.

"Is Troy Powell around tonight?" he whispered to Lyn.

Her face flushed. "He was here earlier but left. He was acting weird."

"What do you mean?" *Suspicious?*

Lyn shook her head and shrugged. "He and Veronica and Dale were arguing or something. I don't know what about. Then he left."

Heath's eyes narrowed. There was more to the story than what she was telling him, but he wouldn't push. At least not right now.

Lyn seemed uncomfortable with almost everything. Was it because she could tell his attention was divided? It was a fine line he was walking: using her as a guise for gathering information while not leading her on.

While at the same time *very much* wanting to lead her on. All the way back to her place, where they could spend the entire night forgetting about janitors and nanotechnology and investigations.

But that wasn't in the cards.

Gathering intel in this sort of social setting was Heath's forte. He knew people. Knew how to talk to them and, more importantly, how to listen to them. He knew how to read lips as well as body language, and his mind was filtering multiple conversations around them.

He'd used innocent people before to get what he needed. But doing it with Lyn left a bad taste in his mouth. He had to force himself to ignore it. Even as he couldn't seem to force himself to stop touching her.

But as the evening drew to a close and everyone got up to leave, Heath knew he was going to have to let her go. He wanted to follow Professor Hudson—see if he really went home or if he was meeting up with the conspicuously missing Troy. Was Troy at the lab right now? The video footage would show that. And Heath had put a tracker on Veronica's car. He'd be able to follow that once he got to his laptop.

Damn it, once again, he needed a team. His attention was split in too many directions—he was bound to miss something.

He scrubbed a hand across his face, tamping down the murmurings growing louder in his head. He didn't have time for them now.

"Are you okay?" Lyn asked softly.

She was worried about *him*. Of course she was. Because she was way too gentle and kind for the world he operated in.

He forced a smile. "Yeah. I'm fine."

"Then I guess I'll see you around campus." She barely looked up from her shoes as they walked out the door.

Everyone else was certainly looking at them, some discreetly, others less so. Like the tall brunette—Heath thought she was from the math department—who had been trying to get his attention all evening. She had pressed a note into his hand as he'd walked by a few moments ago.

Call me later if you decide mousy bookworms aren't your type.

It was already crumpled and bound for the trash.

Lyn might be quiet and a little bookish, but Heath didn't need an advanced degree to figure out she was beautiful in all the ways that mattered, inside *and* out. Reserved, maybe, but beautiful. And there wasn't a damn thing wrong with her soft curves.

She was still studying her shoes, obviously aware that they were the center of attention. "I'm glad you came out with us tonight. I hope you had fun."

He wanted to protect her from her colleague's prying eyes. Wanted to sweep her up in an embrace that would put to rest all doubt that he was legitimately here with her. A kiss that would burn that crumpled note in his pocket to ash.

Screw it.

He pulled Lyn against him, tilted her chin back by threading his fingers through her hair, and kissed her as if he wanted her more than his next breath.

Which was pretty much true.

She was surprised but didn't pull away. After a moment, her soft lips parted under his, and she gave herself over to the kiss, wrapping her arms around his waist.

Mousy bookworm his ass.

His thumb brushed along the silky softness of her jaw, and he wanted to devour her, nosy colleagues be damned. His tongue traced her bottom lip, then slipped inside.

After a few heated moments he forced himself to pull away, the action much harder than he'd expected. But he had to. Not only did they have an audience, but he was undercover.

Undercover, Kavanaugh, remember that.

He put his forehead against hers. "Okay, we're obviously going to need to talk, but not here. And as much as I want to, I can't do it right now."

"O-Okay." Her bottomless brown eyes shone in the streetlamp's soft glow.

"I'll see you tomorrow on campus, okay? Are you safe getting home?"

She nodded. "Yes, I only live a couple of blocks from here." She mumbled an address.

Heath didn't want to let her go alone. He didn't like the thought of her walking by herself even that short distance.

"Where's your phone?" he asked.

She dug it out of her bag and handed it to him. He programmed his number into it. "Text me as soon as you get home so I know you're okay. If I don't hear from you in fifteen minutes, I'm coming to search."

"Do you have to go back to work?"

Heath looked over at Veronica and Professor Hudson, who—now that the show was over—were saying their goodbyes.

"Yeah, I've got to get back to work." He knew she meant his custodial duties back on campus, but he didn't correct her.

"Thanks for coming tonight. I know you said you couldn't, so I really appreciate that you did." With that she turned away and walked down the street.

Heath was torn. He wanted to go with her, *stay* with her, bask in the blistering heat that kiss had started. But he couldn't. Even if this entire situation had left her bewildered. *Especially* because of that.

He made his way to the parking garage along with some of the others, now focused on the job. It was getting late, after eleven. Maybe Hudson was the perp and would make a move tonight.

Now Heath had more than one incentive to finish his undercover work.

Hudson had worked as a professor at the university for more than a dozen years, first as an assistant professor, then as an associate after a few years. But even with tenure, maybe he felt like he wasn't being adequately compensated for his work and had decided to make extra cash by selling parts of the technology the government had commissioned him to design.

Tailing anybody from the department would be trickier now. He'd done it before but had been sure they wouldn't recognize him. He no longer had those assurances since he'd spent time socializing with them.

He waved as he drove by Veronica and Hudson in the garage and they waved back. He watched in the rearview mirror as he made his way toward the exit.

And wasn't that interesting? Hudson pulled Veronica toward him in an embrace before they both got into his car together. They were having an affair.

That could explain some of their odd behavior—calls that were suddenly disconnected when Heath had walked by in the hallway, suspicious looks over their shoulders. They were trying to hide a relationship that the university would frown upon.

Were they trying to hide more?

Heath pulled out of the parking garage, stopped his car on a curve half a block away, and turned out the lights. He knew where both Hudson and Veronica lived. He would bet they were going to Hudson's house. It was much nicer.

He hoped they would meet someone or that someone would join them there. Anything that might clue Heath in that they were the ones trying to sell the nanotechnology.

But nothing. He followed them to Hudson's house and sat in his car the rest of the night, watching the house for anyone else. Nobody came, nobody left. The highlight of the night was Lyn's text letting him know she'd made it home safely.

Another day finished, and Heath had nothing to show for it but gritty eyes.

The sun was coming up when his phone buzzed on the seat beside him.

"Yeah, this is Heath." Only Craig or someone from Linear would be calling on this phone.

"Hey sunshine, hope I didn't wake you. It's Gavin."

"Nah, sweetheart, I'm already awake. Wishing I was in bed, but I'm camped out in front of a suspect's house."

"Anything interesting happening there?" Gavin asked.

"If you consider the fact that my professor suspect brought his pretty young graduate assistant home with him and she hasn't left all night interesting, then yeah."

"Aw, jealous that you don't have a graduate assistant of your own, Shadow?"

Lyn's soft smile came to mind, her lips parting under his. He had to shift in the seat to get comfortable. "No, Hudson can have this one. I've always been more into languages than engineering."

"You holding up okay?"

He couldn't hold back a yawn. It was going to be a long day after this all-nighter. "I'll be honest. This is more than a one-person job."

"Craig and I were talking a few minutes ago. He filled me in on the elevator situation. He says you need help but still isn't sure who to trust from his office. I thought I might call my cousin Noah and see if he could spare a few days away from the ranch to help you."

Heath had only met Noah a couple times but knew he'd been in the Special Forces with some of the Linear guys. And honestly, at this point, Heath would take anyone who was trustworthy and had a pulse. "I could definitely use the help."

"Okay, consider it done. He'll have to be careful not to run into Jackie, but—"

Heath scrubbed a hand across his face. "Crap, Gav. I know you asked me to check on her, but I haven't had a chance."

"Don't worry. I talked to her yesterday. All is well in the world of hospitality academics. Like Craig said, her building is on the opposite side of campus. And you've got your hands full."

"I'll be glad to have Noah here."

"Craig also wanted me to pass along some info about a graduate assistant you're looking into. A Troy Powell."

That woke Heath up. "Yeah? What about him?"

"Powell's name came across Craig's desk from a hospital report. He was beaten pretty severely sometime in the past few hours and is in a coma."

Different ramifications floated around in Heath's mind. "That's pretty damn interesting given what happened with the elevator yesterday. Maybe that malfunction was meant for Powell. Things are definitely escalating."

Gavin whistled through his teeth. "Something's going down, that's for sure. I'll get Noah to you immediately. You might need more help than just him."

"Maybe. I'll keep you posted if anything changes."

"Heath," Gavin said. "Be careful. It's getting crazy around there. It can turn ugly quick."

Heath thought of his scorching kiss with Lyn.

Yeah, things were definitely getting crazy.

CHAPTER SEVEN

The next morning, Lyn was still trying to process everything that had happened the night before.

She'd been kissed.

By two different men.

In the same evening.

That had never happened in her entire life.

Although she'd wanted it, she hadn't been expecting Heath's kiss any more than she had expected Troy's. Heath had seemed to be having a fine time with her university colleagues. And they'd certainly been having a fine time with him—especially the women.

But . . . somehow it had all felt so clinical. Like the whole situation was some sort of science experiment to Heath.

But who was she to talk? She regularly drifted out of social exchanges in order to study the linguistic patterns.

And maybe Heath had just been nervous. Although, goodness , he hadn't seemed so. He'd talked so easily with everyone. More like a CEO than a janitor. Someone totally comfortable interacting with people. He'd been attentive to her, and okay, yeah, she'd been thrilled with how he always seemed to be touching her: his knee brushing hers, his hand on the small of her back, poking her in the ribs with his finger when she said something vaguely entertaining.

But it was everyone else he'd been studying. Almost like The Brothers whenever they went out somewhere—looking for danger or potential threats or whatever. Nothing awkward. Just observant. A little suspicious even.

To think Heath was acting the same way just proved she was crazy.

By the end of the evening, she'd been ready to shake his hand and tell him she'd see him around. It was obvious that the two of them were too many worlds apart to ever be a couple. She could feel everyone around them watching.

Was someone as masculine, as handsome, as *sexy* as Heath really on a date with Lyn, the plump, dowdy, librarian type?

Not that Lyn didn't know what she brought to the table. She was smart, focused, hardworking. Just not the type to attract someone like Heath.

She wouldn't have been surprised if her colleagues had been taking bets on how the evening would end. Handshake? Hug? Either of those were what would Lyn would've bet on.

The kiss had surprised her. Had curled her toes and scorched through her, but also surprised her.

And if she weren't mistaken, it had surprised him too. Maybe the heat between them? Heath had looked as shaken as she'd felt.

Which was kind of hot, if she were honest.

She brought her fingers up to her lips. She wasn't sure where this *situation*—because she certainly couldn't call it a relationship—with Heath was going. There was so much about him she didn't know. Not that she judged career choices, but there had to be a reason a man of Heath's caliber chose to be a custodian. She was pretty certain that if he put his mind to it, he could be anything he wanted.

She drove into campus and parked. Normally she would've stopped by her office, had another cup a coffee, been more prepared for her day, but she was late.

Might have been the late night. Might have been staying up the rest of the night remembering what Heath's lips had felt like on hers. Might have been plotting ways of avoiding Troy altogether. Whichever it was, it still stunk that she was low man on the totem pole and had to teach an eight-a.m. class on a Friday.

As far as freshman sections went, it actually wasn't too bad. The only difficulty was that it only met once a week, so it was nearly three hours long. And today it seemed to drag. By the time it was over—she finally gave up the fight and let them out an hour early, much to their joy—she hoped her students hadn't realized how scattered she was.

That was unacceptable. No matter what was going on, she had to keep focused on her studies and work. Not on Heath's lips.

Not on Heath's lips, damn it, and when she would see them—*him*—again.

She climbed the stairs slowly—her least favorite physical activity, but she still wasn't quite ready to take the elevator—the three floors up from the classrooms to her office. At her door, she slipped her key in the lock, hoping it wouldn't give her a hard time today. The door slid open before she'd even turned the key.

Why was her office door unlocked?

Lyn walked cautiously into the space. "Hello?"

Her office, like those of most graduate assistants, was

small, maybe twelve feet square. There was barely room for her desk, a bookshelf, and another small worktable.

Nobody could be hiding in here unless they were under her desk. She walked quickly around to look.

Nothing.

Of course nothing. She was letting the fact that she hadn't gotten a decent night's sleep take another toll on her. She'd just left her office unlocked. It happened.

Okay, she didn't ever remember doing that before, but it could've happened.

She set her two bags full of books and class materials down on her desk and shrugged off her sweater. She needed some coffee and something to eat to combat her overactive imagination. She could find both in the break room down the hall.

It was her favorite place on this floor, and she'd been delighted when she'd found it a couple of weeks ago. Yes, because of the microwave and fancy coffee maker. But mostly because of the stacks of books everywhere. There were bookshelves in rows, almost like it was its own library. The large, freestanding shelves were haphazardly placed all over the room, almost creating a maze.

People put all of the books they couldn't fit in their office here. And they were everywhere: on shelves, floors, tables, windowsills.

She'd always loved books, and she loved these, even if most of them had to do with biomedical engineering. The books gave the room character, so hanging out here was never a problem.

She made her froufrou coffee, scalding her tongue when she couldn't wait to take a sip, warmed up leftovers, and headed back to her office, still trying to shake her spooked feeling. But between what had happened in the elevator and the lack of sleep last night, she just couldn't get rid of it. Normally, she loved that no one was around on Fridays. Today it made her nervous.

She'd eat her lunch then go home. Forget about her posted office hours. Students never came by during office hours anyway. And this way, she wouldn't have to worry about running into Heath or Troy.

Walking faster with her new plan in mind, she turned the corner to find her office door cracked open.

She *knew* she had closed it when she'd left for the break room.

"Hello?"

She pushed the door open all the way. There was a man standing behind her desk. All her desk drawers were open and the textbooks she had brought up from the classroom were spread out all over.

She kept herself close to the door so she could run if needed but relaxed marginally when the man had the same green coveralls Heath normally wore.

"Can I help you?" she asked. She set her lunch and coffee on the filing cabinet.

The man moved behind her desk slightly. "I'm with maintenance. Just a routine search of offices for any pests or rodents."

"Oh. I didn't know you guys did stuff like that." Or know why he would be looking through her drawers for them. "You're not the normal guy who works this floor."

The man's eyes narrowed. "No, I'm not normally on this floor."

She studied the guy for a long minute. Why did he look familiar?

"Yeah, Patrick usually works here. Where's he today?" She prayed there was no actual Patrick who worked here, but she'd never seen anyone but Heath working on this floor. Lyn didn't know why she'd lied. All she knew was that this guy was lying too.

He shrugged. "I talked to Patrick a few minutes ago. He'll be up here to help with some of the other offices in a second."

She needed to get out of here, to call security to figure out what was going on, but her cell phone was in her cardigan pocket, hanging on her chair. Right next to scary dude.

She smiled as best she could. "I'll go work somewhere else. Get out of your hair so you can do your job. Can you toss me my sweater?"

The man turned his back to her and reached down to get her sweater off the back of her chair, but when he turned back around, instead of handing her the jacket, he had a gun in his hand.

She took a step back.

"Where's the chip?" He made his way around the desk, the gun still pointed directly at her.

"What chip?"

"You're Lyn Norris, right? This is your office?"

"Who are you?"

The man took a step forward and grabbed her arm, eyes flinty. "Where is the microchip?"

Lyn had no idea what he was talking about. "Listen, I know I work on a floor with mostly engineering faculty, but I'm a linguistics student. I don't know anything about microchips or stuff like that."

He took a step toward her, arm raised to strike. They both heard the bell of the elevator chime and the creaky wheels of a cart.

Heath.

The man quickly peeled off his coveralls and grabbed her by the arm again. He kept his gun pointed at her ribs, the clothing covering it from view.

"You're coming with me. If you say anything to anyone as we leave, I will kill that person and shoot you in your kneecap. Got it?"

Oh crap.

Lyn nodded, not trusting herself to talk. She took a couple of deep breaths. Her heart was doing okay. She needed to keep it that way.

He led her out of her office, closing the door behind them.

Pushing his cleaning cart ahead of him, Heath ambled down the hallway toward them.

"I have to say hi to Patrick or else he'll get suspicious. We always say hello to each other."

As they neared Heath, the man gripped her arm tighter. Heath was whistling, although he stopped when he saw Lyn and the man.

"Hi, Patrick. Have a good weekend, okay?"

Bok. Was she making the situation worse by calling Heath by the wrong name? There was no reason he would think something was wrong; he would just think she was crazy.

She prayed he wouldn't bring up last night or their kiss. She glanced up at his brown eyes. His face remained neutral, but his eyes narrowed just slightly.

"See you later, Dr. Norris. Have a good day."

She fought not to expel a relieved breath. Heath had caught on that something wasn't right. He never called her Dr. Norris, only Dr. Almost.

But what was he going to do, squirt the bad guy with window cleaner? The man had a gun. Heath had a custodial cart. She nodded at Heath as they passed and kept walking.

Lyn didn't know what microchip the man wanted, but she didn't have it. And she knew leaving the building with him would be disastrous. She'd have to take a chance that the man wasn't willing to shoot her since he thought she had something he wanted. Or maybe Heath would figure out to call security and someone would stop the guy downstairs.

But as they continued walking, she knew she couldn't take that chance. If this guy got her out of the building and away from other people, Lyn wasn't coming out of this alive.

They approached the break room. It was the only room on this floor Lyn knew of that had two doors, and because it was on a corner that let out into two different halls. It was her best bet.

She pulled away from the man just as they passed the door. She hadn't provided any resistance so far, so he wasn't expecting it now. She threw her head back, cracking him in the nose, and elbowed him in the gut at the same time.

Guy let out a howl of pain.

Lyn ran. He lurched for her but missed. She sprinted into the break room, pulling down a huge pile of books on the table by the door. Maybe that would slow him down some.

She ducked behind one of the large shelves, planning to make her way around it and dart out the door she'd come through. After a moment, she dipped her head around one side and didn't see the guy, so she stepped all the way around the shelf.

He was standing right there. And he was pissed. Blood dripped from his nose. "Going somewhere?"

He grabbed her hair, yanking her head back. Lyn recoiled as his fist came flying toward her face—

Only to stop mid-punch as his whole body went soaring.

Heath covered him, having managed some sort of silent side-tackle.

Lyn scrambled back. "Be careful, he has a gun."

She wasn't sure how she could best help Heath. His opponent was obviously a trained criminal.

But it didn't take more than a few moments to realize Heath didn't need much help. He was giving as good as he got.

"Get out, call security," Heath muttered between taking a punch in the gut and flipping around on the ground so he could elbow the guy in the face.

Lyn turned to run, but the thug grabbed her ankle and pulled hard, sending her sprawling on the ground. She scampered away, but the battle between Heath and the guy knocked into the bookshelf, toppling huge piles of books onto her. She couldn't stop her cry of pain as the heavy texts cascaded over her.

She watched as the entire shelf leaned in her direction.

"Lyn!" Heath let go of the guy and dove for her, deflecting some of the books with his arm. He caught the falling bookshelf, arms straining from the awkward angle where he lay on the floor, giving her time to get out of the way.

The man took advantage of Heath's distraction and fled.

Heath pushed the falling shelf in another direction, then jumped to his feet to steady other shelves as they began to wobble also.

"You okay?" he asked once they were secure.

"I think so."

"I'm going after him."

"But—"

She swallowed her words as Heath pulled a small gun out of a holster at his ankle and took off after the thug.

"—that guy's dangerous."

No one heard her words; Heath was gone. Running after the bad guy.

No. In *pursuit* of the bad guy. She had to call it what it was.

Her world spun, but it had nothing to do with the books that had hit her. One thing she knew for sure: *Heath Smith* was not just a janitor.

CHAPTER EIGHT

By the time Heath made it into the hall, the guy was gone. He chased down the main hall toward the elevator but didn't see him. Damn it. There were three sets of stairs he could've taken. And Heath wasn't about to risk leaving Lyn alone in case the guy doubled back.

He had no idea who the man was. Definitely not someone who was regularly in this building.

He got out his phone and sent a message to Craig. Somebody needed to gather any evidence from the break room. Craig was going to have to decide if he wanted the local PD to do it or send someone himself.

What the hell did that guy want with Lyn?

When Heath had first seen them walking down the hallway, he'd immediately tensed. And not even because he was doing his damned job and concerned about possible danger. But because seeing Lyn that close to another man had raised his hackles like he was some Neanderthal.

He didn't like it. And he was so caught up in not liking it that he might've missed she was in danger altogether if she hadn't clued him in.

The moment she'd called him Patrick, it was like everything shifted and fell into place. Heath saw the jacket strategically draped over the guy's arm concealing a weapon. He saw Lyn's pinched face.

He tried to reassure her, but would she even remember he normally called her "Dr. Almost"? And even if she did, would she figure out he understood she was under duress?

It had been smart of her to make a play at the break room, but all those damn books were dangerous. His heart had caught in his chest at the sight of them falling over on her. He jogged back down the hall now to make sure she was all right.

She had made it off the floor and was wisely hiding behind another shelf when he entered.

"Lyn?"

"Oh holy *merda*. Are you okay? I wasn't sure what I should do. I called security." She hesitated the slightest bit.

He wanted to smile at her Italian curse but couldn't. His cover had to be blown. It *had* to be. She was too smart not to have figured it out when he pulled his weapon. But he still tried to keep his words neutral. "I've also called some people to have this place processed and checked for prints. The guy wasn't wearing any gloves."

"His gun is over there too." She pointed toward a row of bookshelves.

Heath nodded. He'd seen it when he'd walked back in. Hopefully, running the prints and the gun would provide some information.

He crossed a little closer to her. "Are you okay? Did he hurt you in any way?"

"Not as much as some of those statistical analysis texts when they fell."

He could already see a large bruise forming on her

forearm where she'd raised it to protect her head. Good thing she had or they'd be on the way to the hospital right now. He reached out and touched the arm she cradled, stroking it gently.

"Better statistical analysis than a bullet," he murmured. All of this could've gone so much worse.

She took a step back, moving out of his reach. "I guess you don't have to clean this up, do you?"

He grimaced. Holy *merda* indeed. "We shouldn't touch anything until the police arrive."

"You know what I mean, Heath. If that's even your real name. You *are* the police."

He sighed. He couldn't give Lyn all the information about the case, but he could at least answer the essential questions she was getting at.

"Yes, I'm working for the FBI." That was basically all the info he could give her. "And yes, my name is Heath. But my last name is Kavanaugh, not Smith."

"Are you here because of me? Did my father send you to protect me or something—like some sort of bodyguard?"

What? "No. I have no idea who your father is. I'm not working for him."

She continued to cradle her arm. "So you're on some sort of a case. That's why you've been working as a janitor." They weren't questions. It seemed almost old hat to her.

"Yes. But I can't go into any details right now."

She nodded. "Does it have something to do with a microchip?"

Heath's eyes whipped to hers. "Why do you ask that?"

"That's what the guy with the gun was asking about. He wanted me to give him the microchip."

"Do you know anything about that?"

She shook her head. "I had no idea what he was talking

about. I figured he had me confused with someone else on this floor. I came into my office, and he was going through my stuff."

Why would he have been searching Lyn's office? It would've only taken the slightest bit of background info to know she wasn't part of the biomedical engineering department.

Heath stepped out into the hallway and began checking office doors to see if they had been forced. Maybe the guy had been hoping to get lucky by searching all the offices. But even as the thought formed, Heath knew that wasn't the case. It would be too sloppy and take too long.

"Do you mind if I take a look at your office?"

She shook her head and led him down the hall. He studied the other doors as they went—none of them appeared to have been tampered with. Everything was pretty empty, but for a Friday around lunch, that wasn't unusual.

She'd interrupted the guy during the search, that was obvious. But something as small as a microchip? It could be anywhere.

"I don't know why he would think I have something like a microchip. I'm not even sure I know what a microchip looks like."

Heath turned and saw her huddling against the doorframe of her office. Her face was pale, eyes too large in her face. She was still holding her arm against her body and honestly looked like she might fall over any second.

Now that the adrenaline was wearing off, she was crashing hard. Heath took a few steps toward her in case he needed to catch her. But she backed farther away.

Not interested in him touching her right now—got it. But he still wanted to be close in case she toppled.

"You okay?" he asked gently.

"Not too bad, I guess." She put a hand over her heart. "I just . . ."

When she trailed off he finished for her. "You're coming down from the adrenaline rush. It can be pretty overwhelming."

"Yeah, I don't feel so good. Plus, I didn't have lunch." She pointed to the leftovers she'd set on a small table by the door. "Or coffee."

He reached for her slowly again, thankful when she didn't shy away this time, then eased her into a chair by her desk and grabbed the plastic container.

"It's still pretty warm. Think you could eat a little bit? That will help regulate your blood sugar. You burned through a lot of calories when your adrenal medulla kicked into overdrive. Cortisol can play havoc with your system."

She stared at him for a long time before taking the food.

"What?" he asked.

"I'm trying to adjust to words about adrenal medulla and cortisol coming out of your mouth, Mr. Custodian."

Heath pursed his lips. Yeah, he deserved that.

His phone buzzed. It was a message from Craig. He was sending local PD to process but was coming to supervise the scene himself. Heath's cover would stay in place. The locals would be told it was a burglary gone wrong.

As long as he could convince Lyn to keep quiet. He rubbed the back of his neck. He wasn't sure he could convince Lyn to do *anything* right now. She wasn't screaming at him, but that didn't mean she wasn't angry.

"The police are going to be here soon. There will be a forensic team combing the break room, then in here. As soon as there's a federal agent available to supervise, I'll come back and get you."

"Will I need to talk to the police?"

"If you don't mind, it would be better if you don't. The official word that will go out to the college and local police is that this was a burglary that I walked in on—we'll try to keep it as low-key as possible in order to keep my cover intact."

She had set her food aside but was sipping her coffee, or at least holding it between her hands like it could ward off bad juju. "I still don't understand everything that's going on here."

She stared at him, her brown eyes impossibly big behind her glasses. He walked over to her—almost not of his own will—and crouched down beside her.

"I know. And I'll explain what I can. But not here."

He expected arguments, demands. Instead, she just nodded like his answer hadn't surprised her at all.

She was taking this like a champ. Or maybe refusing to process it at all.

He stood and touched her shoulder as his phone chirped again. Local PD was here. He needed to get to the break room.

"Stay here until I come back to get you. I have my keys, so don't open the door to anyone."

"Do you think someone might come back for me?"

"No, but I want to know you're safe." He had to know she was safe. Seeing that bookshelf fall toward her was going to plague his nightmares for a long time.

The microchip mattered, this case mattered, but Lyn mattered more. Hopefully, someone had just gotten their intel wrong and had mistakenly come after her. But Heath wasn't taking any chances.

He waited until she nodded then left, closing the door behind him.

CHAPTER NINE

Lyn sat staring at the closed door for a long time.

Heath had been right about the cortisol and the adrenal medulla and the crashing stuff. Fifteen minutes ago, she'd felt like she could leap over a building.

Now she was struggling not to collapse out of her chair.

She'd taken one of her antiarrhythmic pills from her pocket as soon as Heath had run off after the bad guy. Taking another one now was probably a good idea. Her heart still stuttered slightly even though her body seemed to have zero energy.

This was what she hated about The Brothers' line of work, and even Dad's before he'd gone into politics. She'd seen the toll danger had taken on them: the adrenaline spikes, the crashes, the mood swings. Soldiers, cops . . . it was the same. Two of her three brothers were divorced, and her two cousins—also in the fighting-danger line of work— suffered from PTSD to some degree.

And yet they all, every single one of them, craved the danger like they were junkies.

Lyn had never been interested in that feeling. She never

would've chosen law enforcement or the military even if her heart could've taken the stress. She'd buried herself in academia, about as far away from her family's chosen careers as she could get.

As far away from *Heath's* chosen career as she could get.

She'd known instinctively from the moment she'd first seen him that he was more than just someone who cleaned classrooms and emptied trash. He'd been too aware, too strong, too *much.*

How he'd handled the situation in the elevator on Wednesday should have sealed it for her. His calm and focus. How he'd systematically worked through the issues and possibilities then figured out what to do.

How he'd reached down and lifted her up as if she weighed nothing.

The signs that there was more to him than met the eye had been present the whole time. Heath had deliberately downplayed those signs, but Lyn had still seen them.

Any other woman would be thrilled that the man who had kissed her senseless the night before was some sort of secret agent rather than a janitor.

Not Lyn. In her opinion, this widened the gap between them. Before, he'd been more physically attractive and better at social situations than she'd been, but at least—considering their two professions—Lyn had thought she had the upper hand a little when it came to education. It had provided her a small measure of assurance.

Given what she'd just found out? She'd probably even lost that upper hand. Obviously, Heath was of more than average intelligence if he was successfully living two lives while keeping everyone else from noticing.

At least he wasn't here as some sort of glorified bodyguard from Dad. He would've already reported back to Dad about her real major.

If Heath worked for the FBI, at least that meant he didn't know anyone in her family. They may have most branches of the military and law enforcement in both Wyoming and Colorado covered, but no one worked for the bureau.

But still. This changed everything.

The excitement about last night's kiss that had been bubbling through her veins all morning fizzled out. That hadn't been real. She didn't have any details yet—didn't know if she was going to get any details at all—but everything that had happened last night must have been some part of his undercover work.

She didn't work for the FBI, but she could see the details right in front of her. Something bad was going down, and it involved the people on this floor—the biomedical engineering people. Heath was here watching them.

He'd come to the bar last night for more observation. That's why it had all felt so clinical.

Because it had been.

Kissing her? That had just been part of his operation.

She set down the mug of coffee she'd never finished. The leftovers she'd heated had grown cold again and held no appeal to her now anyway.

Heath had told her to wait here, but Lyn grabbed her stuff. Wait here for *what?*

She knew enough from her family to know how law enforcement worked. She understood that it was better for her to stay out of Heath's way.

Staying here meant that he'd feel obligated to make sure she was all right.

She was all right.

A little shaky, but she'd be fine.

Like Heath had said, the guy who'd grabbed her hadn't even been looking for *her* in particular.

Wrong place, wrong time. Her bad luck.

She didn't have any microchip thing. She could barely remember to back up her dissertation data onto a hard drive. Whatever bad-guy dude was looking for, he was going to have to find it somewhere else. Lyn didn't have it.

And if she had to keep this whole thing a secret and not talk to the police, she was getting out of here.

She needed to be away from guns, plummeting elevators, and FBI agents.

And sexy janitors. Even ones who had probably saved her life from falling bookshelves.

She'd work at home. Put some hours in on her dissertation. Avoid reality. Avoid *danger* and leave that to everyone else.

It had always worked for her in the past. She'd damn well make sure it worked now.

Processing crime scenes always took longer than anyone planned. This one, unfortunately, wasn't an exception.

Longer, since all Heath could think about was getting back to the office and wiping that resigned look off Lyn's face. He couldn't explain much, but he could tell her that the past three weeks of coffee and donuts and learning new curse words had been real to him.

That last night's kiss had been real to him.

The young uniformed officer who Craig had sent obviously wanted to do more than sit around and wait for a forensic team to show up and take over. Fortunately, Heath kept him out of the room and occupied by giving him his "statement" about what had happened. Heath conveniently left out the parts about the gun and Lyn—made it sound like the guy had been trying to steal some computer equipment or something.

Craig would give a full report to local law enforcement later if it was deemed necessary. Right now, Heath gave the young cop some information, none of it truly relevant to the bigger case at hand.

Every minute seemed to creep by with agonizing slowness. Talking to the cop, usually something Heath didn't have any sort of problem with, was like pulling teeth.

Was Lyn okay? Had she eaten?

Was she sitting in her office thinking he was the biggest jerk on the planet?

That wouldn't be completely wrong.

He forced himself to draw out yet another unimportant detail about the "break-in" so the cop could write it in his notebook and feel useful.

When the forensic team arrived, Heath stayed as close as they would allow. He didn't want to contaminate the scene, but he also wanted to know if they discovered something before Craig got here.

Fortunately, Craig arrived within the next thirty minutes, along with two other agents—a man and woman, both looking fresh out of FBI preschool. Heath faded back as Craig talked to the local cop, flashing his bureau ID and explaining that he was comparing this to some other burglaries. Not trying to take over.

The cop ate it up, now much more interested in what had happened since the feds were also interested. Craig introduced his agents, Samuel Rodriguez and Olivia

Collins, to Heath, sent them inside the break room with the cop, and pulled Heath out into the hallway.

"This makes two pretty big incidents in one week. Is your cover secure?" Craig asked.

"I think so. With everyone but Lyn Norris. Perp threatened her with a gun. Was asking her about a microchip."

"This is twice she's gotten wrapped up in something. I'm going to run her when I get back to the office so we're sure we didn't miss anything."

"Fine. Let me know if you find anything interesting." Except for some really bad luck, Heath was betting there wasn't anything to know about Lyn Norris at all.

"Is she going to keep your cover under wraps? All it takes is for her to start chatting with some of her colleagues on this floor and the whole case is down the drain."

"She won't. I'll explain as much as I can, especially the importance of her cooperation."

"This is the same woman you were kissing last night?"

Crap. Heath didn't want to know how Craig knew that. But honestly, he wouldn't be surprised if the man had an informant reporting back to him.

No point lying about what Craig already knew. "Yeah, it was."

"Part of your cover?"

"No."

Craig crossed his arms over his chest. "I know the bureau is paying you, but you don't officially work for me, Kavanaugh. That said . . . what we're doing here is important. Critical. We've got to stop the sale of the nanotech data and, just as importantly, get a grip on who's trying to buy it."

"I haven't forgotten my mission." Heath flinched as the

gibberish decided to ratchet up the volume. Not at all what he needed right now.

"This woman has the potential to cause a lot of harm. Especially if she decides to start running her mouth. I suggest you stay away from her."

He was right, of course.

And yet, all Heath could think about was getting back to Lyn, worried that she was upset. About today's danger and last night's kiss.

It shouldn't matter, especially about the kiss, but it did.

The thought that Lyn might not talk to him anymore, might not give him any more of her shy smiles, might not study him when she thought he wasn't looking actually made his gut clench.

He rubbed his brow and took a breath, nodding at Craig. "Yeah, I'll stay away from her." Right after he talked to her and made sure she was okay. It would be simple. She was one brain cell short of completely brilliant. She would understand.

He couldn't give her many details about the case, but he could at least explain that she wasn't part of it. That he hadn't been using her.

Except for last night at the restaurant. He'd kind of been using her then. And when he'd talked to her about the biomedical staff over the past couple of weeks to find out if she knew anything.

Heath winced. Okay, maybe this wasn't going to be as easy as he thought.

"Rodriguez and Collins are going to stay here to help out however you need them. They think you're on loan from another office. Gavin told me his cousin Noah should be here in the next few hours too."

Heath looked away from the hall leading toward Lyn's

office, ignoring his need to leave this entire conversation behind and go there immediately, and back to Craig. "Yeah, I've met Noah a couple of times. He's a stand-up guy. Solid."

Craig grimaced. "I don't like using so many civilians for a case like this, but I trust the Special Forces training Noah's had. And at least I know he's not the mole on my team."

"And the two toddlers you're saddling me with?" Heath jerked a thumb toward the break room.

Craig rubbed his eyes. "Collins and Rodriguez are definitely green but, again, definitely not the mole."

"It's fine. Between them and Noah, at least I won't be stretched so thin. I'll send them to stakeout Dale Hudson. He and Troy Powell are my two main suspects."

Craig nodded. "Doctors think Powell should come out of his coma soon, maybe even as early as today."

"Let's put Noah on guard duty at the hospital. If Troy knows something, there might be another attempt on him." He glanced down the hall again. He'd been gone from Lyn a long time. "Look, I'm going to go. Send the Wonder Twins over for surveillance on Hudson. I'll be in touch soon."

"You're going to talk to that woman, aren't you?"

Heath didn't even try to deny it. "I'll stay away from her, but she deserves whatever few answers I can give her first. She's not part of this, Craig."

"Fine. But I'm still going to run her."

"Feel free." Heath started down the hallway.

"Heath."

He turned.

"Thank you for what you're doing. Don't think I don't remember that you're helping me out of a jam here." Craig's eyes were sincere.

"We're going to catch these guys. The sellers and the buyers—you have my word."

Craig nodded. "I'm counting on it."

Heath turned back down the hall as Craig went into the break room. When he made it to her office, he knocked on the door, then used his master set of custodial keys to let himself in when nobody answered.

Lyn was gone.

Crap.

He checked to see if there was any note, then looked at his phone for a message.

Nothing.

He immediately dialed her number from last night. After a few rings, it went to voice mail.

Lyn's sweet voice. *Hi, you've reached Lyn. You know me, I probably have my nose stuck in a book somewhere and didn't hear my phone. So leave a message.*

Heath left a message for her to call or text him. But she wasn't going to. He'd known that from the resigned look on her face when he'd left her here.

She deserved answers. And more than that, the guy who'd tried to take her was out there. If he thought she was a part of the biomedical engineering faculty and had the microchip, she was still in danger.

Heath needed to find her. Now.

CHAPTER TEN

After she got to her car, Lyn found herself automatically pulling into the parking lot of a nearby bakery.

Then immediately pulling back out again.

She couldn't go into the place she'd been going for weeks to get donuts and coffee for her and Heath. Everything about their conversations led to more questions now. Like every time he'd casually mentioned one of the faculty members or doctoral students on her floor. Had he been searching for information?

And what the heck had been up with him learning new language stuff from her? How could that have helped his case? Why would he have spent that time with her at all?

She wasn't going to spend any more time thinking about Heath. This week had been crazy. She should stop and get a salad at the café across the street, but instead she drove a couple miles down to one of the best burger places in Reddington City.

She was going to treat herself, and falling elevators, guys

with guns, and men who kissed her—who may or may not be undercover—be damned.

She got the house burger with extra bacon and sat outside to eat it. Usually, she spent a few hours on Friday afternoon outside anyway, weather permitting, grading papers, reading, or working on her dissertation.

She'd do that. It was time to get her life back to normal. Normal meaning Heath Whatever-his-last-name-actually-was had no part in it.

But even after a good burger and sunshine, she still wasn't able to concentrate on the work in front of her. She finally gave up. Getting up from the table, she put her items back in her bag. When she grabbed her phone and walked to the car, she saw she had a message.

From Heath.

She wanted to listen to it but wouldn't allow herself to. He was concerned that she'd left and probably wanted to talk stuff out. Maybe wanted to make sure she didn't mention anything to anyone.

She knew better than most not to talk about ongoing investigations. He didn't need to worry.

She would go home. Take a nap. Bury herself under the covers and not think about anything that was happening.

And she wouldn't think about Heath. Again.

She drove home and walked up to the steps to her doorway, reaching for the doorknob before she realized something was wrong.

Her door was ajar.

Like her office door had been.

Reddington City had its share of problems, for sure. But her small townhouse was in a relatively safe, if urban, neighborhood. Her dad and The Brothers had wanted her to live farther out in suburbia, but she'd wanted to be closer to campus.

Because she lived alone, and because her family would skin her alive if she didn't, Lyn was always sure to double-check her locks. She had when she'd left this morning too.

But now her door was open.

Lyn backed down the stairs. Her heart began an unsteady rhythm. Within a few seconds, she was feeling lightheaded.

Damn it, she could not pass out right here, leaving herself helpless. She needed to call the police. Or should she call Heath? She had to do something.

She forced herself to cough hard—a vagal maneuver that often helped reset her rapid heartbeat. She did it again, and the dizziness thankfully passed.

As she put her bag on the ground to dig her phone out, two men across the street caught her attention. They were big, bulky, but she couldn't make out their features with ball caps pulled low on their faces.

Ball caps, even though they had suits on. Great. Not suspicious at all.

And they were staring right at her. Why?

She needed to get out of here. She grabbed her purse and walked toward her car.

She jumped and shrieked when a hand landed on her shoulder. She spun, trying to remember the self-defense moves Gavin had taught her a few years ago.

"Easy there, sweetheart. It's just me."

Heath.

Thank God. She grabbed the front of his black T-shirt—no janitor uniform right now—and held on, unable to get words out.

Jeez. Her heart was getting a ridiculous workout this week.

"What's wrong?" One look at her face and he immediately pulled her closer. "Lyn, what's happened?"

She pulled one of her pills from her purse and downed it with no water.

"Is that your anxiety meds? Did something else happen?"

Not really anxiety meds, but she didn't want to explain her heart condition right now, so she nodded and shrugged at the same time.

"My front door is open," she finally stammered out. "I know I locked it when I left this morning. I *know* I did."

He sped up the steps to her front door, pulling her behind him. At the door, he reached behind him with his arm, wrapping her to his back.

"You're sure it was open when you got here?"

"Yes." She nodded even though she knew he couldn't see her. "Like my office."

Heath reached down and pulled the gun from his ankle holster the way he had in the break room. He didn't let go of her, and she grabbed on to the back of his shirt this time as he took a few steps inside.

She heard his muttered curse and peeked around him and couldn't stop her shocked gasp. Everything she could see had been gutted or toppled over.

"Robbery?" she whispered.

"Or a search for something."

Of course. "That *kuradi* microchip," she muttered.

He squeezed her hand, and she could've sworn he gave the slightest chuckle. But how could he possibly recognize the *f* word in Estonian?

"Stay right here," he said. "I'm going to check the rest of the house. Make sure there's no one still around."

Lyn nodded. She looked out the door for the men who had been watching from across the street, but they were gone. Had they even been watching her at all? Why would they have been? Was she blowing everything completely out of proportion?

The chaotic mess in front of her wasn't out of proportion. Her plants had been toppled, the contents of her drawers scattered all over the floor. A glance into her kitchen showed even more damage.

It was only stuff. That was the important thing.

Although it didn't feel like that right now.

Her townhouse wasn't that big—a few moments later Heath was back. He put his gun back in its holster.

"Are you okay?"

She shrugged, stepping away from the wall and walking farther into her townhouse. Pictures had been removed from the wall, backs slit open. He furniture had been turned on end. Lamps broken.

Her gut clenched as she walked into the living room and saw the bookshelf with all her personal favorite paperbacks and hardbacks— books she'd collected over the years — had been tossed all over the floor. Many of them destroyed.

Of everything in her place, these books probably had the least monetary value. But to her, they were precious.

She turned away, tears filling her eyes. She blinked them back. She couldn't fall apart right now. Not yet. "This has to be the same guy, right? He thinks I have some sort of microchip."

"Yes, although probably a team. They've mistaken you

for a biomedical engineering faculty member and are convinced you have the chip for some reason."

She leaned back so she could look at him. "That's your case, isn't it? Whatever you're undercover for has to do with the protection or recovery of this microchip or something."

He nodded. "Yes, basically."

There was more, she could tell. She didn't know if he wasn't at liberty to say or just didn't want to. She stepped away, and he let her go. She wrapped her arms around herself—not nearly the same comfort.

"How did the guy have time to do this since he grabbed me on campus? I stopped to get a bite to eat on my way home, but this had to have taken longer."

"You were supposed to wait for me, remember?"

Lyn studied her shoes. "I needed to get away from that whole situation. Honestly, I thought it was just a fluke and you wouldn't really need me anymore." She thought about the two men across the street. Now the fact that they were watching her didn't seem so unrealistic after all.

He moved closer, rubbing a hand down her arm. "If it helps, I think this was done earlier today. Probably while you were in class. The guy with the gun came on campus after he couldn't find the microchip here."

"Do you think they're searching the homes of everyone in the biomedical engineering department?"

Heath shook his head. "It's possible, but unlikely. We've been watching some of the main faculty and doctoral students and none of them have had any problems." Heath paused. "Except Troy Powell."

"What happened to him?"

Heath paused. "He's in the hospital."

"What?"

"He was attacked last night. He's in a coma."

Lyn looked around her house. First Troy was attacked, then someone came after her thinking she also had something to do with the microchip.

"Will Dale and Veronica be okay? Is someone protecting them?" They weren't exactly her friends, but she didn't want anything happening to them. "And the other people in the department?"

"We're watching key players. But I'm not worried about their safety, I'm worried about *yours*."

"Surely by now they've figured out that I don't have the microchip thing they're looking for."

"Thank goodness you weren't here when the perps came to search this place. You . . ." He stopped, shaking his head, looking around.

"I what?"

He took a step closer. "I don't even want to think about what could've happened." He ran a finger down her cheek almost as if he couldn't help himself. "I just want to make sure you're safe until all of this is over."

"Should I start cleaning this up?"

He shook his head. "No. I'll send someone to process this as soon as they're finished with the break room. This is a crime scene too. They'll make sure the perps didn't leave anything useable behind."

Damn it, she was going to have to call the family and let them know about this. As soon as her address got into law enforcement's computers, they would know anyway. She rubbed her eyes.

Heath put his hands on her shoulders. All she wanted to do was lean into him. "How are you holding up? I know this is a huge personal violation for you."

"Honestly, I can't even wrap my head around all this right now. I need to call my father and let him know what happened. He always finds out about everything."

"You mentioned him before. Are you guys close? How does he find stuff out? Is he law enforcement too?"

"Retired." She didn't want to get into the fact that her father was the governor. "And we're pretty close, but it's more that; he's really protective of me. My whole family is."

He pulled her against his chest, and Lyn didn't even try to resist. She wanted to be there. "I mean this in the least chauvinistic way possible: you're worth protecting. And if it helps, this probably won't go into any local police systems for a little bit since it's also part of a bigger case that we're trying to keep under wraps for a while longer."

She nodded. She understood the nuances of working cases, although she'd never known them from this point of view. The *victim's* point of view.

She didn't like it. And right now, she was just tired.

She glanced around one more time. If she couldn't start cleaning up, she should leave. Standing around looking at the mess wasn't going to help her possessions or her peace of mind. "I guess I'll need to get a hotel tonight."

"That won't be necessary."

"Where am I going to stay? I can't stay here, even if you didn't need me out of it for forensic purposes."

He stepped closer so that he was very definitely in her personal space. "You're staying with me at my apartment. There's no way I'm leaving you alone."

CHAPTER ELEVEN

Heath wished he had a nicer place to take Lyn to. Not a two-bedroom furnished rental that looked like . . . exactly what it was: a generically furnished bachelor pad.

His concept of home had always been a fluid thing. He'd lived all over the world in his adult life, rarely staying in one place too long. He'd made his abode in tents in the jungle, five-star hotels, and damn near everything in between.

Home had always been, literally, wherever he hung his hat.

He'd been a surprise and an only child to parents who'd had him in their forties. They'd treated him as a little adult from as early as he could remember—conversing and reasoning with him rather than playing or punishing.

It was probably why Heath had made a career out of talking his way in and out of pretty damn dire situations.

He'd loved his parents, but they hadn't been close. Both of them had died not long after he'd graduated high school. He'd been nineteen years old and studying languages here at Wyoming Commonwealth University when the US government had recruited him for the CIA based on his skills in languages and reading people.

But not as an active agent. He'd spent most of his time watching screens—listening for nuances in conversations, usually not in English, that would help active agents in their missions.

Timothy Holloman had read Heath like a book, contacted and enticed him into Project Crypt by promising Heath what every twenty-one-year-old wanted: action. Crypt would train Heath to be an active agent, to do more good. To go on important, dangerous missions.

Conveniently leaving out that Heath would be working for the very enemies of the country he'd been trying to protect. And that they'd be putting things in his head he couldn't get rid of or figure out.

This undercover assignment had at least kept his mind off all the Crypt hopelessness. Crazy gibberish still played in his head almost constantly, but it was easier to ignore when he focused on the case.

Even easier when he focused on the woman in front of him, clutching a small overnight bag. They'd gotten the bare minimum of clothes and toiletries because her townhouse had been completely wrecked and because he'd wanted to disrupt the scene as little as possible.

After Heath's call, Craig escorted the forensics team to Lyn's townhouse.

Lyn looked around.

"Not fancy, but it's my place at least while I'm on the case."

She nodded, walking forward. "So you don't normally live here."

He took her bag and put it on the kitchen table. "No. I'm not from Reddington City."

She nodded. "Are you from Wyoming at all?"

"No. I was raised in Seattle, but I've been all over the world with my job."

"With the FBI?"

"FBI and different . . . agencies." A thought struck him. "Are you concerned I'm not who I say I am?" It wouldn't be an unreasonable fear for someone in her position.

"No, I believe you're law enforcement. I can't believe I didn't put it together before. You were always too aware of what was going on around you. Too . . . I'm not sure what the word is. Forceful, maybe?"

He grunted. "That's not good in terms of me blending in. I was trying not to draw anyone's attention."

"I don't think it was obvious to anyone else. I was raised around law enforcement. And . . ." She trailed off, her face turning a bright red before she looked down and away, her hair hiding her from his view.

Whatever she was thinking was sexual in nature.

This woman was such an intoxicating mixture of sexy and sweet. It was all he could do to keep his hands off of her. He should leave it alone, but he couldn't.

He took a step toward her. "And what?"

She still didn't look at him. "I-I was just really tuned in to you. Which was completely one-sided and stupid, I realize now."

He reached out and touched her arm. "Lyn—"

She eased away and walked through the small living room to the window, staring out it as if it had a gorgeous view rather than a postage-stamp-sized yard with nothing but grass. "No, it's fine. I understand. I was part of some undercover work. A job. Whatever happened last night with that kiss was just part of your cover."

Damn.

He could say it in different languages too, but it wouldn't change anything. What he had done had hurt her.

Craig's voice drowned out the other babble in his head. *You need to stay away from her.*

Heath couldn't. "It wasn't like that."

Lyn shook her head, then turned, those brown eyes taking up half her face.

A face that could only be described as sad. Resigned.

"It's okay. You don't have to placate me. I get it." That tragic little smile was breaking his heart. "Really, I do. I may have my nose in a text most of the time, but I know how the world works. Someone like you would not be interested in someone like me under normal circumstances."

Heath's eyes narrowed and his jaw set. He slowly and deliberately slipped off his jacket and hung it over the kitchen chair, trying to give himself time to recover. To back down from what he knew he was on the verge of doing.

Proving to Lyn Norris how wrong she really was.

He heard Craig's voice in his head again. And the man was right. Damn it, Heath should walk away. Make a joke. Ease her down gently about how the job really was important and maybe they could go out some time after this was all over.

Heath was good with people. Good with words—in multiple languages. He should be able to do this.

But Lyn wouldn't believe him. He knew it.

And more than that, he didn't want to ease back or make a joke. For months, he'd been living on the edge, first with hunting Holloman and then on this case.

He wanted Lyn. Wanted her with a ferocity he hadn't let himself admit. Wanted to surround himself with someone who was soft and kind and not a part of the ugly, hard world he lived in.

And he wanted to show her how much he wanted her.

She looked at him with those eyes and had no idea how close she was to being pressed up against that window while he did things to her that might get them both arrested for indecent exposure.

"Placate you?" he finally said, raising a brow.

"Yes. It means—"

"I know what it means. You know, you're an incredibly smart woman," he said gently, softly, giving away none of the predatory instincts coursing through him except to take a slight step toward her.

But she felt the danger instinctively. Not that he would hurt her, but that he was coming for her. She backed up a step, not that she had any place to go.

"Thank you?"

"But I don't think you're seeing things clearly."

"It doesn't take a genius to know that you and I are on two different playing fields, Heath. Look at me."

"Oh, I am, Lyn." He took another step toward her. A sexual wariness, followed quickly by confusion, flashed in her eyes. She couldn't figure out what was happening. Poor sweetheart. "And I'll say it again: you're an incredibly smart woman. Definitely too smart to say something so dumb."

"What?" She took another step back and ended up against the window.

"You think you don't have much to offer a man, but you couldn't be more wrong."

"What?" she parroted again.

He took another step closer. "I have been keeping away from you for many reasons. I'm on an undercover mission. I didn't want to bring any danger your way, although it seems to have found you anyway."

Another step. He was right in front of her now. "But

none of the reasons I've kept my hands off you for the past three weeks have anything to do with not being attracted to you."

"They don't?" Her statement was barely a whisper.

He eased himself against her body, trapping her between himself and the window. He reached down and trailed his fingers from her hands all the way up her arms to her shoulders until he was framing her face.

"I'm attracted to damn near everything about you. I couldn't act on it before. Hell, I shouldn't act on it now, but it's true."

"But—"

He didn't let her finish. He kissed her to shut her up but found himself pulled under by the kiss. Just like last night, the heat took over. He pressed up against her, tilting her head back so he could have complete access to that full mouth.

Lyn was still for a moment before her arms worked their way around his shoulders, her fingers clutching at his back. She gave every bit as good as she got with the kiss.

The soft moan she breathed into his mouth was almost his undoing. He slid his hands into her hair and nipped at her full bottom lip before soothing the spot with his tongue. What was it about this small, quiet woman that had him so twisted in knots?

He knew he should slow down, take things more gently, more easily. But he didn't know how. Not that it seemed Lyn would let him, even if he could find the strength to do it.

"I want you right here against this window," he murmured against her mouth. "And we'll get to that. But right now, I want you in my bed where we can do this right."

He reached down to swing her up into his arms.

"No, Heath, put me down. I'm too heavy—"

He kissed her again. She didn't weigh enough for it to even be a factor. "Like I said, for a smart woman, Dr. Almost, you can say some pretty dumb stuff," he said against her mouth. "I'm attracted to everything about you. Your gorgeous body, your stunning mind, your pretty face."

She wrapped her arms around his neck and kissed her way down his chin and over to his ear as he walked her back to his bedroom and lowered her onto the bed. He groaned when she untucked his shirt and slid her nails up over his abs and chest.

"I can't believe I stayed away from you this long," he said. "I've wanted you here since that first donut and coffee."

She giggled, the sound musical. He pulled her shirt over her head as she kicked off her shoes.

She was shy, a little uncomfortable with him being so close to her bare skin. She truly had no idea how beautiful she was.

"Wait." Her voice was a little uneven.

"What do you need, beautiful? We can wait as long as you want."

He eased back from her, "I just need to cough."

Okay, that was a little weird that she was announcing it, but maybe she didn't want to catch him off guard. "Go right ahead."

She coughed hard once and then again. He leaned back so he could see her face. "Feel better?"

"Yes. Thank you. Much better. I . . ." She trailed off and shrugged. "Never mind. I don't want to talk about this right now. Can we continue what we were doing?"

He smiled. "Any particular parts?"

"*All* the parts. I want you, Heath."

"Good." This woman was ridiculously sexy—feminine and alluring in ways he was going to need a long time to discover to its fullest. "You're so *čertovsky* gorgeous, Almost."

"Czech." The word turned into a sigh as he pulled her closer.

"In *every* language."

CHAPTER TWELVE

Heath woke up the next morning, a luscious, sleeping Lyn in his arms. He'd been prepared to feel some guilt over his complete lack of control. But honestly, he didn't.

Because hell, what was Craig going to do, fire him?

It wouldn't have made a difference even if this were Heath's official job. There was no way he was going to stay away from Lyn. Not after last night.

At least he didn't have to keep secrets from her anymore. Craig had been on him from the beginning to get this done as soon as possible. Now there was nothing Heath wanted more.

Last night changed things. He wanted to get to know this woman better without anything hanging over their heads. Oak Creek wasn't so far from Reddington City that they couldn't make something work.

She stretched up against him and yawned. His body got hard again like they hadn't already had sex three times in the past twelve hours.

"I can almost hear you thinking over there. Is it the case?"

"It was until somebody started stretching like a little sexy kitten on top of me."

She kissed his chest and stretched again. "Nobody's ever called me a kitten before and definitely not a sexy one."

"And you hang out with all these PhD-type people? Just goes to show that book smarts aren't everything."

"I'm going to take a shower. Want to join me?"

"Uh, hell yes—"

His phone chimed. He looked over and saw it was Craig. "Crap. I really need to take this."

She didn't seem fazed at all. "No problem. Rain check. I'll go ahead and take the shower so you can talk freely."

He couldn't take his eyes off her naked form as she crossed the room. Might not have been able to if someone had a gun to his head. He brought the phone to his ear without taking his eyes off her.

"Hey, Craig."

"I'm just now getting back to my office after keeping the forensic team at Ms. Norris's apartment all night. They're quite sure they've never gotten so much overtime for what seems like an ordinary break-in."

"Sorry for your late night. Find anything?"

"Not at the townhouse. We've got a usable print from the break room that I'm running now. It'll take a few hours."

Heath sat up and swung his legs over the side of the bed. "The bigger question is why are they after Lyn? I could understand how the perp possibly grabbed the wrong person at the college, but ransacking an entire house? That takes time. You would make sure you have the right person's house first."

"Believe me, as soon as I get a cup of coffee in my

system, I'm going to find out everything there is to know about Lyn Norris. Until then, we probably need to put some sort of protection detail on her."

"That's not currently necessary."

"I disagree. Whether they're mistaking her or not, she's still in danger."

Heath let out a sigh. "No, I mean it's not necessary to put someone on her. I've already got that handled."

A long silence. "You and I have completely different definitions of *stay away from her*."

Heath chuckled. "I know. But I wasn't leaving her alone. You would've done the same thing." Well, hopefully not the *exact* same thing.

"Fine. Keep her stashed somewhere safe until we have a plan in place. Definitely don't let her go back to the school. Her townhouse has been cleared, but she probably shouldn't go there alone either."

"Roger that. Safest place for her right now is right where she's at." Maybe not *right* where she was at, given that he was about to go molest her in the shower.

"You're lucky you can't be fired, Kavanaugh."

Heath chuckled again. "I was thinking that exact thing earlier."

"I'll contact you with any interesting results of my search. Hopefully, Troy Powell will wake up today and give us some sort of lead."

"Treat yourself to some real coffee, Craig. I'm buying."

Craig muttered profanities—in boring old English—as he disconnected the call.

Heath stood, about to walk to the shower, when from the other bedside table Lyn's phone played the *Mission: Impossible* theme. He chuckled, remembering her comment about watching the movie so many times growing up. She walked out of the bathroom, wrapped in a towel, and smiled at him as he picked up the phone to hand it to her.

And saw Gavin's face on the screen.

"Do you know Gavin Zimmerman?" The *Mission: Impossible* theme continued.

She rolled her eyes. "Do you?"

Heath nodded slowly and she continued, "Is it because he's the acting sheriff of Oak Creek? Or did you do some sort of training at Linear Tactical for the FBI? They do that stuff all the time. He's my brother."

She took the phone from him and walked back into the bathroom, already talking.

To her *brother*.

Gavin was her brother.

Heath had spent half the night making love to one of his best friends' *little* sister.

No, that couldn't be right. Gavin's sister's name was Jackie or something like that. And her last name would be Zimmerman, not Norris. He must have misunderstood.

His phone chirped in his hand, and he looked down to see an email from Craig.

You are right. Don't have to worry about Ms. Norris being one of the bad guys. Thanks for the coffee offer, this was much better.

He opened the attachment to find the brief on Lyn.

The first few lines confirmed everything he needed to know. He was going to get his ass kicked.

Jacquelyn Norris-Zimmerman. Known aliases: Jackie Zimmerman, Lyn Norris.

Keppima. Ficken. Jebati. Tā mā de. Faen. He didn't need Lyn—Jackie, Jacquelyn—here to give him any curse words. He was so, so, so, so, *so* screwed.

What was he going to do?

His phone chimed again, and he almost dropped it like it would burn him.

It was Noah this time.

Lyn's *cousin*, for crying out loud. Another person who was going to kill Heath.

Powell is awake. I think you should get over here and talk to him right away.

Heath could hear Lyn having some sort of heated discussion with Gavin in the bathroom.

Settling this, explaining this to Lyn, was going to take more time than he could give right now. If Powell knew something, and there was some sort of sale about to happen, time could be critical.

Lyn stormed out of the bathroom and threw her phone on the bed. "My brother pisses the hell out of me some-times. Most of the time, actually."

Heath had no idea how to handle this. "Did he hear about your townhouse?"

"No, thank goodness, or he'd already be here. This was just his weekly"—she dropped her voice two octaves to do an impression of Gavin—" 'there are bad people in the world and don't forget to take your medicine' call."

"Your anxiety medicine?" No, Gavin had said some-thing else about her, but Heath couldn't remember what.

Lyn pulled on her clothes. "No, I have a heart condition called Wolff-Parkinson-White syndrome. I take daily medication for it and sometimes have to take more if my heart is beating too fast."

"Crap, Lyn. We *really* need to talk."

"Yeah, I guess so. I guess I should tell you that my full name is Jacquelyn. Most of my family calls me Jackie, although I prefer Lyn." She walked over and stood up on her tiptoes, planting a brief kiss on his lips.

"I wasn't trying to keep secrets from you. And I guess I should tell you that my dad is the governor of Wyoming."

Heath scrubbed a hand over his face. He'd known Gavin's father was the governor, so, of course, yeah, that meant Lyn's dad was too.

Dréckt. What a damned brouhaha.

H e gave her the tiniest smile. "We really need to talk, but I can't do it right this second. I've got to go to work."

"Janitor work or other work?"

"Other work. Actually, I'm going to the hospital to question Troy Powell. He woke up this morning."

He expected concern or even distress. What he didn't expect was for Lyn to flush and turn away. "Oh."

He had no right to know what that was all about, especially since she didn't know he was a Linear Tactical employee and had known Gavin for years.

But screw that. "*Oh?*"

She shrugged, pulling her shirt over her head. "It's nothing."

"Is there something between you two?"

"No." She turned away, then sighed and turned back. "Really, no. It's just, before you got to the restaurant on Thursday, Troy kissed me."

Now it was Heath's turn. "Oh."

"But he didn't kiss me because I wanted him to. He was acting all weird."

She wasn't telling him all of it. In light of everything he'd learned in the past five minutes, her kissing someone else shouldn't even matter in the slightest.

And, yet . . . "I see. Did you like it? Is that what you're all flushed about?"

"No!" The word squeaked out of her immediately. "I just . . ."

"Yes?"

She sighed. "I hadn't been kissed in years and then was kissed by two men in the same night. Not my normal Thursday evening."

Heath relaxed a little. She wasn't interested in Powell, just a little overwhelmed by the attention. Still shouldn't be important. But . . . it was.

He hooked an arm around her. "I'm amazed complete strangers aren't coming up to kiss you all the time, as appealing as this mouth is."

She rolled her eyes. "Yeah, right."

"You try to hide behind glasses and books, but it doesn't take much to see how sexy you are. I think most men are intimidated."

That adorable nose crinkled. "By me?"

He grinned. "By the fact that you can sometimes be so caught up in your books, or papers, or whatever you're doing that you don't even really see men who might be interested in you. You're focused on other things. Competing with that concentration can be intimidating."

"I saw you."

"Thank goodness." He pulled her closer. "We'll continue this later, okay? I've got to deal with Powell first. And I'm glad you don't like him. Because it looks like he's probably one of the bad guys."

"Really?"

"Unfortunately. Someone is setting up a sale of the microchip the bad guys keep thinking you have. Powell would be a good candidate." Heath didn't want to mention

Veronica or Professor Hudson as suspects in case he was wrong.

"But someone attacked him."

"And I'm about to find out why."

She nodded. "I guess I should go home."

"No, I think you should stay here. Nobody knows where I live, so you'll be safe. And we really do need to talk when I get back."

She gave him the sweetest smile that had him cursing the fact that he knew Gavin Zimmerman at all. "Hurry back."

CHAPTER THIRTEEN

Heath shook Noah Dempsey's hand outside of Powell's hospital room.

"Good to see you again," he said. "I appreciate you coming out to help. We need people we can trust."

Noah didn't look a lot like his cousin. Gavin had a more of lean swimmer's build—quick and deadly— where Noah was more muscular. Gavin was darker, Noah more fair. But Noah definitely had the same awareness and heightened senses as the rest of the Linear Tactical team.

Noah had served in the Special Forces but had gotten out a few years ago. Heath knew the man struggled with PTSD, though not nearly as badly as Dorian, who had spent five weeks being tortured in Afghanistan. But Noah had his own demons.

Still, he could be trusted, and that's what mattered.

"I'm glad to be here. I've been reading Franklin's brief on what happened yesterday at WCU and the apartment break-in. Interesting stuff."

"Yeah?"

Noah held up his phone so that Heath could see the picture on the screen.

Lyn.

Noah raised an eyebrow. "I'm going to assume none of my cousins know that Jackie was at the center of both incidents. If so, Gavin would already be here. Tristan and Andrew too, if they were in the country."

Heath already knew Gavin was going to kick his butt when he found out what had happened with Lyn. He hoped he wouldn't have to fight Noah too.

"I knew Gavin's sister went to school here, but he told me she was a hospitality major. This person"—Heath tapped the phone screen—"who goes by the name *Lyn Norris*, with no Zimmerman anywhere in sight, is a linguistics doctoral student. I just found out she was related to you guys this morning."

To his relief, Noah laughed. "Good for Jackie. Sometimes the only way to deal with Uncle Ronald is to go around him. Let everybody think she's doing what they want when she really has her own plan. They never liked her studying linguistics, especially when she first started talking about traveling overseas for jobs."

"Her whole family thinks she's studying hospitality?" It made sense.

"Yup. She was smart to use her mom's maiden name on her official school stuff. The Zimmerman name is too well known to get away with much. But is she okay? That had to have scared her."

"Yes, actually, she's at my place."

Heath tried to keep his face neutral. The fact that it was early morning and Lyn was at his apartment didn't necessarily mean something had gone on between them.

Noah wasn't fooled for a second. He chuckled, shook

his head and put his phone back in his pocket. "Gavin's going to kill you."

"It's not like that."

"You didn't sleep with Jackie?"

Heath scrubbed a hand down his face. "I slept with Lyn Norris. Who I had no idea was related to Gavin in any way. Gavin made her sound like she was one step above invalid."

Lyn was very definitely not an invalid in any way. Heart condition, okay, maybe—which would explain the pills. They weren't anxiety meds, but medication for her heart condition. But she definitely wasn't anywhere near as frail as Gavin had made her sound.

"They've always been too protective of her. Gavin, the twins, her dad . . . none of them could see how much it was stifling her." Noah shrugged. "Gavin's still going to kill you though. Sorry, man."

"She might kill me first. I only found out who she was two minutes before I walked out the door. Didn't have time to explain that I worked for Linear Tactical or that her brother is one of my best friends. So, let's talk to Powell and see if we can get any useful information so I can get back to Lyn."

"The guy is definitely scared." Noah reached for the door handle. "I talked with him for a minute, in case he woke up wanting to spill his guts. To be honest, I think he feels like he's in over his head."

Heath pitied the younger man. "Fine. Then I'll get whatever info I can from him, and hopefully the bureau can help him get out."

"I'll stay out here and keep anyone else away."

Heath nodded and entered the room. Powell, twenty-four years old and with a good future ahead of him until he'd gotten greedy with these buyers, looked much worse than the last time Heath had seen him on Wednesday.

Someone had done a number on him. No wonder he was scared.

One of his eyes was completely swollen shut, the other side of his face covered with scrapes from where he'd been held against some hard surface. One arm had been broken and rested in a cast.

Powell obviously wasn't expecting Heath to walk through the hospital room door. And, because he hadn't seen Heath in his street clothes on Thursday, Troy didn't place him right away.

Heath walked over and stood silently beside Troy's bed. "Do you know who I am?"

Despite the beating and the painkillers in Troy's system, it didn't take him long to place Heath. "Wait, aren't you the janitor?"

"Among other things, yes."

"You're a cop."

"I'm working with law enforcement. Yes."

"When that other guy came in here, I thought he was just fishing for information. I didn't think the cops were actually onto me." Troy shifted and winced in pain. "I guess you know a lot more than I thought if you've been working undercover as the janitor."

"We know you're in way over your head. You need to tell me what you know and how deeply you're involved. Let us help you."

Troy looked away for a long moment before finally turning back to him. "Last year, when I finally was given full access in the lab, a man contacted me who wanted to know if I was interested in making a little side money."

"Who?"

Troy shrugged, then winced. "I don't know. We've only ever communicated via phone or email, never face-to-face."

Heath wasn't surprised. "What did he want you to do?"

"Nothing terrible. Bits of information here and there. Nothing that was of critical importance or top secret."

"And you gave it to him?"

Troy looked away. "I needed money. I have nearly a hundred thousand dollars in student loans from undergrad. He paid well for stuff that really wasn't important. I figured he was reverse engineering some stuff and needed the data to make it easier. But I swear, none of what I sold was government secrets."

If that was true, and Troy hadn't let it progress any further, then he wouldn't be in real trouble with the feds. Theft was bad news, but not nearly as bad as selling government research secrets. That would be considered treason.

But minor theft wouldn't have left this kid so badly beaten and in the hospital. There had to be more to it.

"But it escalated," Heath prompted.

Troy nodded. "That earlier stuff . . . I don't think it was what the buyer wanted at all. I think it was just to reel me in, to force me into a place where I couldn't say no when something big like the microchip became available. And I don't think I'm the only one he's got in his pocket."

"Veronica Williams? Dale Hudson?"

Troy shifted slightly on the bed. "Both of them had access. Especially Professor Hudson. Veronica's a grad student like me, but Professor Hudson would have complete access to everything."

Plus, Hudson was having an affair with Veronica. Were they working together? Was Hudson keeping Veronica close to prevent her from figuring out what he was doing?

Rodriguez and Collins had been assigned to surveil

Veronica and Hudson. If either of them did something odd, the newbies would report it immediately.

"I haven't told you everything," Troy whispered.

Heath's eyes locked with Troy's. "What?"

"The microchip is dangerous."

"I know that. It's why I'm here." Heath didn't need to know the specifics to know it couldn't fall into the wrong hands. Whatever the microchip did, it was dangerous.

"Okay. But without the initial algorithm, the info on the chip is pretty useless. There's no baseline for the microchip to begin its progress."

Heath's eyes narrowed. "So it takes two parts in order to make it work."

"Eventually, it won't need the separate algorithm. That's part of what we're working on in the biomedical engineering lab. But yes, right now, two parts."

Heath nodded. "Okay. What's the problem?"

"I realized on Thursday the algorithm had been replaced with a fake. I came across it accidentally. Whoever switched it out obviously meant to do so undetected."

"So one of the two parts needed are already gone." Damn it.

Troy's look was even more pinched. "Actually . . . both parts are already gone."

Heath moved closer. "What exactly are you saying, Powell?"

"When I noticed the algorithm switch, I took the microchip. I know it doesn't seem this way, but I was actually trying to do the right thing. Keep it out of the buyers' hands."

"Do you have it now?" Heath asked.

"No. I went out for drinks on Thursday. Veronica and Professor Hudson were there. I wasn't sure what to do about the wrong algorithm or the microchip. There was a slim chance the algorithm change could've been due to human error. But when I brought up the error, everybody got mad."

Heath nodded. "Okay." That had to have been just minutes before Heath arrived. "Tell me more about that."

"Veronica was defensive since she was the last one to set the algorithm. So if it was an error, it was hers. She didn't like that. Professor Hudson wasn't thrilled with me bringing it up either."

Again, that could be because Hudson was sleeping with Veronica.

Troy shook his head. "I told them I thought we needed to up security. Professor Hudson told me not do anything rash like report it. He would look into it himself and take the necessary measures."

"But you didn't think that was enough."

"No."

Heath wiped a hand down his face. "Yet you didn't really want anyone looking into security because it was going to uncover the other things you'd done."

"Pretty much." Troy nodded.

"So you decided to handle it yourself? What? Go back and get the microchip?"

"No. I went home. I walked, which was a stupid idea. I never made it. I was attacked."

Heath balled his fist. This didn't make any sense. What purpose would it serve for the buyer to attack Troy?

"What was it, a warning? To back off about the security or to scare you into stealing the microchip for the buyer yourself?"

Troy shifted in his bed, looking away again. "No. I'd already taken the microchip before I went to the restaurant Thursday."

"*What?*" Did this mean the chip and the algorithm were already gone? "Did the attacker know that?"

Troy nodded.

"So the buyer already has the microchip," Heath muttered.

Damn it. He reached for his phone. He needed to get Craig and every other available trustworthy FBI agent on this. Like right damn now.

"No," Troy said, barely more than a whisper.

Heath took a deep breath. "Finish, Powell. *Now.*"

Troy started talking quickly. "After I had the argument with Professor Hudson and Veronica, I got nervous. They were acting weird. Plus, two big guys were hanging around that I'd seen around before. So I handed the microchip off to someone else."

"Who?"

"Someone not in the biomed department. I kissed her and slipped it into her sweater pocket while she was distracted."

Heath could feel his teeth grind together. "You gave the microchip to *Lyn Norris?*"

"She was the only one I knew for sure wasn't in on this. I couldn't trust any of my biomedical engineering colleagues."

Events from the past twenty-four hours snapped into place. No wonder someone had trashed her apartment and tried to abduct her from her office.

She *did* have the microchip.

"And you told whoever attacked you that you gave it to her." Heath could feel rage pooling in his blood.

"I only said some girl named Lyn. I don't think the thugs who hit me meant to put me in a coma, I just hit the wall wrong."

Heath had no doubt that if Troy had remained conscious, he would've given up every detail about Lyn, and she'd be dead or badly hurt and the microchip in the buyer's hands.

"Is there anything else?" he asked the younger man, who now had a sickly cast to his skin.

"No, that's it." Troy's voice was small.

"People did come after her, Powell. It's a good thing for you she wasn't hurt." Or else Heath might be finishing what the thugs had started.

"I'm sorry. I was trying to make up for the other bad stuff I'd done. Make sure the wrong person didn't get his hands on the microchip."

Heath nodded. Troy was done in the graduate program. He'd be lucky if he didn't actually do some prison time. But Heath believed Troy had been trying to do what he'd thought was right in this situation.

Thankfully, Lyn was safe at Heath's apartment. No one knew where he lived. The name and address listed at the university was totally different from his real apartment.

Noah opened the door and tilted his head toward the hallway. "Can I see you out here?"

Heath nodded, then looked at Troy. "I'm not sure how this is all going to play out, but I'll be sure to let people know that you were trying to help."

Troy nodded and Heath walked out with Noah.

"Collins just reported in. She tried contacting you but didn't get a response," Noah said once the door was closed. "Veronica Williams slipped her tail about thirty minutes ago."

"Deliberately?"

Noah nodded. "Very deliberately. As in she had some sort of hired muscle that knocked Collins unconscious."

"I need to get back to my place. It ends up Lyn does have the microchip. Troy planted it on her."

Noah raised an eyebrow. "On Lyn?"

"It's a long story." He grabbed his phone to call her and saw he had two missed texts from about twenty minutes ago.

Hey, I forgot my charger at my house yesterday. Phone is about to die so I'll see you when you get here.

But the next one had him running down the hospital corridor at a sprint.

Veronica Williams called. She's coming over to chat.

He called Lyn's phone as he ran, but her battery must've already been dead. It went straight to voice mail.

Lyn was at his apartment alone and had no idea Veronica might have plans to hurt her.

Heath ran faster.

CHAPTER FOURTEEN

ey, where ARE you? Two kisses on Thursday from two different guys and then I get NO details. Need a girls chat, stat.

Lyn made a face at Veronica's text. Lyn wasn't really into girl chat, and while Veronica seemed friendly enough, Lyn definitely didn't want to talk about kissing either Troy or Heath.

But she also wanted Veronica to be safe. So if that meant inviting her over here so whoever was searching for the microchip wouldn't hurt her . . . Lyn would make do.

Her phone battery was about to die, and in her rush to get out of the townhouse last night, she'd forgotten her charger.

Heath had made it sound like it would be quite a while before he returned. Might as well get her over here so he wouldn't have to worry about protection detail at two different locations.

I'm at Heath's. He's out for a while. Want to come over?

HECK YEAH. I'll bring coffee.

She gave Veronica the address, then texted Heath to tell him the plan. She waited, a little disappointed when he didn't respond right away.

Was it just her, or had he been acting a little funny this morning? Not that she could blame him . . . finding out she was related to Wyoming's governor tended to be a little overwhelming. Not to mention, Gavin was almost a celebrity in his own right when it came to law enforcement. Groups from all over the country came to train with the guys from Linear Tactical. It wasn't surprising Heath knew him.

She hadn't been trying to lie to him about anything. It was so much easier to be Lyn Norris sometimes than Jacquelyn Zimmerman.

She'd make sure he understood that when he got back. That she hadn't meant any deceit.

Surely, he would understand. She'd sort of been on her own version of undercover.

Because she definitely didn't want to let this come between them. Last night had been beyond amazing. Yesterday, she might have doubted that he truly found her beautiful, but she could not possibly have those same doubts this morning. She could still feel him everywhere. If she closed her eyes, she could feel his lips skimming over her throat and shoulders and beyond.

But that wasn't the sort of stuff she wanted to share with Veronica. That was private. Personal. She didn't want to share those details with anyone. Would Veronica push? Had she made a mistake inviting her?

Maybe she should tell her not to come. Surely her safety wasn't in too much danger. She glanced down at her phone and found it off—completely out of power.

Girls' chat it was.

Lyn had barely finished getting dressed in what she'd brought from her house—yoga pants and a long-sleeved shirt —and braiding her hair down her back when the doorbell rang. That was quicker than she'd thought.

Lyn opened the door, and Veronica bounded in.

"Hey, sweetie." The taller woman threw her arms around Lyn, even with coffee cups in both hands. "Look at you, here in a man's house so early in the morning. There must have been some naughty deeds going on last night!"

So much for Veronica not pushing. Lyn returned Veronica's enthusiastic hug a little awkwardly. She wasn't much of a hugger. "Hi, Veronica."

Veronica released her, and they walked into the kitchen. Lyn added some milk and sugar to the coffee cup Veronica handed her, because it needed it, but also to gain a little space.

"Rewind to Thursday and start with Troy. Is there something going on with him? I had no idea. And now Janitor Hottie?" Veronica was firing out the questions faster than Lyn could answer them, not that she wanted to.

"No, there's nothing going on between Troy and me. He kissed me at the restaurant totally out of the blue. I had no idea he was interested in me like that."

"That doesn't seem like Troy. There must be more between you than you're telling me."

Why did Veronica want to talk about Troy? They were sitting here in *Heath's* apartment. Obviously, Lyn hadn't chosen Troy.

Lyn gave the best smile she could manage, then took a sip of her coffee. "There's not much to tell. It was pretty awkward."

And now he was in the hospital and possibly part of

some illegal scheme to sell government secrets. Definitely awkward.

But Veronica was not to be deterred. She moved closer and bumped Lyn with her hip. "How did Troy do it? Move in fast? Slow? You guys were outside, right?"

As much as Lyn hadn't wanted to share intimate details about her night with Heath, she *definitely* did not want to talk about her kiss with Troy.

She took a gulp of her coffee, burning her mouth, and moved to the other side of the table. "Heath's kiss was much more interesting, no doubt about it." Surely this would get Veronica off the topic.

Nope. "But you've known Troy for a while, right? Do you guys have a past? There's more than you're telling, isn't there?"

Lyn shook her head, taken aback. "No. Never. Let's change the subject, okay? Talk about other girl stuff."

Veronica studied her from across the table as if looking for clues. Is that how girl chats normally went? If so, Lyn hadn't been missing much over the years. This was decidedly uncomfortable.

Finally, Veronica smiled. "Okay, no past history, and Troy just came up out of the blue and kissed you. Did he say or do anything weird?"

"Besides a very public, unprovoked kiss? Um, no." Wasn't that enough?

Veronica took her phone out of her pocket and texted someone. This entire situation had become super weird. Lyn was used to most social interactions being awkward, but this went even beyond that. Veronica finished her text and looked up from her phone.

She didn't even look like the same person.

All semblance of the friend who had come to the door a

few minutes ago was gone. The person sitting across from her now was cold, calculating, unfeeling.

"This is your last chance, Lyn." Veronica leaned forward on the table. "Tell me what is going on between you and Troy. Are you partners?"

Lyn sat up straighter in her chair. "Nothing is going on between me and Troy. Something happened between me and Heath, but you don't seem to care about that."

"The janitor? No, we definitely don't care about him. Although he was quite problematic at the school yesterday."

We? Who was *we*? And why did Veronica know about what had happened on campus?

Lyn stood. "I think you need to leave, Veronica."

Veronica stood also. She was taller than Lyn, probably stronger. Could Lyn get around her if she ran? A knock on the door interrupted Lyn's thoughts.

Heath? No. He wouldn't be knocking on his own door.

Even worse, Veronica didn't seem surprised by the knock at all. She grabbed Lyn's arm, pulled her to the door, and opened it.

There stood the man with the gun from yesterday and another guy, bald. Maybe even the one Lyn had seen at the restaurant. Veronica let them into the apartment, obviously friendly.

Finally, common sense broke through Lyn's stupor. She snatched her arm from the other woman's hold, sprinting toward the back door. But the first man caught her halfway across the living room. He thrust her so hard into the bookshelves lining Heath's sidewall that half of them fell over.

What was it with this guy and trying to kill her with books?

He backhanded her; pain exploded through her face, sending her stumbling to the floor.

Maybe he planned to kill her by any means necessary.

"You should've just told me what you know about Troy, Lyn." Veronica tsked and shook her head. "Max here isn't known for subtlety."

Lyn could taste blood in her mouth where her teeth had cut the inside of her cheek. She slid away from Max. The bald guy stood guard by the front door.

"I don't know anything about Troy." She pointed at Max. "And I don't know anything about the microchip this jerk was talking about yesterday when he grabbed me."

"We know you have it," Veronica said.

"Why do you think that?" Her voice sounded weird from the swelling in her mouth. Her heart thumped in an uneven gallop. She needed her pills. They were in Heath's bedroom. "You know I'm not in your department. Why would I have a microchip?"

"Troy gave it to you," Veronica said.

"No, he didn't. We aren't partners in anything. He's in the hospital. How could he have given me anything?"

"He gave it to you Thursday night, Lyn."

Lyn froze. That kiss. Troy's weird behavior. He'd given her the microchip, slipped it into her purse or something.

"That's right. Or did you really think he'd kissed you because he was interested?" Veronica smirked and looked over Lyn as she lay sprawled on the floor. "I still can't believe the janitor wanted you. Especially once I saw him in street clothes."

Lyn ignored the crack about her and Heath. "If Troy gave me the microchip, he never told me about it."

"Before he decided to go into a coma like a little whimp, he admitted he'd given the microchip to someone named Lyn. That's obviously you." Veronica leered at her. "Max tried to find the microchip at your townhouse, then your office. He planned to question you, but your janitor boyfriend got in the way. I tried to call you last night to see if I could get any closer, but you didn't answer."

Max was obviously fed up with the talking. He leaned down and got into Lyn's face, his breath hot and putrid. "Where's your purse?" He grabbed Lyn by the shirt. She cringed, preparing for another blow.

Veronica intervened. "Max, relax. Let's not have another coma incident. Her purse is in the kitchen."

Lyn whimpered as Max grabbed her by her hair, pulled her up, and dragged her into the kitchen. He threw her against the refrigerator—the same refrigerator where Heath had kissed her so thoroughly last night when they'd come out for a midnight snack—and watched as Veronica dumped everything from her bag onto the table.

How long would it be before Heath returned?

She knew the microchip was important. Heath had been working undercover for weeks to try to catch the perpetrators. She needed to do something, but what? Even if she could get the microchip, there was no way she could get around Max.

"It's not in here," Veronica said after she checked every section of Lyn's purse and sorted through all the contents.

Max grabbed both of her arms and rammed her against the refrigerator. "I am tired of playing games. Where is the microchip?"

Tears welled out of Lyn's eyes, and her heart stuttered harder, making breathing difficult. "I don't know. I swear I don't know."

"What clothing were you wearing on Thursday, Lyn?" Veronica said. "Think. Could he have slipped it in something you were wearing?"

She'd worn jeans and a blouse. Nothing special. Nothing Troy could've slipped something into except . . .

"Maybe my sweater. It's the only other place. It has deep pockets."

"Is it here?" Veronica said.

"The bedroom," Lyn wheezed. She forced herself to cough hard—another vagal maneuver to try to get the fluttering under control.

She hoped that it would be just Veronica who came with her into the bedroom. Lyn would use some of the self-defense moves Gavin had taught her and make a run for the window.

But Max followed too. There was no way she could take them both down.

Think, Lyn.

She stalled as much as possible, pretending to look for the garment even though it was peeking over the chair in the corner. The room was a mess; she hadn't even had a chance to make up the bed. The delay at least allowed her to get her breathing and heart rate back under control.

"You guys did have a good time in here, didn't you?" Veronica snickered. "Always the quiet ones."

Lyn lifted the comforter, looking under it. Then the pillows.

She needed to figure out something and fast. Because once they had that microchip, they might decide that keeping her alive wasn't smart. She could identify them.

And if Heath came home, it could get even worse. He might be an FBI agent, but he wouldn't know there was danger.

Nobody was bulletproof.

"Maybe it's out in the living room," she finally said, turning back toward them from the corner after searching under a couple of throw pillows that had fallen to the ground last night.

But Veronica was at the chair, picking up the cardigan for herself. "I think we've got your dowdy little sweater right here."

CHAPTER FIFTEEN

"Lyn invited Veronica to my apartment, not knowing she was behind this," Heath told Noah as they both ran down the hospital hallway. "Call Rodriguez and tell him to breach Dale Hudson's house. We need to know if he's in on this or not. Then get Collins and have her meet us at my apartment."

Noah shook his head. "Veronica led her out of town before getting the drop on her. I doubt Collins will make it back in time to help us."

Heath dialed Craig as he ran. "Veronica Williams is definitely one of our perps," he said without any greeting.

"I know," Craig responded. "Collins updated me."

"Troy Powell also admitted to planting the microchip on Lyn, and Veronica knows about it. We're on our way there now. This could be really ugly."

"I'll work on getting locals there."

"They can't go in sirens blaring. That could be a death sentence for Lyn."

"I'm on it." Craig hung up without another word.

They reached the car, Noah still on the phone and

barking orders at Rodriguez. He got into the passenger side as Heath slid behind the wheel.

His apartment was twenty minutes away. He hoped Craig could get some uniformed officers there before that. Because once Veronica and her hired muscle found the microchip, Lyn's life wouldn't hold much value.

Heath was barreling down the on-ramp to the interstate when Noah finished his call.

"Rodriguez is preparing to knock on Hudson's door right now. Collins is still too far out to do us any good."

Heath grimaced. "If Craig can't get uniforms there in time, we might be going into a situation where we have no tactical advantage and very little surprise."

Noah came from good stock; Heath had no doubt the man would be cool under pressure. But that didn't change the fact that they would probably be outgunned and outmanned, along with a civilian who may or may not be injured.

Because there was no damn way he was going to think of Lyn as dead.

Noah's phone rang.

"Actually, I'm not sure if you're going to want to thank me or deck me for this one, but . . ." Noah pressed the receive button on his phone, putting it on speaker. "Hey, Gavin, I'm in the car with Heath and have you on speaker. We've got a little situation."

Crap.

Gavin's voice was granite. "Damn it, Kavanaugh, you told me you hadn't talked to my sister at all."

Heath's hands tightened around the steering wheel. This wasn't how he'd wanted Gavin to find out about this. "You didn't tell me that your sister went by the name Lyn Norris."

Gavin's curse was long and foul. "Her house got broken into, and she was held at gunpoint by someone involved in your case? What the hell is happening?"

"Gavin, we've got bigger problems."

He could almost hear the focus come over his friend. "What?"

"Lyn is in danger. Someone planted the microchip on her, and the perps found out about it. Noah and I are on our way to my apartment now, where Lyn is, but we're going in blind, and unless Craig has already sent in the cavalry, we're going in alone."

"Oh no you're not. My ETA to your address is five minutes."

"Told you they were overprotective," Noah whispered. "I called him before you arrived at the hospital. He was on his way ten minutes later."

Heath would have to deal with the beating coming from Gavin later. Right now, he only had one thing to focus on: getting Lyn safe. At least he knew that was a priority for Gavin and Noah also.

"Fine, we can use all the help we can get." The tires squealed as Heath took the off-ramp way too fast. "I think our best bet is to infiltrate my apartment from two locations at the same time. I hope you brought some firearms, Gav."

"Have you ever known me to go anywhere without them?"

"Two of us should go through the back door," Heath continued, "and then let the third be a surprise. I know for a fact my bedroom window is open unless Lyn closed it after I left this morning."

Silence filled the car.

He had to give it to Gavin, he stayed on task, not

bringing up the question of why Lyn might have been in Heath's bedroom.

But he had no doubt his friend was not going to forget it.

"I'll take the window. Get eyes inside and report. You guys take the door," Noah said.

"This is not a great plan." Heath's knuckles turned white on the steering wheel. Not a great plan was the understatement of the century. There were holes in this plan big enough to drive a car through.

"Jacquelyn has a heart condition. Arrhythmia. Stress can trigger some bad effects for her." Concern was clear in Gavin's voice.

"J-Lyn has been dealing with her heart issues for a long time," Noah said. "She'll be okay."

"I refuse to call her J-Lyn," Gavin grumbled.

"Might I remind you that if you had called her J-Lyn like she wanted to be called, your bestie over here might've realized she was your sister before, you know . . . *stashing* her in his apartment?"

Noah smiled as Heath rolled his eyes. Let Noah stir the pot. At least it was keeping Heath's focus off the fact that the guy who'd held Lyn at gun point and tried to bury her under a ton of books yesterday probably had her in his clutches again.

And overprotective or not, Gavin was right. She did have a heart condition.

"We're pulling up now," Heath said.

"I'm right behind you." Gavin's voice was tight. "Noah, give us a ten-second warning text when you're in position."

Heath parked a hundred yards short of his apartment complex in case anyone was looking out the windows. A few seconds later, Gavin pulled up behind him. Heath pointed out which unit was his.

"You carrying?" Gavin asked his cousin.

Noah looked offended and pointed at Heath. "Remember how you felt when he asked that question?"

Gavin handed Heath a Glock, and the three of them ran toward the apartment, keeping close to the building so they wouldn't be as noticeable.

"You and I are going to have a talk when this is over and my sister is safe."

"Deal." He would take any *talk* he had to if Lyn was safe. Maybe Gavin would even let him get a word in edgewise, but Heath doubted it.

They waited at the back door for word from Noah. It was all Heath could do to keep from breaching immediately —even knowing the best odds came from sticking with the makeshift plan they'd come up with. He was never going to forgive himself if something happened to Lyn.

Finally, the text from Noah.

I'm in and have eyes. Two big guys and a female. All armed and moving. Lyn scared but not hurt.

As they stepped up to the door, ingrained training took over for everyone. Heath didn't have a key to the back door with him so they would have to break it to get in. He knew as soon as they slammed into it, all hell would break loose.

Ten seconds.

He motioned to Gavin, and they hit it together on the hinge side. A bolt would often hold against brute strength, but hinges rarely did.

Heath saw the two big guys immediately. One was from the university yesterday.

"Police. Put your hands in the air," Gavin called out.

Both bad guys reached for their guns instead. Heath and Gavin scattered and dropped to the ground to divide their targets as both thugs fired their weapons.

Heath felt the burn of a bullet graze his shoulder as the television smashed into pieces behind him.

Too damn close.

He ignored the pain, pushing himself quickly to his feet as he squeezed off three rounds. The guy who had tried to take Lyn yesterday groaned before falling to the ground.

A few seconds later, Noah blazed out of the bedroom in a hail of gunfire, sending a bullet into the bald thug as he was about to take another shot at Gavin. The force spun him around.

"Drop the weapon or the next shot won't just wound," Noah told the man.

The man grimaced but dropped the gun to the floor. Noah kicked it away.

"Down on the ground," Heath told him. The man dropped to his knees.

Where were Lyn and Veronica?

Heath only had a second to wonder before Veronica walked out from the kitchen using Lyn as a human shield. She had her in a chokehold, a gun pressed to Lyn's temple.

"Now, now, boys. I'd hate for anyone else to get hurt. Especially Lyn here."

All three men swung their weapons toward Veronica.

"There's no way you're going to make it out of here alive, Veronica," Heath said.

Veronica shot one eyebrow up. "That may be true, but you can damn well believe if I'm going out, she's going out too. So everybody put the guns down."

Heath lowered his weapon, as did Gavin and Noah.

"Now, put them on the ground."

They all reluctantly did so.

"Look at you, all secret agent," Veronica sneered. "I should've known when you showed up at the restaurant, kissing on this one, that you were on some sort of under-cover job. As if you'd be interested in her otherwise." She jerked Lyn tighter.

Heath looked at Lyn. Her breaths were short and labored as she tried to breathe around Veronica's arm across her throat. Terror radiated from her eyes.

Hold on, sweetheart.

"The reverse beauty and the beast story was too good to be true," Veronica continued. "When I realized I was being tailed today, I knew law enforcement was closing in, but I didn't think it was you."

"She means nothing to me, Veronica. Just part of the case, like you said. And while I'd hate for any innocent life to be lost, there is no way I'm letting you walk out with that microchip. That's worth more than any one life."

Heath forced himself not to look at Lyn as he said the totally untrue words. Acid burned in his gut at the thought of playing on Lyn's insecurities. Even if it meant saving her life.

In his periphery, Gavin, arms still upraised, squeezed his shoulder two times before touching his elbow. To anyone else—Veronica included—it would look like nervous movements brought on by the stress of the situation.

But it was a signal to Heath.

Two squeezes meant twenty seconds, the touch to the elbow meant Gavin would be using his backup weapon.

Heath still had his hands held up by his head. He crossed his fingers, signifying he understood, then gently tilted his hand forward. He would dive for them.

Gavin's fingers crossed also—he understood. Then he made a slight fist. The countdown started now.

Heath automatically kept the seconds counting down in his head as he looked at Lyn's face. Her eyes had narrowed and darted back and forth between him and Gavin. She'd seen the nonverbal code and knew they were working in tandem.

Of course she had. She was too brilliant and observant not to.

"Let me go, and everybody gets to live. It's a simple choice, Heath. If that's even your name."

Heath moved to the side, an appearance of moving farther away but really just at a different angle. "Fine, Veronica. You know what? You can—"

Twenty.

Heath pounced. This plan would only work if he and Gavin were perfectly in sync and trusted each other. Gavin might beat him up when this was all done, but Heath trusted him without hesitation now.

Heath's movement startled Veronica, and she instinctively swung her gun toward him, drawing it away from Lyn's head and leaving herself open. Gavin fired with his hidden backup weapon in that instant.

Veronica fell backward as the bullet hit her in the shoulder at the same time Heath pulled Lyn away from the other woman, his arms wrapping around her as they both went flying to the ground.

Gavin immediately moved in on Veronica, kicking the gun out of her reach. Noah grabbed his weapon and kept the other two thugs on the ground.

"Everybody okay?" Gavin called out.

"Good," Noah said from the other side of the room before muttering something threatening to one of the bad guys.

"I'm okay." Heath turned to Lyn. She slid away from him, eyes huge, but at least her breathing seemed regular. "You okay, Almost?"

Sirens blared outside as cops pulled up in time to be of no use at all.

Lyn leaned back against the wall, looking from Heath to Gavin to Noah, then back to Heath. "Yes, I'm okay. But you're hurt," she finally said.

Heath looked down at his arm where the bullet had grazed him. Blood oozed from the wound, but nothing serious. "I'll need to get it looked at, but it's really more a burn than anything else. I'm okay."

He reached toward her, wanting to run a finger down her cheek, to assure her it was all going to be okay. She had a bruise on the side of her face and marks on her neck. And she had to be in shock.

But when she flinched away, Heath stopped. "Lyn . . ."

"You know my brother. Know him well. There's no way you two could've communicated like you just did without having worked with each other for a long time."

Crap. "Yes. I'm actually part of Linear Tactical."

"You told me you were FBI."

"I am. They brought me in under special circumstances . . . it's complicated."

Gavin took the microchip from Veronica, cuffed her, and sat her on the ground. He walked over to Lyn, helping her up from the floor. Heath stayed where he was since she didn't want him near her right now.

"You need to take your pills," Gavin muttered. "And come over here and sit down on the couch. We've got an ambulance on its way."

She shook her head, a mutinous press to her lips. "I don't need my pills, Gavin. I've been managing my own health for a long time."

"You still need to go to the hospi—"

"*No.*" Lyn all but roared the word. It was the loudest

Heath had ever heard her speak.

Everybody got quiet.

Until Gavin got stupid. "Damn it, Jackie, or should I call you *Lyn?*"

Her eyes narrowed. "If memory serves, I asked you to call me that years ago, but you all refused."

"Told you," Noah muttered.

"Whatever." Gavin threw both hands up in the air. "Jackie. Lyn. Norris. Zimmerman. Whatever you want to be called. You've been through a lot. You need to go to the hospital."

Heath could see Lyn try to pull herself together. To find some sort of reasonable tone to deal with her brother—obviously something she'd had to do before.

"I'm not going, Gavin. I'm fine." Her voice was remarkably even.

Gavin shook his head. "If you don't go to the hospital, I'm going to . . ."

"Tell Dad?" she finished for him.

Noah let the paramedics and police officers in the door. Agent Rodriguez followed them in.

Gavin looked like he was about to tear his hair out by the roots. "Damn it, Jackie. Quit acting like a child."

Movement was going on all around them, but Lyn stood completely still, her voice low. "You're right. I have been acting like a child. That ends now."

She turned and walked toward the door.

"Lyn—" Heath reached for her, but she deftly side-stepped him.

"I'll need to give a statement, so send someone over to my townhouse. I've had enough of . . . everyone. I'm going home."

She turned and walked out the door.

CHAPTER SIXTEEN

An hour after Lyn stormed out, Heath was ready to set fire to his entire apartment.

At least that would get everyone out of here.

"I'm not cut out for law enforcement, man," he said to Noah.

They stood at the back of the living room—only a couple feet from where he'd kissed Lyn last night—trying to stay out of the way of the horde of officers and agents inside his apartment.

The only thing he really wanted to do was go after Lyn and try to explain to her what was going on. But Craig needed him here, and Lyn looked like she might need a little time to cool off.

Roughly three and a half decades, if he had to guess.

He'd already called her a dozen times, leaving more than one message.

He'd texted her twice that many times. Just asking if she was okay. Asking if she'd give him the chance to explain the situation a little better.

Read.

Every single message gave the tiny little notification: *Read*.

She'd seen them all but hadn't responded.

The thought that he'd lost her before he'd even gotten the chance to get to know her ate at him.

"Same here," Noah responded. "My brother, Tanner, is the cop in our family. He ropes me in to helping him every once in a while, but I'd rather be on my ranch with the horses."

"Can't blame you there. Way too many rules and red tape with law enforcement. I've been working overseas for Linear for five years. A lot of kidnap and ransom situations, corporate security type stuff. So it's sort of like this but without all the red tape."

A Sublette County detective argued with Craig over jurisdiction. Both Heath and Noah rolled their eyes. Who the hell cared as long as the bad guys were off the street?

"You going to stick around Oak Creek or go back to international work?"

"I was mostly international because I was trying to stay off the radar. Long story short, I was concerned I might be messed up in the head." Hearing voices in a gibberish language certainly qualified as a little crazy.

"PTSD? That's an issue for me sometimes."

"No. Just straight-up regular crazy for me. But I think I'm ready to stay in Wyoming for a while. Teach some classes."

Learn to live with the voices in his head.

Convince Lyn that Reddington City wasn't too far from Oak Creek, and that they needed to give whatever was between them a fair shot.

If she ever spoke to him again.

Heath was surprised to see the locals leading Veronica

and her two henchmen away. Evidently, Craig had lost his argument about it being his arrest. He made his way over to them, not looking happy.

"Let's go. The locals are going to take them into custody."

Heath and Noah shot each other a glance, then followed Craig out the door.

"Is this going to mess up your case?" Noah asked.

"They're in custody, that's what's matters. Right now, I want to turn our attention to the buyers before they go to ground."

"What's your plan?" Heath asked.

"We use Powell. We'll get him to contact the buyer today. Convince the buyer he's had a change of heart and that he wants to meet tonight."

"There's no way Powell is going to be healthy enough to do any sort of sting operation." Heath pulled the passenger side door open and Noah got in the back.

Craig started the car. "You're right. That's why I'm hoping you'll be willing to impersonate him since you've been around him the most."

Heath knew how much catching these buyers meant to Craig. "I'm willing to try. Powell said they never met face-to-face, so it could work."

It was a long shot, but possible.

They drove to the hospital to talk to Powell, who seemed more than willing to set up the exchange if it meant he might be looking at less jail time. He texted his contact with the proposal, then waited for instructions. A few minutes later, he got a text back.

Powell spun his phone around toward them. "Okay, I'm supposed to meet the buyer outside the all-night waffle place at midnight."

"Great," Heath said. "Midnight."

Noah nudged him. "At least it's not an abandoned warehouse."

Craig talked to Powell a little longer, trying to make sure the younger man didn't have any other useful information, then they all left.

"Noah and I will be keeping a tight eye on the place tonight," Craig said as they got back in the car.

Heath looked out the window. "I'm not doubting my own skills here, but don't you think you might want to bring in some real feds for this op instead of those of us on loan?"

"I'm still not sure who I can trust in my office, but I will get everyone I can to make sure we have significant backup. Believe me, catching the buyer is my number one priority."

Heath nodded. "I'll do this, Craig, but then I'm out."

Lyn's frightened face as the gun was pressed to her temple flashed before his eyes. The bruises, the scratch marks.

"There's somebody who never signed up for any of this who ended up paying the biggest price. I need to make that right."

By the time midnight rolled around, it had been a long damn day. Heath wished he could go back to how it had started—in bed with Lyn.

Not with another dozen messages left *Read* but with no response.

Currently, Heath stood in front of the waffle diner at the northwest corner of a strip mall parking lot. There were a few people in the diner, and the overall outdoor lighting around the building wasn't great.

In other words, the buyer had picked a good location.

"And you look cute in the skinny jeans," Noah said into the transmitter in Heath's ear. He was in a surveillance vehicle somewhere in the parking lot. "Quite the hipster."

Noah knew Heath couldn't respond and had been teasing him about his outfit for the past few minutes.

Powell's clothing choices leaned much more toward the latest trends than Heath's. And since Heath was supposed to be Powell . . . he had the dubious honor of slipping on skinny jeans and a button-down Oxford shirt.

Heath could feel eyes on him. Some of them belonged Craig and Noah and whatever ragtag team Craig had pulled together, but there were others.

He had Troy's phone in his hand, checking it periodically. Would the buyer meet him here? Send more instructions? Not show up at all because he'd figured out Heath wasn't Troy?

After fifteen minutes of standing outside, he turned toward the diner's door so his face would be more hidden. "I'm going to go inside. Staying out here makes me too conspicuous."

Craig's voice sounded in his ear. "Roger that."

Inside, Heath studied the patrons—an older couple in the back booth, two students at the table near the door, and a man sitting alone drinking a cup of coffee.

That could be the mark.

"Sit anywhere you like," the waitress said as she breezed by on her way to the couple in the booth.

Heath chose a booth where he could easily see the rest of the diner. Nobody else seemed to be paying any attention to him.

Was this all for nothing? Had the perp spotted someone and decided to take off?

Yet . . . there was something going on, Heath could feel it. He didn't ignore his gut when it came to stuff like this.

But what was it?

On one hand, he wished Gavin were here. The man was uncanny when it came to spotting things other people missed. But on the other hand, Gavin wasn't taking any chances and was staying with Lyn.

Or he was at least parked in front of her house since she wouldn't let him in.

Heath took a sip of water, wincing when the gibberish started whispering in his head.

Now wasn't the time.

He rubbed his head as it got louder.

"You okay, Kavanaugh?" Craig asked.

Heath covered his mouth with his hand. "Yeah, just a headache."

The girl sitting over in the corner with her boyfriend stood up and walked across the restaurant toward the bathroom. The door had barely closed behind her before her boyfriend walked over and slid into the booth across from Heath.

"You Troy Powell?"

Damn, this was not what Heath had been expecting. The kid barely looked twenty years old. "Who wants to know?"

The kid shrugged. "Take the item you brought into the kitchen. There's someone waiting for you there."

The kid stood up without another word and walked to the front of the diner to pay the bill, meeting his girlfriend as she came out of the bathroom and escorting her out.

Heath covered his mouth again. "Did you guys hear that?"

"Roger," Craig said. "We've got eyes on the back door.

You're clear to go back there. Noah, you follow the guy and his girlfriend."

"Roger that," Noah said.

"Heading back to the kitchen," Heath whispered.

He kept his hand near the waist holster tucked under his shirt as he walked past the waitress, who seem too tired to care that he was going somewhere he wasn't supposed to go.

Everything in the kitchen looked normal, but Heath didn't let his guard down.

"You Troy somebody or other?" one of the cooks asked, not even looking up from the grill.

Jeez. This couldn't be the buyer. "Yeah."

"Dude said to meet him on the other side of the parking lot, over by the food truck, and that you've got one minute before he's gone. Said he'd be in a black and white shirt."

"Thanks."

Now the cook looked up. "Don't bring your business to this diner again."

Heath nodded and headed out the back door.

Craig's voice came on in his ear again. "We're moving in that direction, Heath, but that area of the parking lot is pretty dark. Be careful. I'll send someone to question the cook."

"Black and white shirt is pretty damn noticeable," Heath muttered as he sprinted out the door. Why go to all this subterfuge if he was basically going to be wearing a neon sign?

"Hey, never interrupt your enemy when he's making a mistake," Noah said.

Heath cursed the damned skinny jeans as he ran across the parking lot. He saw someone leaning up against the darkened food truck as he got closer. He hoped Craig and his team were nearby if this went south.

"Hey . . ."

"Stop there." The words rang out as Heath came under the streetlight about ten yards from the dark food truck. Heath stopped but knew he was at a disadvantage. The man could see everything about Heath, but Heath couldn't get any details. Plus, he was close to the corner, able to slip away if needed.

If Craig was smart, he was coming up from the other direction.

"Are you ready to do this?" Heath asked. He needed to give Craig more time.

There was no answer from the man in the dark.

"Listen, dude," Heath said, shrugging. "Just give me my money so I can go, instead of looking like a dumbass out here in the middle of the parking lot. I've got your microchip right here."

"You're not Troy Powell."

Oh no.

"Dude, who else am I going to be? Do you want the microchip or not? I don't have time for paranoia. I've got to get rid of this thing and get out of town."

"Not Troy Powell at all. But I do recognize you from somewhere."

This wasn't working. The guy must have seen him at the college. Heath dropped the pretense and pulled out his weapon. "Why don't you hold still now?"

The guy did exactly what Heath expected and instantly slipped backward around the corner where Heath didn't have him in his sights.

"Craig, the buyer made me and took off around the back

of the food truck. I'm in pursuit." He immediately ran after the guy. How far could he get in a black and white shirt?

"Okay, we're closing in from the other direction."

They had him trapped.

He heard Craig's curse just before he made it to the corner.

"What?" Heath yelled.

He stepped around the corner and immediately saw what the problem was.

There was the man in a black and white shirt.

Actually, there were *thirty* men in black and white shirts, having all come out of the bowling alley across the street, making their way across the parking lot—some toward the diner, others to parked cars.

There was no way to figure out which man was the one who'd just been talking to Heath. They were all laughing and joking with each other—no one stood out.

The buyer was gone.

CHAPTER SEVENTEEN

"You and me. Sparring mat. Nineteen hundred."

The low words giving the time and location were all Gavin had said to Heath when they'd both been in the Linear office this morning.

Heath had been back from the microchip case for three days. Once they'd missed their chance to catch the buyer, there hadn't been much point in Heath sticking around.

He didn't know what he could've done differently. The man knew—without question—that he wasn't Troy. It probably hadn't been hard to find a picture of Troy online.

Craig took it all pretty well, considering how desperate he'd seemed to catch the buyer. Probably because at least they'd stopped the sale of the microchip. Veronica hadn't been able to provide any more useful information about the buy, even after being arrested. Like Troy, she'd never talked to the man face to face. Professor Hudson hadn't been in on it at all, although definitely wouldn't be teaching again at WCU given his illicit relationship with a student who had used him for further access to the lab.

All in all, a dead end. Craig was frustrated but had

decided to turn his attention to finding the mole in his department.

And Heath was back in Oak Creek. No more case to keep him distracted from the gibberish in his head.

And no more Lyn.

She still hadn't returned any of his calls or messages. At this point, he was starting to think she never would.

Not that he could blame her.

He filled his time as much as possible here, taking on every available class. Since Dorian Lindstrom and his wife, Ray, had had to move away, there was plenty for Heath to take over.

Heath had never been Special Forces like a lot of the other Linear team. But he'd worked plenty of kidnap missions over the past five years that had required surveilling and sometimes rescue attempts in jungles—both the wild and concrete kind—all over the world. He definitely knew enough wilderness survival skills to teach them to civilians.

Actually, Heath wouldn't mind being alone in the wilderness for a few days right now. Better than the tension around here.

Gavin hadn't come straight back to Oak Creek after the case. Lyn hadn't been interested in talking to Gavin any more than she had Heath.

Which had added to Heath's sins in his friend's mind.

Heath wasn't about to try to explain to Gavin that it wasn't his fault Lyn had been studying something entirely different than what she'd told her family, although he did wish he could stand witness to the fact that she was so passionate about linguistics and languages. You only had to be around her for a few minutes to see that. She *loved* it.

Heath was never going to understand Sahidic and

Bohairic or any of the dead languages of Egypt . . . but there was no doubt she loved it.

And he wasn't giving up. She'd been on his mind every second since he'd left Reddington City, and he was going to find a way to talk her into at least hearing him out, and hopefully giving their relationship another chance. A real chance.

But first he was going to have to face an irate brother.

Heath got to the sparring mat early, not wanting to take a chance on making Gavin even angrier. When he walked into the barn the Linear guys had converted into a training area, Noah was sitting on one of the benches.

Heath walked over and shook the man's hand. "I'm surprised you're still around."

"I was going to leave today, but then I thought I better stay around an extra day and make sure my cousin doesn't kill you."

Heath began a series of isolated stretches he always did before a particularly brutal workout.

This was definitely going to be a brutal workout.

"I thought maybe you were here to help hide the body."

Noah shrugged. "That too. You know, family first."

Heath wasn't one hundred percent certain Noah was kidding.

Heath dropped down to stretch out his hamstrings. "I know the bro code, but I have nothing but respect for Lyn. Yeah, the two of us got a little caught up in the endorphins flying because of the attacks on her life, but she always meant something to me." And the fact that she wouldn't talk to him now was killing him.

"Gavin will figure all that out. Don't worry."

Heath twisted at the spine to deepen the stretch. "Before or after he rearranges my face?"

"After," Noah chuckled. "Much, much after."

That's what Heath was afraid of. "You got a girlfriend, man?"

Noah looked away and grunted.

Now it was Heath's turn to laugh. "That means yes."

"It's complicated."

"Complicated like she's a spy for a different country and you're not sure if you can trust her? Or complicated as in Facebook profile 'it's complicated'?"

"Complicated as in she's a single mom who has an ex who is all sorts of trouble. Violent."

"That sucks. I'm sorry."

Noah scrubbed a hand across his face. "I'm not sure I'm the right man to even go near her. I've got dark history myself. I'm a loner. I can be gruff. Marilyn and her kids need someone . . . who's not me. But still . . ."

Heath shrugged. "Sometimes we don't get a choice in the person we can't stop thinking about. It's not always convenient. Which is why I'm about to spar with my best friend."

Noah stared off toward the door. "Hell, I don't like people at all. Yet somehow, I can't stop wanting to be around her. Her and the kids."

"Sounds like you might be fighting *her* big brother soon."

"I wish she had a big brother. Hell, anybody who would've protected her from what she's been through." Noah stood and slapped him on the shoulder. "Speaking of . . . the grim reaper cometh, my friend."

Gavin stood just inside the doorway, staring at both of them. Of all the Linear guys, Gavin tended to be the most serious, the most upstanding. Not that he didn't know how to have fun, but he'd been given the codename Redwood for a reason.

Gavin saw things in black and white. Heath had always existed in the grays—the shadows. But despite the differences in how they tended to operate, they'd been close friends for years.

Everyone always knew where they stood with Gavin. The man didn't play games.

Heath knew exactly where he stood with his friend right now.

In big damn trouble.

"This really isn't necessary, Gavin. If you'll take five minutes, I can explain the misunderstanding."

"Get your gear on, Kavanaugh."

At least they were using gear. So, less likely that Heath was going to end up at the hospital.

He slipped off his jacket and track pants, leaving him barefoot and in just a pair of gym shorts. As he walked over to the ring and donned his mouthpiece and protective head-gear, Gavin did the same. Noah helped them both strap on their mixed martial arts gloves.

Noah nodded at them as they stood in the middle of the ring. "Okay, boys, let's keep this a fair and clean fight. Or as fair and clean as it can be, given that Fighter A slept with Fighter B's little sister."

"Thanks for the reminder, Noah," Heath muttered. As if Gavin needed it.

Noah hadn't even stepped two feet away before Gavin flew at Heath in a flying tackle.

Gavin wasn't here to play.

They fell hard onto the mat, Heath twisting out of Gavin's grasp before he found himself in a choke hold that would end this fight before it had even started. Both men kipped up onto their feet, and Heath barely got his arms up to block a series of kicks Gavin launched at him.

Not fighting back wasn't an option. Heath threw his own kick-punch combination, pushing Gavin back slightly.

And so it began.

And continued.

Heath and Gavin had always been a good match for each other in the sparring ring. Neither of them was as overtly big or strong as Finn and Dorian, but both of them were quick and agile.

A fight like this could go on for a long time.

And it did. Heath kept his mouth shut and his focus on surviving Gavin's onslaught.

He was beginning to wonder if this was ever going to end when Gavin finally spoke between attacks.

"You slept with my sister."

Heath dodged two jabs, then grunted as Gavin caught him with a knee to the midsection. "I slept with Lyn. I had no idea she was your sister. Hell, every piece of information you gave me about her was wrong: wrong name, wrong major."

Heath shifted his left foot and swung around with a roundhouse kick with his right. It made solid contact with Gavin's head and would've knocked him to the ground if it weren't for the protective gear. As it was, the other man stumbled back a couple steps.

Both of them stood staring at each other, breathing hard.

"Would you still have slept with her if you'd known she was my sister?"

Yes.

Heath didn't say it, but he couldn't deny the truth. He'd wanted Lyn with a single-minded focus that night in his apartment. There had been a lot of good reasons not to sleep with her, and he'd ignored all of them. Knowing she was a Zimmerman probably wouldn't have made a difference either.

His lack of an answer was answer enough. Gavin flew at him again with a midsection tackle that took them both to the ground. Once again, Heath had to roll quickly to avoid getting pinned.

They both got back to their feet, exhaustion becoming a factor. "I can't believe you could treat my sister like this. Disrespect her in that way."

Oh hell no.

Now it was Heath's turn to dive at Gavin in a rage. Gavin wasn't expecting the intensity of it and didn't roll away fast enough. Heath got him in a headlock.

"Listen to me, you hardheaded idiot. I have nothing but respect for Lyn. She's strong, smart, beautiful . . . So don't you dare make this into me not respecting her. You want to pound on me for breaking the bro code, fine. But this has nothing to do with me not respecting Lyn."

He let go of Gavin and pushed him away. They crawled to separate corners and struggled to get up onto their feet.

He was tired.

But Gavin wasn't done. He raised his arms back up into a fighting stance and walked over so he was right in front of Heath. "She almost got killed because of you."

Heath saw the blow coming but didn't even raise his arms to block it.

This blow he deserved.

It spun him around and onto the ground. He got up onto all fours, waiting for a kick or another punch—he deserved that too. Because he *had* almost gotten Lyn killed.

But it never came.

Breath heaving, Heath looked up over his shoulder at

Gavin. "I'll see that gun at her head in my nightmares for the rest of my life."

Gavin dropped his hands. "I will too."

Heath made his way to his feet. He wasn't sure how much longer he would be able to go on like this. But he would until Gavin felt like he'd gotten his pound of flesh.

"I never meant to hurt you or her. Yes, I should've waited until the case was done before I . . . asked Lyn out. But I never dreamed she'd get pulled into it like that." He raised his hands into a sparring stance again.

Gavin's eye's narrowed. "She's not talking to me because of you."

Noah spoke for the first time. "Actually, in Heath's defense, that may be because she got tired of your overprotectiveness ."

All three of them came to a shocked standstill as Lyn's voice echoed from the doorway. "Actually, I'm tired of a lot of things, but first and foremost is my refusal to stand up for myself and what I want."

CHAPTER EIGHTEEN

"Someone want to tell me exactly what is going on here?" Lyn walked the rest of the way into the gym.

"Sparring," all three men said at once.

"Does sparring always leave everyone looking like they might need to be escorted to the hospital?" Both Gavin and Heath looked like they might fall over at any moment.

"I thought you were in Cheyenne with Dad." Gavin walked over to Noah for help taking off his sparring gloves.

She glanced over at Heath as he grabbed the Velcro's straps with his teeth and pulled one glove off, then the other, then his helmet. Never once did he stop looking her up and down as if he was trying to ascertain whether she was really okay.

Her face was still bruised, now an ugly yellowish-green color instead of the slightly less hideous purple, and there was a bruise against her temple where Veronica had rammed the barrel of her gun.

Lyn finally looked back at Gavin. "Dad and I said everything we needed to say, so I left."

"Like what?" Gavin asked. "Like how you've been lying about your name and your major and it almost got you killed?"

The silence in the massive training facility was pretty loud. Heath and Noah both stepped farther away from Gavin, like they didn't want to get caught in the crossfire.

That just proved they were smarter than her brother.

Gavin didn't understand lies. She knew that. For most of her life he'd been her hero, confronting any problems head-on. He couldn't even grasp why someone would feel the need to hide the truth.

Gavin was never scared. She, on the other hand, was always scared.

"No. Like how I've been hiding that info because it was easier than standing up for myself and what I wanted. But that wasn't why I almost died."

Heath visibly flinched from where he stood in the corner of the ring, slipping on his shirt. "Lyn . . ."

She held up a finger. "I'll get to you in a minute."

"Yes ma'am."

See? Smarter than her brother.

Gavin had a lot more to say, so Lyn deliberately looked over at Noah. "Hey, cuz. How are you? How's Tanner and Cassie?"

"They're good. I'm going back to the ranch tomorrow. Tanner met a woman named Bree. She's amazing and exactly what he needs. He's probably going to ask her to marry him. Gavin actually met her a few months ago."

Lyn raised an eyebrow at Gavin. "You did?"

"Only for second. It was a covert op. We didn't even mention to Bree that I was related to Tanner."

She turned back to Noah. "Give everybody in Risk Peak my love."

"Absolutely." Noah smiled. "And I'll take it as a personal favor if you don't kill either your brother or my friend Heath. Not that either of them doesn't deserve it."

"Can't make any promises," she said. "Even for my favorite cousin."

Gavin took a long sip of water, then stepped closer. "Why are you here, Jackie? You should be resting and recovering. You should still be in Cheyenne."

She counted to ten in three different languages, trying to find patience. "Well, for one, I go by Lyn now and have been asking you all to call me that for at least two years."

"J-Lyn." Gavin rolled his eyes. "Like some sort of teenage pop star."

She was seriously about to use some of the self-defense moves Gavin himself had taught her *on him*. "I said J-Lyn because you big babies said you would never be able to remember to call me Lyn. I thought it could be a middle step. And actually, that proves my point. I'm here because I'm a twenty-six-year-old woman who has been catering to your and Dad's delicate needs for too long."

Gavin threw the boxing gloves down on the ground. "Delicate needs? Worrying about your heart condition and wanting to keep you alive is now defined as delicate needs?"

"I'm an adult. I'm aware of my limitations, and I'm the one responsible for them."

Gavin shook his head. "But Mom wasn't aware . . ."

Lyn took a step forward and fought the urge to stamp her foot. She wasn't going to fight Gavin about this. The same way she hadn't fought with Dad. She was going to tell them how it was going to be.

"I. Am. Not. Mom. I have to live my life how I want. I don't want a hospitality degree, and I don't want to work in the governor's mansion. I want to finish my dissertation on my beautiful dead languages and then accept the position that's been offered to me in Egypt."

She almost felt bad for Gavin as she watched the blood drain from his face leaving him a sort of sickly pale that looked so unnatural on his normally tan skin. " You can't be serious, Jackie. You need to stay here near your heart doctors."

She should've eased him into this. The Cairo job had been on her mind for a long time, but it was a completely new concept for Gavin. Just because she wasn't hiding it anymore didn't mean they were ready to hear the entire plan. Dad had nearly had a heart attack himself when she'd mentioned Egypt.

"Gavin, look. We can talk about this more, okay? I've still got a year's worth of work to do on my dissertation before I'm going anywhere. It's going to be okay."

Gavin looked like he wanted to argue but thought better of it. But she had no doubt she hadn't heard the end of this. Her brother was nothing if not strategic. "Fine."

"I'm actually here to talk to Heath. Mostly because my phone company wanted to know if I needed more voice mail storage since I had eighty-seven messages from him."

"Lyn . . ." Heath took a step toward her.

She held out her hand again to stop him, not because she didn't want to talk to him—she had driven across the state to talk to him—but because the things they needed to say needed to be done in private.

Especially since it looked like Gavin had already come close to killing both of them in defense of her honor.

"I'll get to you," she said again.

Heath nodded.

Gavin didn't like that either but wisely refrained from

saying so. "Where are you staying? Not at . . ." Gavin turned deliberately to Heath, then back to Lyn. " . . . a hotel. You can stay with me."

She managed to refrain from rolling her eyes. "Thanks, bro, but Peyton invited me to stay with her and Jess."

That at least got the scowl off her brother's face. He jumped out of the boxing ring, walked over to her, and wrapped his arms around her. She couldn't help but hug him back.

This was the biggest part of the problem, wasn't it? Gavin loved her. All The Brothers and Dad loved her. Everything they did, every overprotective measure they took, was because they loved her. And she loved them. Which was why it had been easier to hide the truth for years rather than just come out and tell them what she was really studying and what she wanted to do.

"I love you. Lyn."

She knew what it cost him to call her that. Gavin was a creature of habit, first and foremost.

"I'm strong, Gav. I can do this."

He kissed her on her forehead. "I know. I just . . . I know." He sighed, let her go, and turned to Noah. "Buy you a beer for doing such a bad job as referee?"

"Referee?" Noah said. "I thought my job was to serve as undertaker."

The two men got their stuff and headed toward the door. "Lock up when you're done, Shadow," Gavin called out from the doorway, then they left.

"I guess that means I'm partway forgiven," Heath said, still inside the ring. He winced again. "At least from him."

She crossed her arms over her chest. "Looks like you and my brother really did numbers on each other."

Heath sat down on the edge of the ring, his legs hanging over the edge, his arms hooked over the lowest rope. He grabbed one of the folded towels and wiped his sweaty face with it. It was tinged with pink when he threw it in the basket. Even with protective gear on, he'd managed to get bloody.

"Well, I deserved it. There's this thing called the bro code."

She smirked. "I work at a college. I know what the bro code is."

"Then you must know that not sleeping with somebody's sister—specifically a friend's *baby* sister of whom he's ridiculously protective—is probably the most primal rule when it comes to the bro code."

"You know, the modern bro code is actually a derivative of some of the concepts within Arthurian legends from the medieval times."

He hooked his thumbs over the rope. "No, I have not, in fact, researched the origins of the bro code."

"It came about because women weren't given a voice to argue for themselves. Could only do what the men in their lives told them to do."

"Archaic."

She had to smile at that. "Yes, I think so."

"Archaic or not, I wasn't trying to deny Gavin the chance to pound on me a little bit. I deserved it. You were almost killed because of me."

"Actually, I was almost killed because some psychopath decided to sell government research to bad guys, then put a gun to my head."

"But if you hadn't been around me, she never would've involved you."

Lyn sat down on the ring, a few feet away from Heath.

"Actually, if memory serves, a busted pipe over in the linguistics building was what actually involved me in this whole mess."

"But your heart condition. I didn't know about that in the elevator or the break room or your townhouse. I thought you were taking some sort of anxiety medicine." He rubbed a hand over his face. "That really could've been ugly."

"But it turned out okay." Yes, she'd had to see her heart specialist before she left Reddington City. And yes, her heart was always going to be an issue. "My heart is my responsibility, and I can take care of it."

"Regardless, I'm so sorry, Lyn. About all of it. About not being able to tell you I was undercover. About you almost getting killed. About the fact that Gavin is one of my closest friends. As soon as I found out who you were, I should've told you I was part of Linear Tactical. I know it doesn't actually make any of it right, but I'm sorry."

She scooted a little bit closer. "I think you said all that in messages one through thirty-four, then again in thirty-six through eighty-seven."

"I didn't say it in number thirty-five?"

"I think that was the one where all you said is, 'I'm an ass.'"

He groaned and laughed just a little. "Now, double ass. For what I did and for leaving that message." He gave her a crooked smile that did crazy things to her heart. "Thank you for listening to them."

"My phone company did tell me I'd have to get a bigger voice mail box."

He groaned again. "I'm so sorry. Believe it or not, I actually have a reputation for being good with people. Not that you could tell by how I screwed things up with you."

She smiled. "In all fairness, it was the fact that I *kept* all the messages that was making my phone company antsy."

"You kept all those messages?" For the first time he slid a little bit closer.

"I know there weren't quite eighty-seven. But, yes, I kept them. Because I knew what they were."

"And what was that?"

"Proof that you really were sorry. That you hadn't been using me."

"I swear, I had no idea you were Gavin's sister."

"I guess I wouldn't be sitting here if you had known. You never would have slept with me—because of the bro code and all."

If Heath had known who she really was, he never would've touched her at all. The thought was unbearable and had almost kept her from coming here tonight to talk to him.

They'd only had one night together. And maybe Heath's relationship with Gavin meant more to him than whatever was going on between him and her.

He looked at her for a long moment before reaching down and sliding up his shirt, pointing to his waist. "Do you see that?"

"Your abs?" Hell yes, she saw them.

"There's going to be a huge bruise there in a few hours. Do you know why?"

She couldn't see anything but perfect skin and defined muscle. "Because you and my idiot brother were fighting?"

Heath chuckled. "Well, this particular bruise is going to be there because Gavin asked me if I would've stayed away from you if I had known you were his sister."

"And what did you say?"

He let his shirt drop down and turned fully toward her. "I didn't answer. Which was answer enough. Gavin took it about the way I'd expected." He touched his side with a wince.

"You still would've wanted me?"

"Getting to know you these past few weeks has definitely been the highlight of the job. If I had known who you were, I might've forced myself to stay away, because dragging you into danger was never my intention."

He slid under the rope and down from the ring, moving until he was standing right in front of her. "But that night in my apartment? It wouldn't have made a damn bit of difference. I would've wanted you even if you'd had your brother's name tattooed across your butt."

She couldn't help her chuckle. "That would've been weird."

"Okay, yeah. That would've been weird. But it's still true." He smiled, reaching up to tuck a strand of hair behind her ear. "We've gone about this whole thing wrong from the beginning. I'd like to take you out on a date, Jackie Lyn Norris-Zimmerman. Lots of dates. I don't mind having to drive to Reddington City to do it."

"Actually, after what happened, WCU gave me a teaching sabbatical for the rest of the semester. I think they were a little afraid I would sue or worse, once the university administration found out who my dad really is. I'm going to use that time to work on my dissertation."

"Oh yeah?"

She gave him a one-shouldered shrug and a little smile. "Thought I might do that here in Oak Creek. Maybe a new location will give me new inspiration."

Heath leaned forward. "I like the sound of that."

"Peyton said I could stay with her as long as I want. I'm

going to help her a little, watching Jess while she works. So yeah, maybe we can go out on a date."

He reached over and kissed her. Softly. Gently. Probably because his face had to hurt. But it was what they both needed.

"That news is worth fighting your brother any day."

CHAPTER NINETEEN

Heath was whistling. He wasn't even sure what the song was, some tune he'd heard on the radio, but damned if he could stop himself. It had been the best three weeks of his life.

He was teaching a bunch of different classes at Linear and had found, a little bit to his surprise, that he was good at it. Even more surprising, he enjoyed it. He never would've pictured himself as a teacher, never would've thought he'd want to come in from the field.

Nor would he have been able to see himself living so happily in such a small town. Admittedly, sometimes he missed the anonymity of the big cities he'd lived in over the years. There was a sort of safety in the knowledge that you could walk around London or Singapore or New York and quickly and easily disappear within the crowds. Nobody paid attention to individuals.

Not in Oak Creek. Everyone knew him here. Went out of their way to say hello. To call him out by name and talk to him. Disconcerting, but also . . . nice.

And then there was Lyn. Seriously, just thinking about

her made his lips curl into such a big smile, he could hardly continue his tune.

He had it bad. He'd laughed as so many of his Linear friends had fallen hard for women over the past couple of years.

He wasn't laughing now. But he was definitely smiling when it came to Lyn.

She was ridiculously smart and kind and funny. And almost always had her nose stuck in her research books. Watching her face scrunch up in thought when something struck her about her dissertation—and grabbing the nearest object for jotting the idea down . . . paper, napkin, even her own arm once.

It was endearing. A sort of awkward charm that made Lyn, *Lyn*. His Almost.

And she was beautiful to the point that sometimes he actually ached when he looked at her.

The past three weeks had consisted of dates, Netflix with each other on the couch, and a whole bunch of sex that had only gotten better from the first night.

The sexy little librarian was quite adventurous.

Of course, Acting Sheriff Zimmerman would've killed Heath outright if he'd caught them, bypassing arrest altogether.

Lyn was still technically living over at Peyton's house, but he'd been able to talk her into sleeping in his arms most nights.

Now if he could only get this gibberish out of his head, his life would be damn near perfect. Or hell, he didn't even have to get it out of his head, just make some sense of it.

"Listen to you whistle. I swear, this town is some sort of love factory," Kendrick said from in front of his computer. "Freaking Jiminy Cricket."

Heath merely grinned as he sat down with the cup of coffee he'd just gotten from Kendrick's kitchen and pushed a second mug in the man's direction. "Your time will come when some girl gets you whistling, Blaze."

"Blaze." Kendrick rolled his eyes. "With that nickname, a woman would be expecting me to show up in a pair of tights, à la *The Greatest American Hero*."

The team had given Kendrick the nickname Blaze since he often explained his ethnicity—half black, half Asian—as Blasian. He'd protested, but the name had stuck.

"Hey, women dig tights. They're sexy."

Kendrick's lips twisted. "Right. I'll take your word for it and stick to my computer."

And nobody could doubt that Blaze was a wiz when it came to all things electronic. Actually, the man was a wiz in general—he'd attended Harvard, majoring in both computer science and East Asian studies, a perfect mix of right and left brain.

"Anything from the hard drive?"

"The damn thing was banged up pretty bad when Dorian and Ray nabbed it. A lot of that info is probably lost forever."

Not the news Heath had been hoping for. Grace "Ray" Brandt and Dorian Lindstrom had acquired the hard drive —the last remaining info about Project Crypt—about four months ago. They'd also both been agents for Project Crypt and, like Heath, had had no idea they were working for the enemy.

"I was able to access some info, but it's mostly what we already know," Kendrick continued. "Stuff about the brain-washing techniques and sleeper missions Crypt used. It definitely would've helped Dorian and Ray if they'd been able to access this info before."

Before.

Before their whole lives had collapsed around them and they'd been forced to leave Oak Creek, at least for the time being.

"I'll make sure they get the info. Rumor is they're coming to the Linear cookout this week."

"You've been in touch with them? How are they doing?"

Heath shrugged. "Ray . . . she still struggles. But she's strong."

"That's for damn sure." Kendrick clicked and brought another page up on his computer. "I found other stuff too. Not helpful in terms of what's inside your head, but I did find Crypt's criteria for the twelve active agents."

"Anything interesting?"

"Criteria included not having any close living relatives, then some other stuff you'd expect: you all scored high on intelligence tests, you each had a particular skill set that would help with missions, you all had way above average physical prowess and endurance."

"Yeah, none of that is surprising. Was there anything about me specifically for my missions that you found?"

"Actually, you're pretty conspicuously missing from a lot of the data."

"Because of the damage to the hard drive?"

Kendrick shook his head. "As best I can tell, no. You just weren't on there. No data about using you for sleeper missions. The only record I could find of you was when Holloman actually pulled you *off* of a couple missions because he deemed them too dangerous."

Heath slid back in his chair. "Why? I mean, I get that I was never one of their best fighting agents. Dorian is much better at almost all types of combat, and Ray is downright wicked with her crossbow, so sending me in for that sort of stuff wouldn't have been the best way to use me."

"What sort of missions did you do?"

"I was used for a lot of talking stuff. Diplomacy, missions that utilized my knowledge of languages and my ability to talk my way in and out of situations. Speaking a lot of languages made me good with people."

Kendrick snickered. "Yeah, I'm sure the fact that you look like Justin Timberlake and Robert Redford's illicit love child has nothing to do with people's natural tendency to gravitate toward you."

Heath rolled his eyes. His looks had always been a part of who he was. A tool he could use. He could play them up or down, the same way he could act like he didn't understand the language in order to better navigate within a mission. "I don't know why Holloman would have protected me from danger."

"He called you his insurance policy." Kendrick clicked on his keyboard, bringing up another file. "That's the most useful thing that I can offer you in what I found."

"Insurance against what? The man was killed two feet in front of me, so evidently I wasn't a very good insurance policy."

"I wish I had more information to give you," Kendrick said. "Have you had any nosebleeds or headaches like Ray?"

"No." Heath rubbed his hand over his eyes. Talking about this wasn't easy. "Only the voices in my head, but they're not saying anything that has any meaning. It's all gibberish. Believe me, I've tried every language I know, and all the ones I don't, and still haven't been able to make any sense of this stuff rumbling around in my head all the time. It has to mean something—some sort of code I can't figure out."

"I'll look again with that in mind, but I've got to be honest with you, man . . . I'm not sure there's anything else viable on this drive."

Heath scrubbed a hand across his face. "Then I'm officially at a dead end."

Kendrick leaned back in his chair. "I want to tell you not to give up hope, but I have tried damn near everything with this hard drive. I don't think we can expect much more from it."

"Great."

"What does Lyn say?"

"Not much." Mostly because he hadn't mentioned it to her. Because he'd been hoping to figure it out without having to involve her in the Project Crypt craziness.

The craziness of what was inside his head.

She'd been through enough already. Had enough on her mind with her dissertation and family pressure and her heart problems. She didn't need to carry his burdens too.

"I'm sorry I don't have better news."

"That's okay. Thanks for spending so much time getting what you could."

Heath wasn't whistling when he left.

CHAPTER TWENTY

"Heath, are you positive you don't mind if I work here? I'm sure Peyton and I can make Jess understand about not 'helping' with my dissertation."

"That kid is amazing, but she can be a little terror."

"I love her. But every time her juice box gets anywhere near my Egyptian dialect texts or my computer, I have a slight heart attack."

Heath flinched at her words before smoothing his features back into their charming mask almost immediately. Damn it, she didn't mean she literally had a heart attack, obviously. She'd made jokes of a similar nature since she'd gotten to Oak Creek—people joked about their hearts more often than most realized—and he'd never had that reaction.

They'd talked about her heart condition. She'd explained about the shortness of breath and lightheaded-ness that could come from adrenaline-induced episodes: stress, panic, or too much physical exertion too quickly. She'd explained about the medication that helped with episodes.

Her heart condition was always going to be a factor in

her life, but it wasn't the controlling factor. She'd thought he'd understood that. It had seemed that he had, like everything was going forward in that exciting way that new relationships did.

Until almost three days ago. She hadn't seen him in two and a half days, the longest amount of time they'd gone without being together since she'd arrived in Oak Creek.

That wasn't necessarily bad, nor did she expect him to spend all his time with her—she didn't. Just . . . she'd always felt like he'd wanted to be with her until a couple days ago. The day he'd called and canceled their dinner plans for that night.

It wasn't a big deal. The Linear Tactical guys and their significant others gathered at the Eagle's Nest for dinner on Tuesday, and she and Heath joined them the past two weeks.

But that didn't mean they had to do it *every* week.

She hadn't really thought anything of it. But then when Heath had called yesterday and they'd chatted for a while, she'd expected him to suggest they do something that evening.

But he hadn't.

Still okay. Right?

She refused to go down the rabbit hole her mind wanted to send her. That Heath was growing tired of her curves. That he'd decided she wasn't what he wanted at all.

It's what she would've done a few years ago. Hell, it was probably what she would've done right up until a few weeks ago, when she was sure she was going to die multiple days in a row.

It was what she'd done with the men in her family ever since Mom died, taking on way too much responsibility for their emotional wellbeing when it came to her.

But she wasn't doing that anymore. Her heart—literally and figuratively—was *her* responsibility. Not theirs. Not Heath's. How she chose to live was just that, her choice.

She was done being cosseted. Even by someone as sexy and amazing as Heath.

"*Heart attack* is only a figure of speech, you know. I'm not going to actually keel over."

He forced a smile before walking into the open kitchen. "Yeah, of course I know. And really, it's fine for you to set up here. I never actually use the dining room table for dining. There's plenty of room."

He was renting Dr. Annie Griffin's house since she'd moved in with Zac Mackay when they'd gotten engaged. It was a little too big for one person, so he was right—there was plenty of room.

But that wasn't the issue, was it?

Lyn stared at his back, while he put away some dishes from the dishwasher, his *Don't go bacon my heart* tea towel thrown over his shoulder.

Three days ago, she would've walked up behind him and wrapped her arms around his waist and trailed her fingernails up and down his chest—just a little hard, the way he liked it.

It wouldn't have been long until *Don't go bacon my heart* ended up on the floor—maybe with the two of them on top of it.

But now she didn't know where she stood. He was distant. That was the only word for it.

She began placing her textbooks back in the box she'd just taken them out of. "You know what? I think I'm going to set all this up at Gavin's place. He's been making a legitimate attempt to understand my dissertation and the linguistics field in general. Him seeing this might be a good idea."

Now Heath turned to her. "No. Lyn—"

She held out a hand in front of her. "Look, I think it's clear you need your space. Our relationship skyrocketed into intense territory pretty quickly."

He grabbed the tea towel off his shoulder and dried his hands, taking a step toward her. "I like where our relationship is. I've liked where it's been ever since you showed up in Oak Creek."

She ignored the excited clench in her heart at his words and the urge to walk over to him. Because there was something going on that she didn't know about. "I wouldn't have doubted that last week, but the past couple of days . . ."

He flinched again. He knew exactly what she was talking about.

"Heath, it's okay if we need to slow down or pause or whatever. I think me getting more into your space right now is a bad idea. I don't think you're ready."

He tossed the towel at the counter. "That's not it. I just have some stuff going on, and I . . . didn't want to involve you in it."

"Is it something I can help with?"

"No." He flung the word in her direction before she'd even finished her question.

"Okay then." She resumed boxing things up once more, blinking back tears.

"Lyn, wait. I'm sorry. I don't want you to go."

She looked over at him. He hovered between the kitchen and the dining room like he couldn't figure out in which room he belonged. "But you don't want me to stay either, Heath."

"*Skit.*"

She raised an eyebrow. "Icelandic?"

He gave a brief nod. "I *don't* want you to leave. I really don't." His voice was gritty. Heavy.

She'd never seen him look so torn. She'd seen him with all sorts of people over the past few weeks—big groups, little ones. Elderly people and children. The guys from Linear Tactical and their significant others. Unlike her, he always seemed to know what to say to put someone at ease or defuse a difficult situation. He was a master at small talk, at finding the right words, at getting people to smile and relax.

But not now. And she almost couldn't bear to see him this way. She put down the manuscripts and walked over to where he seemed rooted. "Why don't you handle whatever it is, and then we can talk." She reached up and cupped his cheek.

He didn't touch her. "I'm not sure that will work."

She brought her hand back down slowly. He still hadn't touched her. "Okay." She blinked away tears from her eyes. "You know what? I should definitely go."

Was this really over?

Keep it together, Lyn. Five minutes.

She turned back to the table and rapidly piled manuscripts back into the box, not using as nearly as much care as she should. She still needed to wind up all the cords to her computer.

She wasn't going to make it out of his house without blubbering like an idiot.

Skit indeed.

"You know what, I'll come back for this later." She turned toward the door without looking at him. "I don't need it today. I—"

Now he touched her.

Both his big hands fell on her shoulders, stopping her progress toward the door. "Lyn. *Almost.* Wait."

"What do you want from me?" She spun around. "I know you have secrets you don't think I can handle. But I can't stay here and pretend like everything is okay."

"It's not that I don't think you can handle my secrets. I don't want you to have to handle them."

What did that mean? She swiped at a tear that had leaked from her eye. "Because what's between us is temporary? Because why would you share your secrets with someone you don't plan to be around long?"

His hands dropped to circle her upper arms. Almost how she liked it in bed. Not forceful enough to hurt in any way, but with enough pressure to let her know he wasn't letting her go anywhere.

The thought was strangely comforting.

"Are you kidding me? *Temporary*? I have done *temporary* my whole adult life, so I am very familiar with what *temporary* feels like. And what is between us is not it."

She stood there trapped in his arms and turned her face up to his. "Then tell me what it is you're not telling me!"

For a moment, as he let go of her arms and took a step back, she thought he was going to refuse.

But she grabbed his hands and put them back on her biceps, wrapping her fingers around his and squeezing until she could feel him applying pressure. She dropped her hands but his stayed, strong fingers wrapped around her tightly as his thumbs traced a tender line up and down.

Yes, now they could talk.

He gave her a pained smile but didn't drop his grip on her arms. "Before I worked for Linear Tactical, I worked for a covert government agency called Project Crypt."

"The same one Dorian worked for?"

"Yes. I'm surprised you know about that."

She shrugged. "I overheard Dorian and Gavin talking

once. That weren't speaking overtly about it, but I was able to put the details together."

He shook his head. "Too smart for your own good. Yes, Dorian worked for Crypt. His wife, Ray, did too." He pulled Lyn closer and kissed her on the forehead. "Crypt was closed down five years ago, but we've since found out that they were corrupt—the missions they sent us on weren't government sanctioned. We were working for enemies of the United States."

She reached up and covered his hands with her own. "That must have been devastating."

"We found out Crypt did a lot of horrible stuff—brain-washing agents, sleeper missions."

"To you too?"

"No. There's no evidence that I was ever used for any sleeper mission, unlike other agents. Crypt is gone now. Someone killed almost all of the agents over the past few years, then Dorian and Ray made sure the files and research Crypt kept about the brainwashing were destroyed."

"Is that what you wanted to tell me?"

"No, it's worse. I wasn't used for sleeper missions, but I was brainwashed in some way. They put something in my head." He lowered his forehead to hers, struggling to find the words.

She was pretty sure he didn't have to. She already knew.

"Sounds. Nonsensical words," she whispered.

He stepped back but still kept hold of her arms. "Yes. How did you know?"

"You say them sometimes in your sleep or when you're doing some sort of menial physical task. And, well, I do almost have a PhD in linguistics. It caught my attention." Now his hands dropped to his sides. It was her turn to grab his arms. "You don't have any idea what the sounds mean?"

"None whatsoever. It's gibberish to me. I should've known you would notice." He shook his head and turned back toward the kitchen. "The problem is, the last of the Project Crypt leaders are gone. Dead. There's nobody left to give me any answers. So I might be stuck with this inside my head forever. I didn't want you to have to deal with that."

Now it was her turn to stop him and spin him around. It wasn't nearly as easy, but he didn't fight her. "How about if you not be one of the men in my life who thinks they know what's best for me?"

He let out a sigh. "It's not that I think I know what's best for you, Almost. Your brain is a crazy smart place. You have so much on you right now, I hate to add my issues too."

She stepped closer and gripped *his* forearms. "If this is going to turn into a real relationship, we're going to have to have to rely on each other more—trusting each other with our weaknesses."

"I'm not good at letting myself be vulnerable around people."

"I'm not *people*. And I'm stronger than you think."

His forehead dipped to hers. "I know you're strong. Just . . . I've accepted that the gibberish in my head is never going away, but now I have to accept that I may never understand what it means. It's always going to be a part of me that doesn't work right. I hate to throw that on you."

She raised an eyebrow. "My heart doesn't work right. Does that make me less appealing to you?"

His arms slipped around her. "No. Never."

"Precisely the same. And I'll admit I haven't been exactly forthcoming with info about my heart condition.

There are things you should know. Things you might be able to help with. The same is true with what's in your head. We'll research and learn and figure it out together."

He walked her backward until her legs bumped against the far end of the dining room table, tilting his head at her computer and documents at the other end. "And you damn well won't be taking this stuff over to Gavin's. You're staying here."

She smiled as he began unbuttoning her blouse. "Okay. But if—"

"No but ifs. I want you here."

All concerns about *everything* else disappeared as he lowered his lips to hers.

Yes. This is right where she wanted to be.

CHAPTER TWENTY-ONE

Lyn woke, sitting straight up in Heath's bed, the new idea for her dissertation's direction all but coursing through her veins.

She'd been thinking of Sahidic and Bohairic, the ancient Egyptian dialects her paper centered around, as an *art*—approaching it with a high respect for the beauty and creative nature of the dead language.

And she'd gotten a little stuck. Attempting to verbally recreate a language that hadn't been spoken for centuries wasn't easy, and it had just occurred to her subconscious sleeping mind that she was coming at it all wrong.

Everything known about the ancient western Nile Delta people suggested that they had been highly practical. Pragmatic. Maybe their language was more scientific in nature than artistic.

She eased herself out from under Heath's arm at her hip, whispered for him to go back to sleep, and padded out to the computer at the dining room table.

Although exactly how she was supposed to work with the memory of what they had done right on this table was beyond her. She was never going to think of everyday panties the same way again.

She dove into her research, pulling up the files and soon lost herself in a language she'd never actually get to hear anyone else speak.

She had no idea how long she'd been engrossed in her research when she heard Heath mumbling from the bedroom, even with the door pulled nearly closed. The gibberish in his head he'd been so loath to tell her about. She walked over to the door and stuck her ear closer so she could hear the sounds more clearly.

She couldn't blame him for not wanting to talk about it. She wasn't sure how he managed to keep his sanity. Constant noise that didn't make any sense? It drove her half-crazy just thinking about it.

They'd talked about the situation for most of the evening. How he'd researched the sounds in his head and eliminated every known language. She could only agree. None of what she'd ever heard him mumbling—like he was doing now—sounded like anything she'd ever heard.

It seemed like made-up sounds—the ones little kids would yell while sticking their fingers in their ears if they didn't want to hear what someone else was saying.

But why would anyone deliberately put nonsense in Heath's head? What purpose would that serve?

He'd told her what he could about the years he'd worked for Project Crypt. Some of it he would never be allowed to discuss, something she understood after growing up in her family. Heath assured her that part of his life was in his past.

But how could it ever really be if a constant reminder of it played in his head on repeat?

Lyn had never envisioned herself falling so hard and so

fast for someone—especially someone from the same alpha-male world she'd been trying to get away from. But watching him sleep now, hearing those mutterings come out of his mouth, she couldn't deny she was falling head over—

He'd said that before, in that exact order.

All her other thoughts came screeching to a halt, and she focused in on what Heath was saying. Had she heard him right? None of his mumblings ever seemed to repeat. And yet that three-second grouping had. She remembered because when she'd heard it before, it had reminded her of some version of modern Egyptian Arabic on steroids.

Not exactly that . . . the sounds he was muttering definitely weren't any form of Arabic. Listening to him a few more seconds proved that.

But something about that particular phrase wasn't nonsense. She would swear it.

They were missing something.

She pulled out her recorder, the decades-old one that still recorded onto mini cassettes rather than directly onto digital format. Everyone made fun of her for using it, but it had been her mom's, and Lyn loved it. Loved the subtle vibration of the tape moving.

Feeling a little bit like a stalker, she stood over Heath as he slept, recording nearly fifteen minutes of his nonsensical words.

Not once did she hear the phrase that had caught her attention again. Maybe she was mistaken, trying to find something that wasn't actually there because she wanted to help him so much.

Finally, she clicked off the recorder and went back into the kitchen. She made herself a cup of coffee, rewinding the tape and letting it play—this time at half speed.

Definitely flowed more like the specific patterns of a language when it was slowed down. But still nothing.

She set her coffee down and reached for her glasses, accidentally knocking the recorder into the sink.

"Damn it." Then she heard the noise she dreaded. The one that made her wish she'd used a digital recorder rather than an analog tape.

The recorder was eating the tape.

"No. No. No." She grabbed the recorder and yanked it out of the sink, quickly pressing buttons to try to stop it from continuing its damage. She cursed again as it made a crazy noise, then started playing the recording backward.

"Oh, come on." She hit the stop button but that only slowed it down.

She was about to rip the batteries out but stopped, snatching her hand back from the recorder and staring down at it as it continued to play backward and at less than half speed.

"*Merde. Palavra. Diarree.*"

That was *definitely* a language.

She listened as a recording played on, years of studying the patterns of word usage coming to her aid. This wasn't a language she was familiar with, but the most important thing was that it was *definitely not gibberish*.

She ran to her computer bag and pulled out her digital recorder. This one would allow her to play recordings backward on purpose rather than by happy accident. She snuck back into the bedroom and recorded nearly an hour of Heath's mutterings before taking it and uploading it all into her computer. She played it backwards and was disappointed when none of her usual databases recognized it as a language . That would've made translation easiest. This language almost had mixtures of Latin in it, like Heath had learned his own dead language.

She sat staring at her screen. Wouldn't that be absolutely brilliant—placing a configuration of a dead language in someone's head? If you had someone like Heath, whose brain was already wired for languages, and you needed to hide information in his mind that he wouldn't be able to understand but that could be decoded when needed . . .

He'd be the perfect storage unit, and a dead language would be the perfect method.

The problem with dead languages was that they were dead. Nobody spoke them anymore. For most dead languages, all researchers and academics could do was make an educated guess as to what they would have sounded like. Generally, it was based on an agreed-upon index. An algorithm, so to speak.

It looked like she needed to study the science of this language also, as well as her Sahidic and Bohairic.

But that wasn't a problem. She knew how to research dead languages. She was almost giddy with the thought that she'd be able to help Heath.

When she found Pictish, a Scottish language that hadn't been spoken aloud since the late Iron Age but that fit the vowel and syllable patterns of Heath's backward gibberish, she knew she was definitely onto something. Now all she needed was some sort of software that could run the patterns, find the correct algorithm, and basically teach her the language so she could translate it.

But that sort of computer expertise was beyond what she could do.

But not beyond what Kendrick could do. She shot off an email to him explaining what she'd discovered and what she thought it meant. She sent him the data she'd downloaded, the basics of Pictish, and what she needed.

She ended the email by asking him not to tell Heath about this until they knew for sure. She didn't want to get his hopes up.

But her hopes were up. This was so logical. So brilliant. So devious. It fit with everything she knew about Project Crypt.

"If you fall asleep at the computer, I'm going to be forced to use that table again like we did yesterday."

She spun around and grinned at Heath, looking so sleepy and rumpled and completely sexy. "Don't you threaten me with a good time, mister."

She couldn't stop smiling. She flew out of her chair and launched herself at him, kissing all over his face.

"Wow." He wrapped an arm around her hips and pulled her closer against him. "I should come interrupt your early morning work more often if it will get me this response."

She just kept kissing him. Hopefully, in the next few days, she'd have some really good news. It may not stop the murmurings in his head, but at least he would know what they meant.

CHAPTER TWENTY-TWO

Lyn yawned as they showed up to the Linear Tactical cookout. Her late-night work had caught up with her.

They pulled up in front of the small house that had been remodeled into an office; quite a few cars were already parked there.

Lyn smoothed her hands down her lightweight sundress. She knew all these people, had met them all over the years when she'd come to visit Gavin and had gotten to know them all better the past couple of weeks, and considered them her friends.

But being here as Heath's girlfriend...that changed things.

"I'm glad you're coming with me today," he said. "I know you don't really like law enforcement."

She turned to him, blinking rapidly. "What? That's not true. Who told you that?"

"Gavin."

She rolled her eyes. "Gavin always wants to make things so black or white. It's not that I don't like law enforcement or the military. It's just there's a cost for being in that line of work that sometimes I don't think you guys realize. Your awareness—that innate sixth sense you have? That comes at a price. A toll."

They got out of the car and he walked around and took her hand. "You're incredibly insightful, do you know that?"

She smiled, loving the way his fingers felt around hers. "Growing up in my family, I've had plenty of practice observing."

They walked toward the back where the festivities were already in full swing. "Well, today nobody should be in alpha mode. We're keeping this to the company and their guests, not the whole town. We got a couple of people who'd prefer we keep it intimate."

"Like Cade Connor?"

The country music star had been raised in Oak Creek and was a silent partner at Linear Tactical. It was his money that had helped the company grow so fast.

"Yeah, Cade likes to keep a low profile as much as possible. But also our friends Dorian and Ray are going to be here."

"They were both in Project Crypt." She'd met Dorian a few times, but not Ray. "They moved away, right? Dorian isn't working for Linear anymore?"

He nodded. "He is but taking a less traditional role right now while they aren't living in Oak Creek. It's hard for them to be around people. We're all used to it with Dorian because of his PTSD. Ray's difficulty being around people has come on much more recently. I was hoping I could help, but . . ."

He shrugged, his features tight. There was obviously more he wasn't telling her, but she didn't press. It all came back to that gibberish in his head.

She squeezed his hand, wanting to tell him about her

findings last night, that hopefully an answer was coming soon. Kendrick was already working on the program. With any luck, it would lead somewhere.

The tension slipped a little from his face as they joined the Linear family in the open space behind the office; the talking, laughing, and the aroma from whatever was cooking on multiple grills a soothing balm.

Everyone simply enjoying one another.

Little Jess ran up to Lyn— Finn's son, Ethan, not far behind.

"Lyn! Lyn! I'm so glad you're here!" Jess hugged her. "I get to roast marshmallows after we eat!"

Before Lyn could respond, Jess ran off giggling. Obviously, the firecracker wasn't mad that Lyn had moved her computer to Heath's house, out of her little fingers' reach.

"I'm glad you're here too." Heath kissed the top of Lyn's head as they walked farther into the fold. "Maybe you'll let me roast your marshmallow later tonight."

She laughed. "That line work often?"

He grinned and waggled an eyebrow. "I'll let you know later tonight."

He kept his arm around her, and Lyn didn't mind that at all as they walked up to the nearest table, where the enormously pregnant Charlie was sprawled, fanning herself even though it was a relatively mild day.

"Damn, Charlie." Heath let go of Lyn to wrap an arm around the tiny woman. "Did you have to swallow the whole watermelon and not leave any for anybody else?"

He jumped back as she elbowed him in the stomach, then rubbed her own belly. "Never make fun of a woman who's four days overdue. I don't even need a weapon to take you out, Kavanaugh." Charlie smiled over at Lyn. "I would blame my violent tendencies on this baby, but we all know I'm just crazy all the time. Good to see you, Lyn."

Heath kissed Lyn on the forehead. "I'm going to go see if Gavin and Finn need any help over at the grill."

Charlie smirked as Heath walked away. "Finn's using the grill as an excuse to stay far away from me. His mama didn't raise a fool."

"So I guess the baby should be coming any second."

"Yeah, he better hurry up and get here." She reached her hand out for Lyn's and brought it to her extended belly.

Lyn's eyes widened as she felt the slight movement under Charlie's loose shirt. "Oh my gosh. That's amazing."

Charlie smiled. "Thanks. Ethan has Jess halfway convinced I have an alien in there. Poor guy doesn't move quite as much anymore . . . he's running out of room." She knocked on her belly. "That's a sign it's time to come out, little man."

She talked with Charlie a few more minutes about baby stuff—not that Lyn knew much. Finn never did leave his perch at the grill a few dozen yards away, but the big man had a pretty constant eye on Charlie. If she needed him, he'd be there right away.

Charlie knew it too, Lyn realized, as Zac and Annie came over to talk with them. Annie, one of Oak Creek's emergency doctors, took Charlie's pulse as they chatted and gave Finn a little nod when she was finished. Charlie noticed and gave her husband a big smile before subtly flipping him off. His laughter rang out.

She talked with the newly engaged Zac and Annie for a while. After all, she was spending most of her nights at the house Annie had rented to Heath.

Before it had belonged to Annie, it had belonged to Zac's late-mother-in-law. His dead wife's mother.

No one batted an eye when Jordan Reiss and her fiancé, Gabriel, stopped by the table to talk to all of them— everyone exchanging hugs all around. Even Zac and Jordan.

Jordan was the woman who'd killed Zac's wife and toddler son in a car accident years ago.

But they'd all made their peace with it.

This was a family, and family was sometimes messy. She knew that firsthand.

Lyn wandered around, talking and watching how everyone interacted with each other—the linguistics of it. Studying was always going to be in her nature. She'd long since given up trying to stop herself from observing and categorizing interactions.

She walked over to sit at one of the other picnic tables and let out another yawn.

"I would ask if you've been having a lot of late nights, but I'm afraid you'd tell me the truth, and I'd have to go pound on Heath some more."

She shook her head at her brother's words as he sat down beside her. "If you're not careful, I'm going to pound on you."

Gavin slipped an arm around her shoulder and pulled her against him. "It's hard for me not to see you as that sickly kid who could never really catch her breath."

"I'm a grown woman who knows how to manage her own health."

He actually ruffled her hair, and she thought she might have to actually punch him. "I'm trying."

"Well, you're not here with a shotgun, so I guess that's a step in the right direction."

"I am glad you're here, sis. And, believe it or not, I think you're a great fit for Heath. He's been struggling the past few months—took some hard hits like Dorian and Ray."

"I know. He's told me about some of it."

He kissed her on top of the head. "Good. I just want you to be safe."

"I am safe, Gav. Heath keeps me safe. I feel safer and more sexy and more capable around Heath than I have in my entire life."

The look that crossed her brother's face was downright comical. "I'm not sure how I'm supposed to feel about that statement."

She smiled. "Then let me help you: 'I'm happy because you're happy, Lyn.' See? Not so hard. I won't even make you call me J-Lyn."

"I am happy because you're happy. But you're still my sister, and you just told me how one of my best friends makes you feel *sexy*. I need a beer. Noah is here. He was purchasing a couple of horses in the area, so he stopped by. He'll understand my pain."

She smiled and let him go. Getting The Brothers and Dad to see her as a fully capable woman was going to take more than a couple of weeks. Dad still called every day to check on her, and she'd had multiple messages from Tristan and Andrew.

They'd all been willing to accept her choice to study linguistics. Getting them to not freak out over the potential job offer in Egypt was going to be different matter altogether. She'd save that battle for another day.

Kendrick was talking to Jess's mom, Peyton, near the corner of a shed out the back of the area everyone was congregated in, and Lyn made her way over to them.

"Hey, you two. You guys hiding over here?" She smiled at them both.

Kendrick grinned back, but Peyton actually flushed. "No. I'm just keeping an eye on that rascal daughter of mine. You know how she can find trouble no matter where she goes. Heck, you had to move out of my house because of her."

Lyn grabbed Peyton and pulled her in for a hug. "It really is a shame you can't bottle that energy of hers. You'd make a fortune."

Peyton laughed. "Don't I know it."

"Why don't you sit down and enjoy the cookout?" Lyn tugged on a strand of Peyton's short brown hair. Her friend looked tired. Then again, she always did. "We'll all take turns keeping an eye on Jess. Plus, Ethan never seems to let her out of his sight anyway."

Peyton nodded, her eyes darting around the area. "Yeah, maybe later. Right now, I need to tell her something. I'll catch up with you guys in a little bit."

She headed off before Lyn or Kendrick could say anything further.

"What just happened?" Lyn asked.

Kendrick shrugged. "She was fine until she saw Cade Conner a few minutes ago. Maybe she has some sort of celebrity crush on him and is all discombobulated."

"Yeah, maybe." But she'd known Peyton for a couple of years now, and the woman had always seemed way too reasonable to become flustered by the mere presence of a celebrity—not that Cade was treated like one here. Here, he was Oak Creek family.

But now that Lyn thought about it, how many times had Peyton turned off a Cade Conner song on the radio?

All the times.

Lyn had thought her friend just didn't like that style of contemporary country music, but Peyton never turned off any other artists. Only Cade.

She watched as Peyton stopped in her tracks as she got

close to the grills, then made an almost military-grade pivot in another direction. A second later, Cade stepped away from the grills where he'd been talking to Finn and his brother Baby and followed Peyton as she headed away.

Interesting.

"I've been working on our little pet project all day." Kendrick nudged her with his elbow, drawing her attention back. "Quite an impressive theory."

"It makes a lot of sense to use a dead language if you've already got someone like Heath whose brain is wired for languages."

He nodded. "I need to go back and filter through the data from the hard drive again. There might've been something about Heath and languages that I missed because it seemed so benign."

"That's the reason it was such a perfect vehicle for Crypt to use. A language that for all intents and purposes is untranslatable for darn near everybody in the world." She looked over at him. "What about the program I need you to build? Will that be a problem?"

He winked at her. "Child's play. I've actually got something running now. Definitely not my most sophisticated work, but I wouldn't be surprised if we had your algorithm by the end of the day."

That would be perfect. The sooner Kendrick's program was ready, the sooner she could use it to begin translating the recording.

She looked over at Heath, who was talking to Dorian and a slender, dark-haired woman she hadn't met. That must be Ray. Dorian had her tucked into his side.

"I'm still not going to say anything to Heath about this until we know for sure. I don't want to get his hopes up in case this is all wrong."

Kendrick nodded. "My lips are sealed."

She reached up and kissed him on the cheek. "Thank you for doing all this. This is above and beyond friendship."

"Look, I watched that man put himself in considerable danger to help out his friends. So I don't mind." He grinned. "But now I'm going to get away from you before your boyfriend comes over and beats me up because he thinks I'm trying to steal you away."

They walked together back toward everyone else and were immediately drawn into a conversation. The rest of the afternoon passed by much the same way. Lyn chatted with different people. Everyone was friendly, and every once in a while, she'd find herself caught up in Heath's arms and spun around for a kiss. Everything was light and happy.

But it didn't take long for Lyn to realize the true purpose of this whole get together.

Dorian and Ray.

Lyn didn't know Dorian well. She knew he'd been in the Special Forces with Gavin and had also broken Gavin's jaw in a PTSD-induced rage a few years ago.

Gavin had never held any ill will toward Dorian, and she didn't either. She'd wanted to break most of Gavin's bones at some point in her life.

Ray was a complete mystery. Evidently, she'd been a part of Dorian's past and had shown back up a few months ago. Lyn wasn't exactly sure what had happened, but they'd had to leave Oak Creek because of it.

Also, something about Ray shooting Dorian with a crossbow?

Lyn wasn't entirely clear on any of it, but there could be no doubt that the huge man was definitely protective of Ray regardless of whether she'd shot him or not.

Everyone here seemed protective of both of them.

Which was a little crazy, given that if they had worked as agents for Project Crypt, then they were more than capable of protecting themselves. Maybe taking down everyone around them.

Although, admittedly, Ray looked a little fragile. She was slender almost to the point of being skinny, and her black hair seemed unnatural with her pale skin. And Lyn had no idea what the giant headphones she'd had wrapped around her neck all day were about. If it was a fashion statement, it was a weird one.

But everyone here was so glad to see them, it was almost a tangible thing.

Which was why it became evident something wasn't right when a man she didn't recognize—but whose jacket and tie and department store loafers fairly shouted FBI—walked around the office and into the party area. The noise level noticeably dipped as people became aware of his presence and then picked back up as they tried to play it off like it wasn't a big deal.

Lyn glanced over at Heath, who'd been talking to Dorian and Ray. Heath and Dorian were communicating without saying anything, using some brief hand motions. They both nodded before separating. Heath headed toward the new man; Dorian and Ray subtly eased back farther away.

Dorian wrapped his arm tighter around Ray's shoulder—her face even more pale and gaunt now. She reached and pulled the headphones that had been around her neck up over her ears.

Fashion statement, Lyn's ass. Something definitely wasn't right.

CHAPTER TWENTY-THREE

E ven though his back was to the other man, Heath was aware of the moment Craig Franklin walked onto the Linear property. He glanced over his shoulder, then back at Dorian and Ray.

Ray stood there, paling, as Dorian signaled his plan without words. He'd be getting out of here with Ray by any means necessary. Heath shook his head. It was better not to make a scene, if possible.

It crushed Heath to see Ray slip her headphones over her ears as Dorian led her away even though he understood why she did it.

But right now, he had to handle the problem at hand. It was important to keep Craig as far away from Dorian and Ray as possible. If Craig found out who Ray really was, things would get ugly quick.

Heath caught Gavin's eye. His friend nodded, and they both headed toward the FBI agent from different directions. Heath upped his pace without making it noticeable and plastered a grin on his face.

"Hey, Craig." He reached out his hand to shake as he

reached the other man. "What are you doing in our neck of the woods?

Craig shook his hand, then did the same to Gavin as he walked up. "Just passing through. Had a couple of questions for you. Didn't realize you were having a Linear shindig."

Gavin grinned. "It's all mostly Charlie's doing. She said it was the only way to get Finn to do any cooking, even with her being 'three thousand months pregnant' as she calls it." He crooked a finger over his shoulder and pointed. "You remember Finn and Charlie, right?"

Heath knew exactly what Gavin was doing—trying to turn Craig's attention anywhere but on Ray and Dorian.

But Craig wasn't necessarily falling for it. "Yeah, I think I know just about all of your team, since most of them were in the Port of Umatilla earlier this year, helping take down that terrorist ring. That's Dorian Lindstrom over there, right? I didn't get to meet him that day."

The FBI getting their hands on Dorian, and especially Ray, that day hadn't been an option. The entire Linear team had made sure it wouldn't happen.

"Yep," Heath said. "That's him. In for a couple of days from out of town."

"Who's that woman with him?"

Heath shrugged. "Just some gal he brought. How about a burger or beer for you, Craig?"

Craig wouldn't be deterred. "She looks like she wants to get out of here. What's up with those giant headphones?"

Heath and Gavin exchanged glances. Everyone here knew why Ray kept her noise-cancelling headphones as close as a security blanket, but it had to seem odd to an outsider.

Gavin chuckled and turned Craig toward the grill, and away from Dorian and Ray, with a hand on the shoulder.

"With this group, are you kidding? Lady probably needs them to keep from being traumatized. That's what Ghost gets for bringing someone he only met last week. He should know better."

Heath fell in step beside them. "It's good to see you, Craig. Everything happened so fast after the failed sting operation, I didn't get much chance to talk to you. I'm really sorry we weren't able to catch your buyer."

Craig grimaced, but at least now he was distracted. Good. If he and Gavin could keep him over here at the tables for a few more minutes, the rest of the team would get Dorian and Ray out into the surrounding woods without it being obvious and raising Craig's suspicions.

And once they were in the woods, there were no worries. No one found Dorian and Ray out there if they didn't want to be found.

"Actually, there's some bad news. Troy Powell was murdered two days ago. He was out on bail awaiting trial."

Heath let out a curse. Dammit, he hated to hear that. He really thought the kid had been scared into going straight and would be okay. "Any leads on who did it?"

"Nothing definitive so far, but it wasn't pretty. He was tortured before he was killed."

Heath scrubbed a hand across his face. Damn it all more. "Revenge for reneging on his promise to sell the microchip?"

Gavin handed Craig a plate of food. "It's possible. Or to see if he had anything else of any value in that head of his. I don't know."

Heath tensed as a small hand slipped around his arm. "Hey guys. Everybody okay?"

He glanced down at Lyn, who'd walked over with Kendrick. Crap. The wrong word out of her could be disastrous. She could unwittingly prove everything he and Gavin had said about Ray to be false.

Gavin realized the same thing. "Hey, sis. Have you met Craig Franklin? He was the FBI agent in charge of the operation at WCU. Craig, this is my sister Jacquelyn and the bald dude is Kendrick Foster."

She nodded. "Nice to meet you, Agent Franklin."

"Please, call me Craig."

Heath nodded. "Craig was just telling—"

"Do you happen to know the woman Dorian brought?" Craig interrupted Heath. "These guys don't know her, but I thought maybe you'd talked to her. You know, woman to woman."

Both Heath and Gavin tensed. Craig was still suspicious. And Lyn had no idea about the potential disaster they were skirting. Finding out who Ray was, and that she was still alive, could trigger a massive manhunt.

"The woman Dorian brought?" Lyn repeated. "Oh, yeah, sure, I talked to her."

Heath wrapped an arm around Lyn, trying to think of a way to signal her without making it so completely obvious.

"Charlie's great," Lyn continued without missing a beat. "I love talking to pregnant ladies. And watching them eat is hilarious."

"Pregnant?" Craig asked.

"Yeah, she was due last week. Bless her heart. That's Dorian's wife, right?"

Heath relaxed. Lyn had figured it out without them needing to tell her anything.

Of course she had. She may not have chosen a profession in law enforcement or trained in tactical awareness like her father and brothers, but that didn't mean she didn't have the same instincts they had.

This woman was *every* kind of smart. Smart in terms of academics. Smart in terms of awareness.

Smart in terms of stealing his heart without him even being aware of it.

"No, silly, Charlie's married to Finn, not Dorian." Heath kissed her temple. "Thank you," he whispered so no one else could hear.

"Dorian's friend is the one with the headphones," Craig said.

"Oh. Yeah." Lyn shrugged and gave everyone a ditzy smile that looked so unnatural Heath almost laughed. "I can't tell everyone apart. No, sorry, I'm not sure who she is."

"Craig gave us some bad news." Heath tightened his arm around Lyn. Time to get this conversation off Dorian and Ray. "Evidently Troy Powell was killed a few days ago."

All traces of ditziness fell from her features. "Oh no. *Troy?*"

Heath kissed the top of her head again. "I'm sorry, Almost."

Craig nodded. "Looks like it was probably some of the bad guys he fell in with when selling the microchip."

"Oh no." Lyn buried her face against Heath's side. "He was my age."

He pulled her close and shook his head at Craig. Lyn definitely didn't need to know that Troy had been tortured. "I know."

Craig pushed his plate away. "I'm sorry. Hell, I wasn't planning on finding a cookout when I came to see you guys. I didn't mean to disrupt."

"No, it's okay." Lyn peeked back out, pulling herself together. "I just hate to hear that about Troy."

Heath nodded. "We all do."

"Look, I'm not going to stay." Craig pulled out his

phone, opened a picture, and handed it to Heath. "I also wanted to see if this happened to jog your memory."

Heath studied a picture of a slender man with dirty-blond hair. "Who is this?"

"Guy goes by the name of Keith Saunders. He's an information and weapons broker the bureau has been after for a while. Big player on the West Coast and is moving east. We think he's the buyer. Stands to reason he's also the guy who killed Troy."

Heath handed the phone back to Craig. "I don't recognize him at all. I'm sorry. I didn't get any visual that night."

Craig nodded. "I knew it was a long shot but wanted to check. Listen, I'm going to go, so you can enjoy the rest of your event. I'll keep you posted if we catch a break in Powell's case."

Heath shook his hand. "Sorry I'm not any more help."

"How is your head doing, by the way? Any better?"

Heath didn't even remember mentioning the gibberish in his brain to Craig, but at this point it wasn't a huge secret. "About the same. Might just have to be something I learn to live with."

Lyn squeezed his hand, and he looked down at her.

Yeah. If he had to learn to live with these voices in his head, then so be it. He'd visit Dr. Diaz, the new shrink in town, some more. See if there was anything he could do to help compartmentalize it better.

Knowing that Lyn knew and would be standing next to him as he learned to adapt made him ready to move forward.

Craig nodded. "Yeah, I guess we've all got stuff we have to learn to live with."

Gavin stood up with him. "I'll walk you out, Craig."

Heath, Lyn, and Kendrick watched the two men go.

"I'll go let Dorian and Ray know he's gone," Kendrick said.

"Thanks, man." Heath nodded but knew Dorian and Ray were probably already out of reach. It had been hard enough for them without Craig showing up—sheer bad luck. But Heath would be surprised if Ray and Dorian didn't surface again for a while.

"Do you think Craig heard about Dorian and suspects Ray?" Kendrick asked.

Heath shook his head. "No. Nobody here would let that information out of our immediate group."

Kendrick looked like he was going to say something but then shrugged and headed off in Dorian and Ray's last known direction.

"Craig seemed awfully interested in them," Lyn said.

"I think he got lucky—just happened to stop by and that law enforcement sixth-sense you were talking about kicked in."

"Do you think he'll pursue it?"

Heath wrapped an arm around her waist and pulled her close. "Honestly, no. Thanks to you pretending you thought Charlie was Dorian's date. Brainiac."

She shrugged and smiled weakly. "Seemed like the right thing to say at the time."

"It was a brilliant thing to say. Really got Craig off the scent."

"I hate what happened to Troy," she whispered. "I was mad that he dragged me into that whole mess, but . . . dead?"

"Yeah, me too."

It pissed Heath off. Maybe he'd give Craig a call tomorrow to see what he could do to help bring this buyer down. They'd stopped Veronica from selling the microchip

—maybe he could do more to help catch the buyer, whether it was this Keith Saunders guy or not.

"I can almost see wheels turning in your head," Lyn said.

He gave her a half smile. "Troy was trying to get out of the game. Killing him"—especially in such a violent manner —"wasn't necessary. Whoever did it needs to go down."

She sighed. "There it is. That toll I was talking about earlier. You're wired like Gavin . . . can't let an injustice go."

"I know you don't—"

She put a finger over his lips. "I'm not saying it's wrong or bad. The opposite, actually. The world needs people like you. The warriors who stand in the gap and fight for those who can't fight for themselves. Pushing their own needs and pains to the side to get the job done. It makes me proud to know you. To be part of your life."

He yanked her to him. "You're becoming the most important part of my life pretty damn fast, Almost."

"Good. Because I like it."

He kissed her—hard and hot and wet. He normally wouldn't put on such a public display of affection in front of family and friends and kids running around, but he could no more stop himself than he could stop his next breath.

"You're amazing, Lyn," he finally whispered against her mouth. "And I—"

"Aunt Charlie, are you okay?" Jess's voice rang out across the entire area. "I think you just peed yourself."

The entire area got quiet once again as everyone spun to look at Charlie. She was still sitting on one of the picnic tables, staring down at her shorts, which were indeed wet.

A few seconds later, Finn was at her side. Charlie beamed up at him. "I think it's time to meet our son."

CHAPTER TWENTY-FOUR

The party moved to the hospital. Little Thomas Bollinger may not have had much interest in coming out of his mother's belly, but once he got on the move, he didn't hesitate.

Kid had Linear Tactical blood in his veins, after all.

Finn rushed Charlie—almost in active labor before they made it off Linear property—to the hospital, Annie Griffin riding with them. By the time everyone else had cleaned up the cookout and made it into town, Thomas had just about made his way into the world.

Even with Annie as a hospital employee, the staff balked at the sheer number of people there to see the couple and baby. The Linear family took up nearly the entire waiting room.

Once they heard both mother and baby were doing fine, most decided to go on home and leave the visiting for the literal family. Lyn held Heath's hand as they walked out to the car in the hospital parking lot.

"Things are never boring around here, that's for sure." An enormous grin split her face as they got into the car.

He smiled too. "I didn't think I'd like a town the size of Oak Creek, but small-town life has suited more than I thought it would."

He drove through town and came to a turn. "My house? Or would you like me to take you back to Peyton's? And, before you ask, I vote for my house."

"My vote is for your house too."

For multiple reasons. Because she'd been ready to jump his bones most of the afternoon. But also because she'd like to get another couple hours of work in on the Pictish. She wanted to be as familiar with the dead language as possible when Kendrick's program was ready to help her begin translating.

She would hopefully have answers for Heath soon. She couldn't wait to share that with him.

"What's that grin about?" he asked as he pulled into the driveway at his house.

"It's a surprise."

"*Blayd*." His handsome grin got downright carnal as he opened the car door and helped her out. "Does it involve more panties?"

"Croatian?" She giggled at his exotic expletive as she walked toward the front door, his hand on the small of her back dipping lower by the second. "I would've thought you'd gotten your fill of panties yesterday."

His hand slid over the curve of her butt. "You obviously do not know how a man's mind works. Showing us something as sexy as that leads us to wanting much *more*, not less. Never, ever less."

"In that case, I better order some—"

Her words fell away when his arm wrapped around her waist and pulled her behind him. And *not* in a sexy way.

The voice that had been low and playful a heartbeat ago was now hard and focused. "Stay behind me."

"What is it?" she whispered.

He pointed toward the door. "That wasn't cracked open when we left here this afternoon."

Keeping a hand on hers, he stepped inside and flipped on the lights.

Someone had broken in.

"Stay right here. I want to make sure no one is still in here."

She nodded as he tucked her into the corner by the front door, then went searching the rest of the house. She pressed her hand hard over her heart in an attempt to encourage it to settle back into a normal rhythm. Her pills were on the kitchen counter.

He was on the phone when he walked back toward her a couple of minutes later. He held his hand out toward her and led her toward the kitchen.

"Looks like a snatch and grab," Heath was saying into the phone. "I don't keep much cash lying around. Firearms were hidden. I assume they were looking for whatever they could take quickly and got out. I've already checked to make sure the building is secure."

Lyn pulled away from him and grabbed her pill bottle next to the sink. She took one, not even bothering with water.

"Yeah, she's with me. We'll wait for you here. Thanks, Gavin."

She slumped back against the counter. "A break-in?"

He nodded, looking back into the living room. "Yeah. Took the flat screen and both of our computers."

Her eyes flew to the table. "Oh no. My laptop."

Had she made an off-site backup for her work on

Heath's Pictish? She'd sent it in pieces to Kendrick but wasn't sure that included all of it.

He squeezed her arm. "Are you worried about your dissertation? Please tell me you had it backed up somewhere besides just your laptop."

"I did. My dissertation is backed up in multiple places. You don't have to worry about that."

"Thank goodness. I know no town is perfect, but I wasn't expecting this. Oak Creek is basically Mayberry. We might still be able to get your laptop back. Was there other critical stuff on there?"

She couldn't keep it from him any longer. "I didn't want to say anything in case it ends up being nothing." But it wasn't nothing, she *knew* that. "Last night I woke up with an idea about my dissertation and was working and you started saying your gibberish in your sleep."

"Crap. I know I do that. I'm sorry—"

She put a finger over his lips. "I recorded it, and, long story short, I accidentally played it backward."

"Backward?" The thought obviously hadn't occurred to him.

"Heath, I don't think it's gibberish at all. I think it's a version of Pictish, which was the language spoken by the Pict people of Scotland."

"I don't know what that is."

"You wouldn't. It hasn't been spoken in two thousand years. It's a dead language. Only studied academically, and even then, not widely."

"Can it be translated?"

"That's the tricky thing. Written, it could be translated immediately. But spoken, it becomes a lot more problematic. It's dependent on certain algorithms for oral usage.

Without knowing that, it could almost be its own secret language."

He stared at her, taking it all in. "Is it possible to decipher with an algorithm?"

"Yes. Definitely yes. It would take me weeks to try to do it by hand, but it could still be done. I sent the info to Kendrick, and he's already started developing some software that can do a lot of the mathematical basis for me—it can help distinguish the pattern used when it was put in your head so I can translate it. We were hoping to have something to tell very soon."

He looked back at the table where her computer had sat. "With your computer gone, is the information lost for good?"

She couldn't stand the look of heartbreak on his face. "No. At worst, it would set us back a couple of days. I would need to try to re-record your gibberish, download it again, filter it through my academic software, and then have Kendrick do his magic. I was so excited last night I'm not sure if I backed up the information to the cloud. As soon as I can get on a computer, any computer with internet access, I'll be able to check."

She hoped she had backed up everything. She had jotted down all her initial thoughts and considerations last night. She wasn't sure she would be able to remember all those exactly.

It wasn't long before Gavin showed up with Noah in tow.

"You both okay?" Gavin asked, pulling Lyn in for a hug.

"We're fine," she said. "This must have happened while we were at the picnic or the hospital."

Heath told Gavin and Noah what had been taken.

When Gavin heard Lyn's computer was missing, he had the same concerns about her research.

"My dissertation is fine. But there was some other data that might've been lost." She didn't want to mention it was about Heath unless he wanted to mention it. "It's not critical, just a hassle."

But evidently, Heath didn't mind sharing. "Lyn might have made a real breakthrough on the crap inside my head."

Both Gavin and Noah turned to her. She shrugged. "Looks like my advanced degree in dead languages might end up being useful after all."

Gavin nodded. "Okay, I'll get the crime lab in here to check for prints right away. But I'll be honest, the chances of us getting your stuff back are pretty slim."

Bon sang. She hated the thought of having to start again. "I'd really just like to get on a computer and see if I backed up the data."

Gavin nodded. "You're welcome to use the one at my house."

Noah smiled at her. "How about if I take you there, cuz?"

She looked over at Heath. "Do you need me here? I'll stay if you do, but otherwise I'd like to see what I definitely have saved."

He shook his head, his lips twisting up into a half smile. "I know what you're like when you're intent on researching something. I wouldn't dare stand in your way."

She stepped up to him and grabbed his shirt. "I hope they can find who did this so you can get your stuff back."

He wrapped an arm around her waist and pulled her closer. "Me too." He looked over at Gavin. "Is Dorian still around anywhere? If the perps went off through the woods, he might be able to track them."

Gavin nodded. "Yeah, he's still around. He and Ray came back in after everyone left for the hospital."

Heath walked her to the door. "Did you mention what you found to anyone besides Kendrick?"

She shook her head, grimacing. "No. I wasn't sure how much of the knowledge was public. I only mentioned it to Kendrick because I needed that program. Was that wrong? I thought since he was already working on the hard drive, he probably knew what was going on."

Heath grabbed her hand. "Yes, he knows, and it's fine. I'm excited about possibly actually having answers. This is a huge step."

She reached up on tiptoes and kissed him. "Well, you go try to find the punks who broke into your house, and I'll try to figure out the voices in your head."

CHAPTER TWENTY-FIVE

Noah and Lyn hadn't been gone long when Dorian showed up at Heath's place. The fact that he arrived through the woods rather than a vehicle didn't surprise anyone.

"D, thanks for coming." He shook his friend's hand. "Is Ray okay?"

"She's staying out of eyesight right now where she's comfortable. Craig showing up spooked her a little, but she's a lot stronger than she gives herself credit for."

Gavin was studying where the flat screen had been dismantled from the wall. "I canceled the call for someone to come run prints. I figured if you were asking for Dorian, you had something else you wanted looked into."

Heath shrugged. "Might be nothing. I know you've only been acting sheriff for a few months, but does Oak Creek have a lot of break-ins?"

"A few," Gavin said. "Not enough to make townspeople nervous, but it does happen."

"You thinking this was more than an ordinary burglary?" Dorian asked.

"I've got a Glock 42 in my nightstand. Two more shot-guns and cases in my closet. It wouldn't take much work to find them."

Gavin walked back into the kitchen. "Guns would've gotten a lot more cash than the electronics. The perp would have to know what he or she was doing to wipe a laptop before it could be sold."

Heath shrugged. "It seems a little suspicious to me that a few hours after Lyn makes significant progress into discovering what this stuff in my head might mean, the laptop containing all the data gets stolen."

Dorian moved closer. "What do you mean *progress*?"

Heath wasn't surprised by the interest. What was in his head could possibly affect Dorian too, and definitely Ray.

"A way to possibly decode it all. She thinks it's a version of some Scottish language . . . Pictish, or something. Nobody in the world still speaks it. It would be the perfect vessel for encoding information in my brain, especially since I'm already prewired for learning languages."

Gavin nodded. "Someone needed Lyn's laptop but didn't want to make it obvious, so they grabbed some other stuff to throw us off the scent."

"You guys having the after-party without me?" They spun toward the voice from the front door, weapons raised.

Kendrick immediately threw his hands in the air. "Whoa. Black man isn't here to hurt the white folk. The door was cracked open."

They all reholstered their weapons.

"Sorry, Blaze," Heath said. "Come on in. Didn't realize word about the break-in had gotten out already."

Kendrick looked around. "What break-in? Someone broke in? Is everyone okay?"

"We're fine." Heath scrubbed a hand over his eyes.

"Nobody was hurt, but Lyn's computer was taken. If you're not here because of the break-in, why are you here?"

Kendrick crossed to the kitchen table and sat down. "Came to ask how well you know that FBI agent Craig Franklin."

Heath looked over at Gavin, who shrugged.

"I met him a few months ago at the Port of Umatilla. He was the FBI agent sent to arrest Dorian and Ray."

Kendrick nodded. "But you've never worked with him on anything for Linear Tactical? He's not part of some secret subsection I should know about?"

Heath didn't like where this was going. "Why?"

Kendrick gave a sigh. "He mentioned that guy Keith Saunders, remember? Showed you the picture, asked if you recognized him?"

Heath nodded. "Yeah, so?"

"I just thought I would help. You know, I have some channels that somebody in the FBI might not be able to readily use, if you know what I mean."

Not quite legal channels. Heath understood.

"And?" Gavin prompted. They all liked Kendrick a lot. He'd been critical in helping Dorian and Ray get out of their situation alive. But he wasn't always one to get directly to the point.

"Keith Saunders is bad news. Not difficult to see why Craig would have a hard-on for taking him down. Guy is into human trafficking, weapon sales, and old-fashioned terrorism. He's on top of everyone's most wanted list."

"Okay. It would make sense that he was after the WCU microchip then," Heath said.

Kendrick nodded. "The big thing about Saunders is that no one actually knows what he looks like. That picture Franklin showed you was a guy named Michael Cinelli.

He's doing twenty years for assault and armed robbery somewhere in Texas."

Heath looked at Gavin again. What the hell did this mean?

"That's weird but doesn't necessarily prove nefarious intent," Gavin said. "Craig could've pulled up the wrong picture by mistake."

Kendrick nodded. "Yeah, I get it. But it was enough to start me looking a little more heavily into Franklin. Dude is not on the up and up."

"How so?" Gavin asked. "We need specifics."

"Franklin was temporarily suspended from the FBI a year ago. Don't ask me how I got this information"—Kendrick looked pointedly at Gavin—"but his suspension centered around his obsession with Timothy Holloman and a defunct government group known as Project Crypt."

Heath ran a hand through his hair. "What the actual hell?"

Kendrick held his hand out in front of him. "When I say obsessed, I'm talking *deeply obsessed*. All his other cases suffered, and he couldn't be trusted to do basically anything."

Heath shook his head. "Crypt wasn't even functioning a year ago. That was when Holloman was busy killing everyone off." Heath looked over at Dorian. Dorian and Ray had been in the absolute middle of that nightmare.

Dorian, who had been listening silently while leaning against the wall, spoke for the first time. "I'm going out to Ray."

"Don't you want to know more details about Franklin?"

"He's not who he says he is. That's all I need to know."

He was gone without another word. His codename was Ghost for a reason.

"Tell us the rest, Blaze." Gavin sat down at the table.

"Franklin came back off of suspension and was given desk duty. Psychological eval and all that. He wasn't even supposed to have been at the Port of Umatilla that day when Ray and Dorian were almost arrested."

Gavin looked over at Heath. "Craig did get there before anybody else, but it was so chaotic I didn't think anything about it."

"But wait, there's more," Kendrick said in his best infomercial voice. "Franklin wasn't authorized for the WCU microchip case at all. He was running that on the down low and out of his own pocket. That's why he said there was a mole, so you wouldn't expect more backup."

Heath began pacing back and forth. "Not to sound like a broken record, but what the actual hell? Those were real bad guys. This wasn't some sort of paid-actor stuff. What about Troy Powell? Is he actually dead?"

Kendrick's shoulders slumped. "Yeah. And he was tortured. So, yes, definitely real bad guys involved. Selling the microchip technology—Veronica Williams and her cohorts—that was real. Do you know what was on the microchip?"

Heath shook his head. "Not really. Something we didn't want falling into the hands of government enemies. I didn't need much more detail than that."

"It was data specifically about synthetic neural inhibitors." Kendrick tilted his head at Heath. "The research is highly controversial and secretive partially because it would make brainwashing easier. One of the earliest experts was—"

"Dr. Timothy Holloman," Heath finished for him. "Who then founded Project Crypt and proceeded to psychologically torture me, Dorian, Ray, and a bunch of others."

He began his pacing again. "Was Craig working with Holloman? If not, why not just tell me what he was doing outright? If anything, I would've helped more. If I'd known any of this might lead to answers, I would've been the first to volunteer."

Kendrick shrugged. "That I don't know. What I do know is that Franklin hasn't been back to work since Troy Powell was killed."

"Damn," Gavin muttered. "Could Craig have killed Powell himself?"

Heath had to resist the urge to slam his fists onto the table. "Is it possible he's trying to mastermind some sort of reboot? That's what Holloman had planned to do. Could Craig have killed him in Rome?"

"But why take a chance on getting so close to you?" Gavin asked.

"He needs what's in my head. He could've been the one who broke in here, stole Lyn's research."

"It's not finished yet," Kendrick said. "I just sent her the finished program she needs to start the translation, but it will all take time. And it will take *her*. She's got the unique skill set to be able to translate it. So if Franklin took your laptop thinking it had all the answers, it didn't."

"We need to find him." Heath was done pacing. It was time for action. "Before he figures out he doesn't have what he needs. He has no reason to think we're onto him, so let's just go to his house and get him. I need answers."

"You got a plan to get those answers?" Gavin asked, eyebrow raised. "What if Craig decides he's not going to roll over and give you every bit of information you want?"

Heath huffed out a breath. "Then I'm going to help him

come to the realization that doing so would be in his best interests. Project Crypt ruined too many people's lives."

"Damn it, Heath, we need to go through proper channels. Use the law."

"People are dead, Gavin." He slammed a fist down on the table. "Dorian's and Ray's lives were damn well nearly destroyed because of whatever Franklin is involved in."

"That doesn't mean that you can torture the information out of someone. There's a price for that, Shadow." The angrier Gavin became, the calmer his voice was. "If you don't believe me, ask Dorian."

Dorian had been on both sides of the torture table.

Rage rose in Heath like a savage black wave. The people involved with Crypt had been pulling his strings like a puppet for too damn long. To find out yet another person had done so was almost more than Heath could bear. "I've got to have some answers, Gavin."

His friend stood and grasped him on the shoulder. "And we'll get them. But we'll get them the right way. We'll figure out a plan and deal with this the way *we* do things. With honor, not by torturing someone who we're not even completely sure is one of the bad guys."

Heath stared at his friend for a long moment, the words finally penetrating his rage. Gavin was right. Solid. Clear-headed. His codename was Redwood for a reason. The man was unshakable.

But it didn't mean Heath had to like it right now. "Freaking *Redwood*."

Gavin cracked a little smile. "It will take us some time to figure out how to find and track Craig, but—"

They all spun toward the door again, weapons raised, as it flew open, and a man came tumbling inside.

With an arrow protruding from his shoulder.

Franklin.

Dorian walked in behind him. "Ray left us a present. He was surveilling the house, maybe waiting to attack. I thought you might have some questions for him. If not, I do."

CHAPTER TWENTY-SIX

Gavin muttered a curse and helped Craig into one of the kitchen chairs.

"Don't worry, there is no real damage," Dorian muttered. "If Ray was really trying to hurt him, she could've."

Nobody knew that better than Dorian. He'd been on the receiving end of one of Ray's arrows before. She didn't miss.

"I can't act like I'm not law enforcement here, you guys," Gavin said. "I'm not going to go after Ray, but Craig needs to go to the hospital. After that, I'll bring him in for official questioning, and we can go from there.

"No." Craig spoke for the first time and looked up from where he was clutching his shoulder. "I don't want to go to the hospital. It's time for us to talk about what's really going on."

Heath sat in the chair next to Craig, getting right up in his face. This man had almost gotten Lyn killed with his little game. It ended right now. "Is that what you think? Because I think we might've figured out quite a bit on our own. Like your ties to Project Crypt, and how the case at WCU wasn't even on the official FBI books."

Craig shrugged with his good shoulder. "I was willing to do whatever I had to."

Heath had always been a people person. The charmer. The good cop to someone else's bad.

But not today.

He grabbed Craig by the collar and got in his face. "For *what*? Who are you working for? Everybody involved with Project Crypt is dead except for three people, and two of the three are in this room right now. Are you trying to relaunch the project? Are you working with Keith Saunders?"

Did that even make any sense? None of this made any sense.

Craig shook his head. "No. Saunders is only a middle-man; someone I'm trying to use. I needed him to tell his boss that you're alive, and the information in your head is still viable. That's why I involved you in the case at WCU. You were always the key."

Heath literally wanted to pull out his own hair. "The key to what?"

"Saunders's boss was the individual who bankrolled Project Crypt once the government shut it down. Holloman went to him, showed him what they'd been able to do in terms of brainwashing, and Saunders's boss basically paid the fee and took it over to use however he wanted."

Heath looked over at Dorian. This explained so much. Crypt had started on the up and up, then unfortunately nobody had notified the Crypt agents when the government had shut them down.

"Who is Saunders's boss?" Kendrick asked. "Who bankrolled it all?"

Craig shook his head, sweating a little. "I don't know."

They all waited for him to say more, but Craig stayed silent.

Dorian took a step forward. "The woman out there who shot you with that arrow? She made sure you'll still have full range of motion with your arm and live through the night rather than bleeding out." D's voice was barely more than a whisper, but it thundered through the room. "That same woman had her life and mind torn completely apart by Holloman and your mystery man and their Project Crypt games. So you're going to tell us what you know right now, or I'm going to escort Gavin out of here, and then I *promise* you're going to tell us what you know."

"Dorian . . ." Gavin's voice was low and urgent.

Things were about to get very, very ugly.

And honestly, Heath wasn't sure which side he was on.

"Mystery man has my sister." Craig's words stopped everyone in their tracks.

"What?" Dorian and Heath said at the same time.

"Saunders's boss kidnapped my sister Jenna a year ago. She's a biomedical engineering grad from MIT. Specialized in—"

"Synthetic neural inhibitors," Heath finished for him.

Craig nodded. "She went on vacation and never came back. I couldn't get anyone invested in her case because a postcard shows up from her every couple of months."

"Proof of life." Dorian wiped his hand across his face.

All the anger had evaporated from the room.

"I managed to pick up a trail that led me to Saunders, but I realized he wasn't the one who had Jenna. I've been after his mystery boss ever since. I thought I was going to catch Holloman that day at the Port of Umatilla. Or at least nab some of the actual Project Crypt agents to get some answers, or hell, just to prove Crypt existed. But it didn't go down that way, did it?"

The Linear guys had made sure no Crypt agents were around to be questioned. "We didn't know there was an innocent involved," Gavin said.

Dorian shrugged. "It wouldn't have mattered even if I had known. I wasn't leaving Ray there."

"Fine. I don't blame you for doing what you had to do. But don't blame me for doing whatever I could to find Jenna." Craig rubbed his eyes with his good hand. "I don't even know if she's still alive anymore. But I can't stop trying."

He turned to Heath. "Saunders led me to you and Holloman in Rome. If I had been ten minutes quicker, I might have been able to stop him from taking Holloman out and gotten some answers. But instead, it led me to you. I knew Holloman had put something in your head, I just didn't know what."

"Join the club," Heath murmured.

"Apparently, Saunders didn't know who you were or that you might be important to his boss. That's why I asked for your help on the WCU case. All I could do is keep throwing you in front of Saunders in hopes the mystery man would see you and come after you."

Heath leaned back in his chair. "And then you would follow."

"It was my only option. I've been waiting in this area for three damn weeks, but nothing. Obviously, Saunders was too stupid to realize your importance. So dead end. Seeing Grace Brandt at the picnic today is the closest I've come to helpful info in three weeks."

Dorian took a step closer. "I don't know what you're talking about. Grace Brandt is dead."

Gavin took a step forward to ward off his friend if needed. Dorian, generally speaking, only fought when absolutely necessary. He'd seen enough violence, had had enough violence inflicted on him, to last five lifetimes.

But when it came to Ray's safety, there was nothing the man wouldn't do.

Craig held out his good hand in front of him in a gesture of surrender. "My mistake. Grace Brandt is dead. Listen, all I want is my sister back. My interest in Project Crypt starts and ends there. Agents who are or are not alive, and what they've done, do not interest me. Only Jenna."

Dorian relaxed slightly.

"Did you kill Troy Powell?" Gavin asked.

"No. First of all, I'm not a murderer. But also, he had no knowledge that was helpful to me. I'm sure it was Saunders, and he might have been looking for info about you, Heath."

Heath grimaced. "I don't think Powell knew very much. Definitely not enough to die in that manner."

"Speaking of knowledge, I just got an email from Lyn." Kendrick held up his phone, big grin on his face. "She *had* backed up all the data, and more importantly she's had a breakthrough using the new software. She's been able to translate some of your gibberish. She still doesn't know exactly what the information means because it looks like it's a bunch of numbers. And that's only the first set. She's going to keep working."

Heath shook his head and sat back in his chair. *Finally.* For the first time in years he was actually going to have some answers. It being numbers was weird, but at least it was something, not just nonsense.

But right now, there was something more important than what was in his head. Craig's sister.

"We can use me as bait." Heath leaned closer to Craig.

"Your plan, just with more help. We'll figure out a way to leak to Saunders that I'm a big deal. Then when he makes his move, you'll follow them and get your sister back."

Heath looked around. Everyone in the room nodded in agreement.

"I don't know what to say." Craig winced as he accidentally moved his injured shoulder. "Nobody in the bureau even believed Project Crypt was real."

"There were some really smart people making sure it stayed that way," Dorian said. "The government itself denied its existence. And then the agents themselves had too much to lose by going public."

"But you still should have been up-front with us," Gavin said.

Craig nodded. "You're right, but I wasn't sure who I could trust, and Jenna would pay the price if I trusted the wrong people."

Gavin gave a wry shrug. Everybody knew how protective he was of his sister.

"Let's get you to a hospital, get that patched up," Gavin said.

Craig shook his head. "No. One of you guys just pull it out. I don't want to waste time with the hospital."

Nobody looked thrilled at the thought of pulling out the arrow.

"Call Annie," Dorian finally said. "She has experience after pulling the quarrel out that time Ray shot me. We need to let Zac know what's going on anyway."

"The way she has to make house calls all the time, we're going to have to put Annie on retainer as Linear's own private physician." Gavin pulled out his phone and walked into the other room to make the call.

"And let's get Lyn back over here where she can work," Heath said. "I want her in my sights."

"Actually, we're probably better off over at my place. I've got the computer firepower to handle whatever she needs," Kendrick said. "If she's coming up with numbers, we might have more decoding to do."

Heath nodded. "Good idea. I'll have Noah pack her up and take her over."

He texted Noah. When he didn't get a response in a couple minutes, he called.

Straight to voice mail.

He tried Lyn's phone, but it was the same. "Something's not right. I can't get hold of either Lyn or Noah."

Gavin turned to Heath. "Lyn might get caught up in what she's doing on her computer, but Noah wouldn't. There's no way he'd be out of communication."

Kendrick looked over at Craig. "Wait a minute. How did you know to steal Lyn's laptop? How did you know she'd made a breakthrough?"

"I was sitting in my car using parabolic mics at the picnic today before I came to talk to you. I heard you discussing it with her."

Kendrick let out a curse. "Somebody's been piggy-backing off of Lyn's emails. When I found you out today, I assumed it was you."

"It wasn't me," Craig insisted. "I don't have the technology available to do that."

Heath turned to Kendrick. "What are you saying exactly? What does piggybacking mean?"

"It means somebody knows about Lyn's breakthrough. And if it's not Craig, then my next best guess would be—"

Heath and Gavin were already running for the door.

They were in Heath's car, peeling out of the driveway ten seconds later.

"Dammit," Gavin muttered. He didn't say anything else, but he didn't have to. Heath knew what he was thinking.

They'd put Lyn right in the middle of danger.

Again.

Because if Lyn had already discovered what was in Heath's head, and the mystery man knew about it, he didn't need Heath at all. He could just take Lyn.

The five-minute drive to Gavin's apartment was the longest of Heath's life. They pulled into the driveway, he ripped the keys out of the ignition, and they both sprinted toward the door, weapons raised. Neither cared that this wasn't the best tactical plan.

They burst through the door and found what Heath had been terrified they would find.

Nothing.

Heath's heart jackhammered against his ribs as they searched each room.

They found Noah unconscious near the back door, a tranquilizer dart still protruding from his back, but Lyn was nowhere to be found.

Gavin looked as distraught as Heath felt, especially when they both glanced down at the open back door.

Gavin muttered a curse.

Lyn's heart pills were spilled all over the floor.

CHAPTER TWENTY-SEVEN

Everyone met at Kendrick's house, and they set up headquarters there.

Kendrick was busy re-creating whatever it was Lyn had discovered.

Annie was busy doctoring Craig's shoulder.

Heath was busy losing his damned mind.

"Once again, Ray did a remarkable job inflicting as little damage as possible," Annie announced as she finished stitching up Craig's wound. "It shouldn't affect mobility at all, just hurt for a while. But I would like to talk to Ray about not using arrows as a method of communication."

"Thank you," Craig muttered as he slipped on a shirt Kendrick had provided to replace his ruined one.

They'd already retrieved Lyn's laptop from Craig's car, although it hadn't contained any more information than what they'd already known.

Kendrick had launched a full-court press. He had multiple online computer friends working with him, including Neo, the hacker who had provided Dorian and Ray the original Project Crypt hard drive. Kendrick had her on speakerphone, but it was like they were conversing in their own language. The only thing Heath could understand was when one or the other would curse or call each other names.

The feeling of uselessness choked Heath. Growing inside him until it felt like it might consume him from the inside out.

He kept seeing those spilled pills.

Gavin hadn't found anything useful at the crime scene and was on his way back over here now. Except for Finn, who was still at the hospital with Charlie, the rest of the Linear team trickled in—ready to help in any way they could.

Which, right now, was nothing.

"You doing okay?"

Annie came and stood beside him where he leaned against the kitchen counter. Between stitching Craig's shoulder and making sure Noah didn't have any permanent damage from the tranquilizers used on him, she'd had a busy night.

"Besides being completely useless?"

Annie gave him a sad smile. "Kendrick will have something for you guys soon."

"Will Lyn make it that long without her pills?"

Annie rubbed the back of her neck. "I'm not going to lie to you. Wolff-Parkinson-White syndrome is a tricky thing."

That was not what he wanted to hear. "Her mother died from it. And as far as I know, her mother was never kidnapped by someone willing to torture and kill others."

"Well, that's two different issues. Lyn's mom wasn't aware of her heart issue. The fact that Lyn is aware of it works to her advantage. Lyn has years of experience dealing with her heart. She probably knows some things she can do if she has an episode."

"But she needs the pills."

Annie nodded. "There's only so much that could be done without them—but there are certain things. Vagal maneuvers to help reset her heart rhythm. I'm sure she knows about them. But yeah, she's definitely in more danger than the average person."

"We've got to find her soon." Fear clamped his own heart. Every breath seemed harder to take.

Annie reached over and grabbed his hand. "I don't know Lyn very well, but we all know Gavin. And if she's got the same strong, stubborn blood flowing through her veins as her brother, Lyn is going to fight. You just be ready to get to her."

"We've got something!" Kendrick yelled. "Lyn was right, the first section only seemed like random numbers but we figured out they're coordinates."

Everyone rushed into the computer room. On the giant screen in front of them was a map. Nine different locations all across the country.

Heath was actually looking at what had been noise inside his head for years. He could still hear the murmurings in his subconscious, but knowing what they meant—at least part of them—made them easier to ignore.

"What are they?" Heath asked.

"Mostly medical research facilities. Various sizes from barely more than a blood bank to multimillion-dollar clinics."

"Any commonalities between them?" Gavin asked.

Kendrick shrugged. "Nothing obvious, but we're still digging. We need a little time."

Time was something Lyn might not have.

Uselessness crushed at Heath again. He hovered over Kendrick's shoulder until the man started giving him dirty looks, so he took a few steps back into the hallway. No point slowing down the non-useless people.

An hour later when there was still nothing, Heath thought he might go crazy. Noah and Dorian herded him into the kitchen when it became obvious his presence was just agitating Kendrick.

Heath questioned Noah about the kidnapping again. As if the man was going to remember anything different the fourth time around. The team that had taken Lyn had been efficient and brutal. Smashed through the door and tranquillized Lyn and Noah before they'd had a chance to react.

It wasn't easy to get the drop on Noah, and the man obviously felt terrible for what had happened to his cousin on his watch. At this point, Heath was glad they weren't dealing with a dead body. A tranquilizer could've easily been a gun with a silencer.

They sat him down at the kitchen table and placed Lyn's laptop in front of him.

"Let's start familiarizing ourselves with these locations," Noah said.

Heath let out a huff of air. "What good is that going to do?"

"It's going to do more good than grunting over Kendrick's shoulder," Dorian told him.

That was true. They began studying the different buildings, looking for any similarities that might give them a clue to what they had in common.

When Dorian stiffened a little while later, Heath was immediately wary.

"What?"

"Ray."

Heath had no idea how the man knew, but sure enough, Ray eased silently through the side kitchen door a few moments later. Her features were pinched and her giant headphones—to be used if she wanted to be able to keep from hearing anything, a fear the Project Crypt scientists had instilled in her—were wrapped around her neck, her hands hovering over them protectively.

He hated to see the woman—his *friend*—who'd once moved with such confidence and fire now so timid and unsure. She walked over to them, Dorian immediately moving to stand protectively near her.

"Hey, Wraith," Heath said.

"Hey, Shadow."

"Thanks for delivering Franklin to us."

A ghost of a smile lit her lips. "Got to keep up target practice."

Dorian slipped an arm around her. "You doing okay? I didn't expect to see you in here."

"I was watching through the window. I . . . I have information that might help. When I destroyed the Project Crypt facilities, there was some data about a couple of those locations. I just didn't know what it meant at the time."

Heath stood, anxious for *anything* that might help, just as Craig walked into the kitchen, talking with Zac and Annie. Ray flinched at their voices, her body jerking almost uncontrollably, knocking into the computer on the table. Heath dove for it to keep it from crashing into the ground.

The movement and noise had Ray visibly withdrawing into herself, her eyes large and blank. She pulled her headphones over her ears and looked up at Dorian.

Noah recognized what was happening and immediately walked over to urge the others out of the kitchen.

But even with them gone, Ray wasn't okay. "I'm sorry. I-

I can't. I have to go." Her voice was unnaturally loud over the noise-reducing headphones. She began walking toward the door.

"Ray, wait—" She couldn't hear him, so Heath reached for her.

Dorian caught his arm before it even made contact. "No."

"D, come on, man. If she knows something, she needs to tell us. Lyn's life may be at stake."

"No. I won't ask her to risk all the progress she's made. She's already done her part. She's done enough."

Crap.

Heath was going to have to fight one of his oldest friends.

Even understanding why Dorian was willing to protect Ray—*agreeing* with it—Heath was still going to fight him.

Even knowing Ray would be out the door into the night and long gone before Heath could get through Dorian—*if* he could get through Dorian—he was still going to fight his friend.

Because he had to. Because, just like Dorian hadn't had a choice but to defend Ray, Heath had no choice but to *try* for Lyn. He took a step toward his friend to push him out of the way.

Dorian raised his fist.

But then Ray stopped and turned around. "D."

He stopped at her soft word and lowered his arm.

Her face was pale and pinched; her eyes darted back and forth. But she slid the headphones off her ears the slightest bit. She'd known what Dorian had been willing to do without having to hear or see it.

"Adil Garrison," she whispered.

"The billionaire?" That didn't make any sense.

But then again, the man had been at WCU when Heath had first started his investigation.

Had gotten a tour of the biomedical engineering labs.

"Have Kendrick look into the buildings with Garrison as a filter."

Her breaths became shallower. Dorian didn't say another word, just reached up to slip her headphones back over her ears, then wrapped an arm around her waist and propelled her out the door.

Heath didn't waste any time getting Ray's information to Kendrick.

"Adil Garrison? The reclusive businessman?" Kendrick asked. "What does he have to do with any of this?"

"I don't know. Just use him as a filter."

Kendrick shrugged and got to work.

Neo's voice came on over the speaker. "I've already started putting feelers out about these medical facilities. It's not pretty."

"What do you hear?" Heath asked.

"That there were calls for people looking to make money if they were willing to undergo testing that wasn't exactly FDA approved. Targeting homeless people."

Heath nodded at Gavin as he walked in.

"The word is, brainwashing," Neo continued. "That people go into these facilities and don't always come back out. And the ones who do come out aren't the same way they began. At best, nosebleeds and headaches. At worst . . . almost brain-dead."

"Cops haven't shut them down?" Noah asked.

"Cops have no idea these subsections of the buildings even exist. The majority of all these facilities are on the up and up. I'm talking to one source right now who says he's been inside one and has seen people kept like zombies."

Craig looked over at Heath. "They could be testing synthetic neural inhibitors."

"If they are, it doesn't sound very successful," he said.

"Oh my gosh," Kendrick said from his computer. "Heath, you were right. Adil Garrison is tied to every single one of these facilities in some way."

Everyone turned toward Kendrick. "He owns them?"

"No, he's way too clever for that. But he's tied to them all. He owns two, but he's linked to the rest. He's on the board of directors for a couple, for one he gifted the building to the nonprofit organization that uses the majority of it. For some, he has overseas corporations that are tied to the buildings. But all of them. He's linked to all of them."

Heath turned to Craig. "Meet your mystery man."

"I walked right by him a month ago at Wyoming Commonwealth," Craig whispered.

Kendrick took Neo off speaker and turned to face the men and women in the room, most pointedly Gavin. "I need to talk to Neo about some things you might not want to hear. Not quite legal things."

"Is it going to help save my sister?" Gavin asked.

"At this point, it's probably the only way to save Lyn. Her and a ton of other people."

Gavin didn't even hesitate. "Do it."

Kendrick began talking to Neo on the phone, discussing the best ways to pull all possible info on Garrison and the facilities. The databases they were talking about hacking were top secret and pertinent to national security. Everyone in the room would be going to jail right alongside Blaze if they were caught, just because they were aware of what was going to transpire.

As Kendrick and Neo began their search—back on

speaker with each other and yelling obscenities—Gavin motioned everyone else into the kitchen.

"Whatever they find on their computers is just going to be gravy for the meat and potatoes we already have sitting right in front of us," Gavin said. "We have the locations where human experimentation is happening. We have the element of surprise on our side and the ability to stop it and bring down someone who's been fooling the public for years."

They all turned as the side door opened, and Dorian stepped inside. "Whatever is going down, I want to help. Ray wants to also, but . . . can't." His eyes met Heath's, shaking his head, the big man's shoulders slumping. "She can't. This isn't her fight anymore. I can't ask her to come back into this."

Heath didn't even hesitate. He walked over to Dorian and pulled the man in for a hard hug. He knew his friend didn't like to be touched, but Dorian wrapped his arms around Heath anyway, slapping him on the back.

"Ray's done her part," Heath whispered to Dorian. "Now let's make sure this ends for good."

They broke apart, and Zac Mackay nodded, stepping forward. He'd been the team leader in the Special Forces, the tactician. "In order for this to work, it's going to require a strategic strike. Every location hit at the same time. If not, Garrison will have the chance to . . . tie up loose ends."

Everyone knew what that meant. Kill anyone who could speak out against him. Including Lyn, and Craig's sister.

Heath nodded. "This sort of strike is more than we can do ourselves. We need law enforcement in on this. Multiple strike teams."

Gavin's jaw was set as he looked over at Craig.

"Between what we've heard here and Lyn being missing, I can get us our warrants. As governor, my father has the connections we need. For Lyn, he would call in favors based on my best guess. And what we've learned here tonight is much more than just a guess."

Craig nodded. "I've still got a few people loyal to me in the bureau and a few who are willing to risk a long shot if it means making a career-catapulting bust. I'll be able to get several teams."

Noah pushed away from the wall. "I'll call Tanner and wake him up. He'll be able to get SWAT together and move on the facility in Denver."

Gabriel Collingwood wasn't an official part of Linear Tactical, but he might as well be. "I've got a few law enforcement contacts also. Once we have warrants, they'll be more than willing to move."

"I'm going to call Dad now," Gavin said. "Everybody reach out to your contacts as if the warrants are a done deal. We need to be prepared to move at dawn."

Everyone dispersed, the team ready to do whatever they had to save one of their own.

For the first time since he'd seen Lyn's pills scattered across the floor in Gavin's apartment, Heath had a sense of hope.

CHAPTER TWENTY-EIGHT

"What's wrong with you?"

Lyn stared at the young woman who'd asked her the question.

What was *wrong* with her?

Besides being kidnapped, knocked unconscious, stuffed in the trunk of a car, backhanded twice, and being worked nonstop for fifteen hours with a gun to her head?

Was that not enough wrong with her?

And with all that danger, it was still going to be her own heart that ended up killing her. She'd managed to salvage one pill; the others had flown from her hand when she'd been shot with the tranquilizer back at Gavin's apartment.. And she'd taken it when she'd woken up and found herself stuffed in a trunk.

Maybe she should've saved it.

"I have a heart condition. It's called Wolff-Parkinson-White syndrome, and it's a type of arrhythmia."

The woman, maybe Lyn's age or a little older, nodded like Lyn as talking about an unfortunate rash.

Then again, this woman had a lot more bruises on her

face, arms, and neck—all at various stages of healing from new and dark purple to old and yellowish green—than Lyn did.

"What's your name? Do you know where we are? Why we're here?"

"Jenna," the woman whispered. "No. And to do whatever they tell you to."

They wanted Lyn to decipher whatever was in Heath's head—had demanded she start working on it as soon as she'd been put into this windowless room.

She'd been stalling as long as she could, not sure exactly what it was she'd been finding. What if it was dangerous? What if it was some sort of nuclear code or the formula for a bomb?

The first group that she'd translated and sent to Kendrick had only been numbers, and she'd had no idea what they meant. The second series she was working on now wasn't just numbers, but it wasn't just words either. It was something she didn't understand. Even as she was becoming more and more familiar with the Pictish, what she was finding didn't make sense to her.

"I'm trying to translate a dead language. I'm a specialist in linguistics. What are you doing?"

"I'm trying to perfect a formula for synthetic neural inhibitors. I'm a biomedical engineer."

Like Troy Powell and the people Heath had been investigating. "I don't know what a synthetic neural inhibitor is. You . . . work here?"

Jenna's soft laughter held no trace of humor whatsoever. "Yeah, like how you work here. Except I've *worked here* for nearly a year."

Which would explain the bruises.

Lyn had to tamp down the panic. She had no idea

where she was, and there was no way for anyone to find her. She was stalling in translating the data from Heath's head, but what good was that going to do if no one was coming to save her?

She had to figure out a way out of here herself. But at least she had a possible ally.

"Jenna, listen—"

Her words were cut off as she was yanked back by the hair and the guard's fist flew into her jaw, knocking her to the ground.

She fought through the pain and dizziness, her heart beginning an unnatural rhythm that stole her breath. She forced herself to cough hard. The vagal maneuver wouldn't work long-term, but it would buy her time now.

Of course, doing it with blood pouring out of her mouth from where her cheek had scraped her teeth didn't make it easier.

She didn't even have a chance to catch her breath before the guard reached down and pulled her back up by her hair.

"No talking. Get your work done."

Lyn put the headphones back on but didn't turn on the translation software. She closed her eyes, trying a different vagal technique—holding her breath and bearing down—not pretty, but working to get her heart back in a normal rhythm.

Jenna slid a tissue toward her. Lyn nodded and used it to wipe the blood dripping from her mouth.

She just needed to survive this moment. Working on some grandiose escape plan was useless if she didn't live through the next five minutes.

She turned on the translation software Kendrick had created and began the tedious task of entering in the phonetic spelling of the language no one could actually speak. Slowly, the software provided more data.

Lyn wrote it all down as it came through, often having to double-check because even the translation seemed to be in a different language.

But at least concentrating on this kept her heart rate even.

She'd been at it for about an hour when Jenna tapped her on the shoulder.

"That's not right." She pointed at the word on the screen.

"What? How do you know? Are you familiar with Pictish?" Lyn looked over her shoulder to make sure she wasn't about to get punched by a guard again, but he was over by the door on his phone.

"No, not the language. What you're translating this into."

Lyn looked at the random letters and numbers she had on the screen. Yes, they were in English, but she still had no idea what they meant.

"This makes sense to you?" she asked Jenna. "Because this is just as much gibberish to me here as it was coming out of Heath's mouth."

"Heath Kavanaugh? Shadow?"

Lyn nodded. "Yes. Do you know him?"

If anything, Jenna looked more frightened. "They have been desperate to get at what's in his head ever since I arrived. It's the same formula they brought me here to re-create. That's what you're translating, what was in Shadow's head?"

"Yes. I figured out it was a dead Scottish language called Pictish. But honestly, I'm not sure I'm doing it right. It doesn't make any more sense to me translated."

Lyn brought up the first segment she'd translated earlier in the evening before she'd been kidnapped. "The first part of it was only a series of numbers." She'd had to filter through all of this again so that she could start on the second segment. "Here's the second. I don't know what any of that means."

Jenna reached over to the keyboard and added tabs between certain numbers.

"That's prettier, but I still don't know what they are."

"They're coordinates. Facilities where different types of brainwashing techniques and the synthetic neural inhibitors I'm attempting to develop are being tested. Mostly against people's wills."

"Project Crypt."

Jenna gave a short nod. "Holloman. He was my mentor in college. Crypt was only the tip of the iceberg."

"What is this other stuff I'm translating? It's not just numbers, but I don't understand what it means."

"You're translating it too literally. Thinking like a linguist, not a scientist. The words 'division' here and here"—Jenna pointed to the screen—"shouldn't be written out as full words."

Jenna grabbed a piece of paper and wrote the sentence Lyn had translated a few minutes before. But instead of writing out the letters and words, she wrote them as . . . an *equation*.

It still didn't make sense to Lyn, but at least it was making sense to someone.

"I see you two have met." Jenna all but jumped out of her skin at the deep voice behind them.

Adil Garrison. Lyn recognized him as soon as she saw his face. He'd been with her father at the governor's mansion more than once.

"You look familiar." Garrison studied her. "Have we met before?"

Lyn looked back down at the computer. "Why would we have ever met? Unless you studied languages at Wyoming Commonwealth University, I'm pretty sure we don't know each other."

Garrison's eyes narrowed. "Lyn Norris. Linguistic doctoral student at WCU."

She nodded without looking at him again. "That's right. Probably should've double-checked that before you kidnaped me. Who are you anyway?"

He was an international businessman with companies across the world. Lyn didn't need him to tell her who he was. But she knew for a fact she'd never walk out of this building alive if he knew she could identify him. He kept a low profile. Not often pictured in the paper, never doing press conferences himself. Now she knew why.

"It doesn't matter who I am," Garrison said. "What matters is the progress you're making on our little project here."

"It's not an exact science. You're asking me to translate a language that's been dead a couple thousand years."

"Yet look how well you're doing. And I knew Jenna would be able to help you piece together the specifics. Isn't that right, Jenna?"

The other woman hadn't said a word since Garrison had walked in. She just nodded now.

"Dr. Franklin is brilliant in her own right, but unfortunately hasn't been able to successfully develop the algorithm for a synthetic neural inhibitor during the time she has stayed with us."

Lyn's eyes narrowed. *Franklin?* As in Agent Franklin? Surely not.

"Translating this will take time, and I'm not necessarily working in the best conditions. Honestly, I'm not sure I'll be able to help you at all."

Garrison gave her a tight-lipped smile and moved closer. "I'm sorry the conditions don't meet your high standards, Ms. Norris. I'll—"

"Excuse me, Mr. Garrison." One of the guards cleared his throat.

"What?" Garrison snarled.

"We've got reports of unusual movement outside of three of our facilities. No confirmation as to what exactly it is, but it's unusual for it to involve three."

Garrison's face morphed into a scowl. "She got off the coordinates before we took her. I was hoping her little team wouldn't figure out what they were so soon. We're going to need to go into emergency protocol. Shut everything down."

"Sir, are you sure that's necessary? It could just be a coincidence."

"No, they're onto us. It's time to go underground." Garrison turned back to Lyn and Jenna. "Ladies, you've got much less time than we thought. One hour, to be exact."

Good. She shouldn't have a problem stalling for that long.

Garrison reached down and cupped Lyn's hand in his. "Ms. Norris, are you right-handed or left-handed. "

"Right, why?"

Before Lyn could even process what Garrison was doing, he brought her left hand up in front of him, grabbed her pinky, and twisted his hands.

She heard the sickening sound of a bone breaking right before the agony burst through her finger. White dots flashed in front of her eyes as she struggled to hang on to consciousness.

"If you're not finished in an hour, I will break something a little more painful. Maybe a kneecap or an ankle—just not anything that would further affect your ability to type."

Lyn wheezed in and out, trying to survive the pain radiating up her arm.

"She has a heart condition," Jenna said. "If you cause her to have some sort of heart attack, she won't be any good to you."

Garrison backhanded Jenna, and she caught herself on the table. "I've obviously been too lenient with you lately. I think it might be time for us to go back to our original state."

Even through her pain, Lyn could see Jenna withdraw into herself. Whatever Garrison was threatening her with was more than the woman could handle.

"One hour."

Garrison turned and walked out the door while Lyn struggled to get her body under control using all the vagal maneuvers she could think of. Jenna was right—there was only so much more Lyn's heart was going to be able to take.

A broken knee or ankle might be it.

"Are you okay?" Jenna reached for Lyn's hand where she had it cradled against her chest, but Lyn pulled it back. It was all she could do to breathe through the pain right now. She didn't want to see what her finger looked like. That would only make everything worse.

"Let's get the rest of this translated. We only have an hour." Lyn coughed hard, ignoring the pain in her hand, trying to bring her heart rate back down.

Jenna shook her head. "His name is Adil Garrison."

"I know."

"He's going to kill us, you know. As soon as he has the formula, he'll have no need for either of us."

Lyn fought to think. Jenna was right, of course. They

had to look past this moment. To figure out a way to survive. It was what The Brothers would expect her to do. What Heath would want her to do.

She'd just found him. She wasn't giving up her chance with him. Not without a fight. "You're right, but we're going to have to figure something out. I can guarantee we are the smartest people in this building. I can also guarantee I have people already looking for me right now. We just need to stay alive."

The words didn't seem to reassure Jenna in any way. "I used to think that too. My brother works for the FBI, and I used to believe he'd come for me. But he never did. I'm sure he thinks I'm dead."

"Craig Franklin? He's your brother?"

Jenna's dark eyes got wider. "Do you know him?"

Lyn didn't have all the facts, but it couldn't be a coincidence that Jenna Franklin's kidnapper wanted the information in Heath's head. This was somehow all tied together.

"Yes, I know him. And he's still looking for you, using every possible tool at his disposal, believe me." Probably including Lyn and Heath.

Jenna's face crumbled. "I used to pray he'd come rescue me every day, but I've been here so long now. Nearly a year. I thought there was no way."

She squeezed Jenna's hand with her good one. "My people have the coordinates. They might have already figured out what's going on and where we are. You heard what the guard said about there being unusual movement outside of three of the facilities? Maybe that's them. Maybe that's Craig and my Heath and their teams."

"But maybe it's not."

Lyn smiled through the pain. "You're right, maybe it's

not, but I'm not going to give up hope. And I'm not going to cave to that jerk."

"But what can we do?"

"You recognized the coordinates from what was in Heath's head. Is one set for here?"

"I think so. But there's no way to notify anyone or send any outgoing messages."

Lyn took a step closer. "But if they're already aware of this location, maybe we can do something to draw more attention."

Jenna bit her lip. "It might not be enough. We're running out of time."

"Maybe." Lyn didn't want to think about that possibility, but she had to. "And if so, then we make sure Garrison doesn't get what he wants. Fool him into thinking he has the perfect formula. Make it so close, but not quite right. We can make it look like it was an error in the original—that he still needs us."

Jenna shook her head. "I don't know if that will work. He might kill us anyway."

"Then so be it. We'll have done what we could."

She thought Jenna might disagree—and who could blame her? There was no telling exactly what sorts of torture the woman had lived through in the past year.

But finally, she nodded. Lyn squeezed her hand.

They worked as quickly as possible. The only thing Lyn was able to access from this computer terminal was her remote data server. She used every bit of the available bandwidth—one thing she could say for the bad guys was that they didn't skimp on connection speed—to download everything and anything in her cloud storage over and over again, including every paper she'd cited in her dissertation.

No doubt someone as smart as Garrison would make

sure the connection from this terminal was anonymous. There'd be no way to trace her connection back to this facility by something as simple as an IP address. But if someone was already electronically surveilling this location *and* her accounts— someone who had a significant knowledge of computers— that someone might notice the simultaneous and equal uptick in data usage at both sources. The breadcrumbs were tiny at best, but maybe, just maybe, Kendrick and Heath would find them. Maybe, just maybe, they'd realize she was here.

While everything downloaded on repeat in the background, they worked, huddled together, as Jenna took the formula Lyn had been translating and tweaked it. Making it close enough to seem perfect but far enough from viability that no one would be able to fix the problem easily.

After an hour, Garrison returned. Lyn's heart began its erratic beat almost immediately. It was fine to talk tough about not giving Garrison what he wanted when he wasn't around, but it was another thing altogether to do it when torture and broken bones were imminent.

"Ladies, for your sake, I hope you have good news for me."

Lyn swallowed her fear. "We need more time. You're asking me to translate something from a language that's been dead for two millennia. It's going to take more than a day to finish this."

She saw Garrison's sneer and his arm draw back for a strike, but the blow never came. Jenna stepped in front of Lyn, obviously not something Garrison was expecting.

"She's telling the truth," Jenna spat out. "If you want her to be able to work quickly and thoroughly, you'll stop with the violent histrionics. It's not going to help anybody get what you want."

"You're right. Hurting her will not speed up the process. But you, on the other hand, have really outlived your usefulness, haven't you, Dr. Franklin? You should've been able to solve this problem months ago."

Lyn screamed as Garrison grabbed Jenna by the hair and slammed her face down into the table, once and then again. She grabbed for his arm but he shrugged her off, crashing Jenna's now-unconscious form into the workstation a third time.

"No!" Lyn dove for them, her only thought to keep Garrison from killing Jenna.

But before she reached them, the power blew, leaving the room in darkness.

CHAPTER TWENTY-NINE

I t was all happening in ten minutes. Coordinated strikes at eight different facilities all over the country.

This was either about to be one of the biggest rescue events in the history of law enforcement or a huge waste of time, not to mention the loss of multiple careers. Ronald Zimmerman, Gavin and Lyn's father, put everything on the line to get these warrants. If this ended up being nothing, Zimmerman was going to owe a lot of people a lot of favors and have nothing to show for it.

Heath had to admit he had some doubts. Especially since he was currently standing in the shadows in front of what looked like a nice house on the outskirts of Reddington City—near Wyoming Commonwealth University—where everything had started for him.

This location had been one of the coordinates inside his head. But it had been deemed a low-priority target, given its size and location—the smallest of all the facilities. The chances of it being used to experiment on unwitting subjects seemed highly unlikely.

But it could possibly hold Lyn. Especially when

Kendrick had informed Heath about some weird data patterns emerging from Lyn's cloud server that matched part of the data trafficking in and out of the facility located here.

They hadn't been able to trace whoever was accessing Lyn's data—Kendrick had used a lot of computer-speak that boiled down to the fact that the bad guys weren't stupid and had covered their tracks well. But what if Lyn had found some other way to get their attention?

Heath wasn't going to ignore the possibility, no matter how small.

Most of the Linear team were assisting law enforcement at some of the medical facilities about to be raided. Heath had been on his way to one in Salt Lake City but had turned around with Noah when they'd gotten the info from Kendrick.

"We've got all sorts of movement on the interior," Noah spoke into the communication units they were both wearing. "Not heavily guarded, but the way three out of the four people inside are rushing around, I would argue that Garrison and his people know there's about to be a move against his facilities."

Heath grimaced. "There were too many people involved for him to not get word of it in some way. We have to let everyone else worry about the other buildings. We're going to have enough on our hands with this one."

"Roger that," Noah said. "We've got a guard at the back door, plus the other three I can see are distracted and won't be a problem."

"Thermal imaging puts two more people in the basement room. They're sort of huddled together."

Again, it might mean nothing. But it might mean everything.

"Let's hope it's Lyn," said Noah. "She has always been stronger than anybody wanted to give her credit for."

Heath believed that. But he also knew there was a limit to what a person could take. "Plan is the same. We blow the power, tranq the bad guys, and get Lyn out if she's there."

"I'll be ready on your mark."

"Roger that."

Heath moved into position. This was another operation that really should be more than a two-man job. The same had been true when he and Dorian had moved in to get Ray out of a bad situation a few months ago.

But you didn't always have the ideal situation. You had to work within the parameters you were given. Heath had the skills to adapt and respond on the fly, to make changes as needed to stay ahead of his enemy.

His training at Project Crypt had taught him that. And he was about to use it against them.

But it still should've been more than a two-person op.

"I'm in position, Phoenix," Heath said, using Noah's codename. From here on out that's all they would use. Not that there would be much talking.

"Roger that. I'm a go."

"Three. Two. Go."

The sun was creeping up, and they didn't have the cover of darkness, but they didn't need it. Heath shattered the front window, then entered through the side door he'd already disabled the alarm on. By the time the thugs inside came running to see what was happening at the window, he'd already flanked them and was able to tranquilize them immediately.

When he heard a thump behind him, he spun, waiting for the sound of gunfire, but it was another tango Noah had neutralized.

"Thanks," Heath nodded to the other man.

Noah nodded back, and they both moved silently through the rest of the house, taking out one other guard on their journey toward the basement.

Some sort of emergency generator had turned on down here, providing dim lighting on the stairs. Why was it so quiet? There had been two prominent heat signatures in this area less than five minutes ago. Had they somehow gotten out?

They paused near the bottom step. They couldn't simply walk out into the open basement and what might be an ambush. Under normal circumstances, they'd throw down a sound grenade or smoke canister.

But with Lyn's heart, they didn't want to take the chance.

Their best option was the set of metal balls Noah had in his hands. Tossing them would only buy them a couple of seconds of distraction from anyone waiting for them around the corner of the stairwell.

But a couple of seconds was all they needed to get away from the stairs.

Heath nodded, giving Noah the go-ahead.

Noah let the balls fly around the edge of the last step, and as they clanked on the floor, both men dove out and away.

At the same time, a woman's mumbled voice yelled, "Watch out!"

Heath landed hard to the right, rolling and coming back up on one knee. The warning had let him know where the danger was.

But the danger wasn't to him.

Adil Garrison held a gun to Lyn's head, hand over her mouth, muzzle against her cheek.

It was like his apartment all over again.

"Both of you put your guns down, or Ms. Norris will get a bullet to the head."

Heath lowered the tranq gun to his side but didn't put it all the way on the ground. Her face was way too pale, the corner of her mouth blue. Heath didn't know what he was going to do, but he needed to do it fast. She didn't look like she was going to last long.

Garrison pressed the gun harder against her temple. "Guns on the floor, now. It's so nice to finally meet you in person, Shadow. Holloman did a good job hiding your identity from me. He always mentioned insurance, but I had no idea it was a *person* who held the information I need. That it was possible to trap so much detailed information inside one brain."

Heath lowered his weapon and saw Noah doing the same out of the corner of his eye. They didn't have any other choice, not with Lyn so close to collapsing.

"It's me you want, Garrison. Like you said, I'm the one with all the info in my head." Heath took the slightest step closer.

"It's only after Holloman died we realized it was a person at all who had the data. Saunders recognized you from Rome that night I sent him to buy the microchip. But it took us a while to figure out who you were since Holloman deliberately misled me. Protected you."

It all was making so much sense now. But that didn't matter. All that mattered was helping Lyn. "You're too late to stop your facilities from going down, Garrison, but with me you can start again. I'll stay here with you. All you have to do is let Lyn and Noah walk out of here."

"Oh, I don't think so. I broke my other toy, so I'm going to like playing with Lyn here very much."

Heath forced himself not to dive for Garrison as he brought his face closer to Lyn's, running his nose up her cheek. She flinched, pulling at his hand like she couldn't get enough air.

"Stay away from her, I'm warning you." He couldn't stop the step he took toward them.

"Better be careful, Shadow. Seems as though I'm taking your girl's breath away."

The sound of Lyn's labored breathing behind Garrison's hand filled the room.

"Heath," Noah whispered.

"Fine. Fine. You can have both of us, just let me help her now."

Garrison grinned. "Oh, I'm going to enjoy this. All of it. If you're going to destroy all my work, I'm happy to return the damage."

Too late Heath realized Garrison may be willing to let him help Lyn, but he wasn't going to do it while there were still *two* people who could come at him from different angles. Almost in slow motion he saw Garrison turn and raise his gun at Noah.

But something struck Garrison from behind as he fired.

Heath heard Noah grunt as the bullet struck him, but he didn't allow that to stop him from throwing himself forward at Garrison. This was the only chance he was going to get.

He dove for Garrison's arm with the gun, also trying to catch Lyn as she collapsed to the ground. He was twisted the wrong way and knew this was it—Garrison was going to get the gun up again, and Heath wouldn't be able to stop him. All he could do was try to protect Lyn from the bullet he knew was coming.

But then a computer keyboard appeared out of nowhere

and crashed into Garrison's head, cracking his skull with a sickening sound, and sending the gun flying across the room. A small woman, face almost completely covered in blood, collapsed beside them, keyboard still in her hands.

"I'm not your toy, you jerk."

Heath looked at the carnage around him. He didn't care about Garrison, so he kicked the man out of the way, then grabbed Lyn to him. She was still making that frantic breathing sound and now had one hand clutched to her heart.

"Here, Almost. Take your pills." He pressed two into her mouth and watched as she swallowed.

And what about Noah? Garrison had gotten that shot off. "Phoenix?"

Noah didn't respond.

The woman who had attacked Garrison was also passed out. She was covered in so much blood, it was difficult to tell how badly she was injured.

Heath needed to get an ambulance here right away, but he wasn't sure he could keep everybody alive until one arrived.

A heavy thumping from the stairs drew his attention. Heath set Lyn down and dove for Garrison's gun. Damn it. He wasn't going to make it in time again, and he was fairly certain there were no more keyboards left to come flying at the enemy.

One of Garrison's henchmen tumbled to the bottom of the stairs headfirst.

And unconscious.

With an arrow sticking out of his back.

Ray.

A moment later, she peeked out from around the stairwell with her crossbow pointed right at them.

"It's Heath, Wraith. It's us. I think the room is secure now."

Ray's hand shook as she lowered the crossbow. In the ten years he'd known her, he'd never seen that, but after what she'd been through in the past year, it was completely understandable.

She gave him a brief nod. "This one was sneaking down. Arrow was a tranquilizer. I'm not a killer. But this is my fight. Our fight."

"Thank you, Grace. You saved our lives. And hopefully, the fight is done now."

She didn't even correct him for calling her by her given name, the name she had no longer felt worthy of. Maybe she was starting to forgive herself.

"Can you check on Noah? He's been shot." He pulled Lyn closer. She was looking a little better after her pills but was still gasping for breath, her lips blue. "Lyn's got a serious heart condition, and blood's pouring out of damn near everywhere on this woman over here. I've got to get an ambulance on the way."

She moved to Noah. "I've got a pulse here. I'm applying pressure to the wound."

Heath dialed 911. He gave the operator the address and explained that there were three people hurt. He didn't want to give too many details, especially about a gunshot wound, which would draw the cops along with the paramedics.

The police could definitely not get their hands on Ray. The consequences would be disastrous. She had to know that, but she was still here.

He brushed the hair off Lyn's face. She was becoming more listless, more pale. "Hey, Almost, you hear me? You hang in there. No way you're getting rid of me this easily."

"Va-vaga . . ."

Wait. Vagal? Wasn't that what Annie had been talking about earlier? "Your vagal maneuvers for your heart? Is that what you're talking about?"

She nodded.

"Is there something I can do?"

She nodded again.

Obviously, Lyn wasn't going to be able to give him instructions. He grabbed the phone again and called Annie.

He barely saw the doctor's face on the video call before he started explaining.

"Annie. I've got Lyn, but she's in real bad shape. Her mouth is blue, and she was trying to say something about those vagal things you and I were talking about. But I can't understand what I should do."

"If she's that bad off, you need to get her to a hospital right away."

"The ambulance is coming. I'm far from help. If I take her myself, I'm not sure she'll survive the drive."

"Okay, then she's right. You don't happen to have a defibrillator lying around anywhere?"

"No. Do we need one?"

"Honestly, it would work best in this situation. But we have other options."

He hoped this didn't involve cutting Lyn open like some sort of tracheotomy. "Please don't tell me I need a knife."

"No, it's pressure points. You're going to do something called a carotid sinus massage. It will help slow her heart rate and allow the heart to pump more effectively. But you are going to be careful not to press too hard. That will reduce the flow of oxygen to her brain."

That sounded very, very bad. This was *all* bad.

"I don't want to make it worse, Annie."

But it was Lyn who reached up and put his hand on the side of her neck.

"Trust. You." Her voice was weak, but her eyes were steady. He could feel her pulse fluttering wildly under his fingertips.

"Tell me what to do, Annie."

"Touch her throat where her Adam's apple would be if she were a man, then run your fingers to the right about halfway back." He did it. "Yes, there. Now tilt her head the other way. Good. Circular motions on that pressure point."

Heath did it, but it didn't seem to be making any difference in what was happening to Lyn.

"You're going to have to put more pressure, Heath," Annie told him. "Like that pulse is a flame and you've got to put it out with your fingers before it spreads and burns everything down with it."

Meaning was clear: get this under control before it became deadly.

Heath put the phone down so he could hold the other side of Lyn's head and put more pressure on the carotid sinus. "C'mon, Almost. I need that heart of yours. Mine isn't going to make it without yours next to it."

Her hand reached up and wrapped around his, squeezing slightly.

"C'mon, Lyn. You're a fighter. You fight this with me."

He panicked for a second as her pulse weakened under his fingers, afraid he was losing her. But her grip on his other hand, despite whatever had happened to her pinky, was firm.

Her pulse was *slowing*, not stopping.

He looked down at Annie's concerned face on his screen. "I think it's working. Her pulse is slowing."

"Good. That's good. She still needs to go to the hospital right away, but she's okay for now."

He looked down into Lyn's brown eyes. "You hear that? You're going to be okay. Orders from a full doctor, not an almost doctor. So it's true."

She gave him a ghost of a smile, the panicked oh-crap-I-can't-breathe look gone from her face. "Help. Jenna."

"I don't need help," the bloody woman next to them said without even picking herself up off the ground. "That bastard can't kill me. I won't allow it."

Heath smiled at the woman. "Your brother has been looking for you for a long time, Ms. Franklin. He's busy making sure they put an end to all of Garrison's operations, but he's going to be overjoyed to know you're alive."

They could hear the sirens in the distance.

"Ray, how's Noah?"

"Grazed him in the head. Bleeding like a stuck pig, and he's out cold, but with medical arriving right now, he'll live."

"You need to get out of here." The fact that she had stayed this long after what she'd been through was a testament to her bravery. "You've done your part."

"I'm sorry I didn't do more."

"You came when we needed you. That's plenty."

Ray stood up and looked at Garrison's body. "This is really it, isn't it? Crypt, the brainwashing, the sleeper missions . . . it all dies with him."

She fingered the headphones around her neck.

"Yes, it does. I don't think you're going to need those anymore. Nobody can ever control you against your will again."

"Yeah."

But she didn't take them off. Only time would heal that wound.

Without another word, Ray was gone, moving silently out of the house.

The sirens were closer now. He realized he still had his finger on the pulse at Lyn's neck, her hand still wrapped over his. Her eyes were closed, but her heartbeat was steady.

That heartbeat was everything to him. There was no way he could live without it now.

EPILOGUE

O*ne year later.*

H eath carried a man purse with him everywhere he
went.

The murse, all the Linear guys had nicknamed it.
Always with a laugh.

Heath didn't care.

He'd had it for a full year, since the morning he'd
received a crash course on carotid sinus massage over the
phone in a basement room.

Lyn had been in the hospital for four days. It had taken
both electrical and chemical cardioversion to get her heart
beating a normal pace again, and it had been touch and go
for longer than Heath's own heart had been able to handle.

Sitting by her side at the hospital, mostly while she
rested and the doctors monitored every breath and heartbeat, he'd researched everything he could about Wolff-
Parkinson-White syndrome. The doctors and nurses, and

Lyn's family—including Noah who had been recuperating in the same hospital and was now fully recovered—had been tired of his questions by the time Lyn's hospital stay was over.

Her heart had taken a hard hit during the twenty-four hours she'd been in Garrison's clutches. The terror, the pain —a broken rib, pinky, and significant bruising and abrasions to her face—along with not having any medication available, had put stress on her heart that her family had been trying to help her avoid her whole life.

But Lyn had survived. Because her physical heart might not be strong, but her will, her zeal, her fervor for life?

None of those were giving up so easily.

Still, every day for a year Heath had carried around a small, portable defibrillator in *the murse*.

Because the carotid massage shouldn't have been enough that day in Garrison's basement. All the doctors had said so. And more importantly, no matter how strong Lyn's fervor or zeal, another episode like that and all the vagal maneuvers in the world wouldn't be enough. And if a defibrillator wasn't nearby, that might be it for Lyn.

So he would carry one wherever he went with her. He hardly noticed it anymore.

Just like his gibberish. It was still there in his head all the time, but easier to deal with and ignore now that he could actually assign meaning to the sounds. When Lyn had explained all of what was inside his brain—not only the co-ordinates to Garrison's facilities but the formula for the synthetic neural inhibitor itself—Heath could hardly believe it.

No wonder Holloman had referred to Heath as his *insurance*. What was in Heath's mind had been of utmost importance to Project Crypt's success, or whatever

Garrison wanted to call the new version. And Holloman had thought he was the only one who could access the information.

He obviously hadn't been counting on someone with Lyn's intelligence and expertise.

But Heath was free now. The gibberish may continue, but he could control the volume rather than it controlling him. For the first time in his adult life, he was able to go wherever he wanted with no need to look over his shoulder.

Which had brought him here to Egypt where Lyn was about to start her new job with the Center for Ancient Languages.

He came up behind her as she put the finishing touches on her makeup in the bathroom mirror of the apartment they'd moved into two weeks ago. "You almost ready? Don't want to be late on your official first day."

She practically glowed. "Yes. I can't believe I'm actually starting today. It's been such a whirlwind."

No one deserved this opportunity more than her. She had saved Jenna's life and her own.

The raids on the medical facilities had been a success. Relatively little loss of life, Adil Garrison notwithstanding, and multiple innocent people rescued.

The FBI had owed Craig Franklin a pretty damn big apology and offered him his job back with full privileges.

He'd promptly told them where they could stuff that invitation.. He'd quit so he could take care of his sister.

"Jenna emailed me this morning—or, last night for her— to wish me luck." Lyn stroked a little mascara on her eyelashes. "She's been doing better. Teaching computer classes at an elementary school."

Heath kissed the top of her head. "Good." The two women had remained friends and talked nearly every day.

"Dad and The Brothers checked in on me too. Again." She rolled her eyes. "Sakhif idiots."

He smiled at the gentle Arabic curse. "You were expecting that."

She grinned up at him. "Of course. I'm a little surprised they're not here now."

Actually, Tristan, one of the twins, was here in Egypt. At least for a couple more days. And he was only leaving because Heath had discovered him tailing them over the past week and threatened to tell Lyn.

Heath had to chuckle when Tristan backed down at the threat.

They were all a little afraid of feisty Lyn now. She wasn't going out of her way to protect their feelings anymore when it came to living her life. She wasn't accepting limits any longer just because someone tried to tell her she should.

Her game. Her rules.

He loved this woman.

If he had the rest of his life with her—and he planned to —he was never going to get tired of her.

"Your first day too." She met his eyes in the mirror.

He'd accepted a job running security for a company here in Cairo. One that happened to be in the same building where she worked. The position would be challenging and a good utilization of his skills.

But hell, he would've worked as a janitor if it meant being near her.

"I know. I'm excited."

She turned and wrapped her arms around his neck. "I love you, Heath Kavanaugh. I know this isn't where you thought you'd be. I know you were ready to put down roots in Oak Creek."

He kissed her plump lips. "Oak Creek and Linear Tactical will still be there if we decide we want to go back that way. Loving you means more to me than any place or job."

Her smile took his breath away. It was always going to take his breath away. "Thank you," she whispered. "For carrying *the murse* around. And for telling Tristan to get lost when he showed up here last week."

He raised an eyebrow. "What? I—"

She pressed a finger to his lips. "I was raised surrounded by all things law enforcement. Please remind my family of that next time they think they can get away with something without me noticing."

"Yes, Doc." He couldn't even call her Almost anymore since she'd gotten her PhD.

"But mostly, thank you for being the caretaker of my heart. In all the possible ways a heart can be cared for."

"Always." He pulled her all the way against him.

And knew their hearts beat as one.

ACKNOWLEDGMENTS

Shadow didn't end up ending up like I originally envisioned it. Heath's story turned in an unexpected direction early on. But I didn't mind, because it allowed me to get back into the heart of what the Linear Tactical books are about: love (and danger!) in a close-knit community.

Family isn't always blood—they're the people you know you can count on to have your back. That's true in my life and true in my books.

A very special thank you to Marci Mathers of Moon-flower Manuscripts editing. She and I first connected years ago because of an earlier version of this story, and she's been an absolute godsend and wonderful source of support ever since. Marci, thank you for all you do. I couldn't ask for a better proofreader.

A huge virtual hug to my alpha readers: Denise, Kaitlin, Susan and Jessica. Your comments and suggestions for this story made it so much stronger! I appreciate your effort and time.

To my ARC Review Team...thank you for providing your reviews and spotting those last couple of pesky errors who tried to make it into the final draft despite everyone's dedication to their demise. I appreciate you and the time you take to review my books. Mwah!

And, as always...special thanks to my hubby and kids who patiently live through my crazy with every book. This one was no exception.

And finally, a special thanks to my readers, who have come with me on this Linear Tactical journey for six books now. I get asked all the time how many LT books there will be. We're at book 6, and I know there are at least 4 more characters demanding their story be written. So never fear... Oak Creek isn't going anywhere any time soon.

Thank you from the bottom of my heart. For reading these books. For making them possible. For allowing me to put down on paper the voices inside my head.

With appreciation,
Janie

ALSO BY JANIE CROUCH

ABOUT THE AUTHOR

"Passion that leaps right off the page." - Romantic Times Book Reviews

USA TODAY bestselling author Janie Crouch writes what she loves to read: passionate romantic suspense. She is a winner and/or finalist of multiple romance literary awards including the Golden Quill Award for Best Romantic Suspense, the National Reader's Choice Award, and the coveted RITA© Award by the Romance Writers of America.

Janie recently relocated with her husband and their four teenagers to Germany (due to her husband's job as support for the U.S. Military), after living in Virginia for nearly 20 years. When she's not listening to the voices in her head—and even when she is—she enjoys engaging in all sorts of crazy adventures (200-mile relay races; Ironman Triathlons, treks to Mt. Everest Base Camp) traveling, and movies of all kinds.

Her favorite quote: "Life is a daring adventure or nothing." ~ Helen Keller.

 facebook.com/janiecrouch

twitter.com/janiecrouch

instagram.com/janiecrouch